DRUG OF DESIRE

He pulled the sheet off the young woman he called Kay and raised her gown to her throat.

Standing back, he admired her in clear uninterrupted light. An exquisite body. Very young. Curvaceous. Smooth. A tan line that was quite exotic. She had been so willing, held so still while he'd painted the hexagon, even quivered with pleasure, nipples hardening, as the stroke of a wet camel-hair brush drew thick oily color over her flesh.

Aroused by that thought, he withdrew the syringe from the wadding in his shirt pocket.

The best part was coming up. . . .

TERROR ... TO THE LAST DROP

Preston A. Pairo III

BRIGHT EYES

AN ONYX BOOK

ONYX
Published by the Penguin Group
Penguin Books USA Inc., 375 Hudson Street,
New York, New York 10014, U.S.A.
Penguin Books Ltd, 27 Wrights Lane,
London W8 5TZ, England
Penguin Books Australia Ltd, Ringwood,
Victoria, Australia
Penguin Books Canada Ltd, 10 Alcorn Avenue,
Toronto, Ontario, Canada M4V 3B2
Penguin Books (N.Z.) Ltd, 182-190 Wairau Road,
Auckland 10, New Zealand

Penguin Books Ltd, Registered Offices:
Harmondsworth, Middlesex, England

First published by Onyx, an imprint of Dutton Signet,
a division of Penguin Books USA Inc.

First Printing, August, 1996
10 9 8 7 6 5 4 3 2 1

PUBLISHER'S NOTE
This is a work of fiction. Names, characters, places, and incidents either are the
product of the author's imagination or are used fictitiously, and any resemblance to
actual persons, living or dead, events, or locales is entirely coincidental.

To my parents and Moira,
for their unending support and encouragement;
and to
Amy Stout, inspiring editor; and
Agnes Birnbaum, tireless agent.

Prologue

Three-fifteen A.M. Jimmy Griffin hid in the shadows of the small front porch, wearing a black T-shirt and jeans. Wool fibers of a ski mask covering his face itched the sweaty stubble of his beard.

A tumultuous summer squall had just ended. Trickles of rain fed through crooked roof gutters and splashed onto unkempt yards of dirt and stone. Storm drains gurgled, struggling to digest the downpour. Waves of steam rose off Baltimore city streets and drifted toward amber pole lights. Now and then a car passed, tires spinning over the wet surface.

Griffin made a final adjustment to the ski mask that concealed his face. The 9mm semiautomatic in his grip was untraceable. He gave final thought as to what he was about to do. Going over it again for the thousandth time. Reassuring himself he had not become a vigilante. That wasn't what this was about.

His back was pressed to the wall. "Okay," he whispered to himself. "Okay."

He turned and broke open the cruddy row house's front door. An inexpensive lock drove through aged molding with a sharp report. The doorknob slammed hard into a plaster wall and rattled the windows.

It was dark inside. No lights except what showed beneath a closed door at the end of a short hall. The air was stale and hot, rifled with the sweet smell of burning marijuana.

Griffin assumed a defensive crouch near the door and covered the room with the 9mm. Looking for movement behind the sofa, two chairs, and the big cardboard box in the living room. Nothing—until glass broke behind the door at the end of the hall. Someone breaking out a window.

Griffin ran toward the noise.

Just before he hit the door, he heard footsteps on the fire escape. His target going out.

Griffin kicked the door open. Splinters of molding sprayed across tattered black and purple sheets on an unmade bed.

A dozen unlit votive candles were scattered atop a cheap nightstand along with roach-clip remains of a burnt spliff. The bathroom door was open; water dripped from the faucet.

At the window, Griffin kicked a sharp triangle of glass that remained like a loose tooth; the broken pane skidded across the metal fire escape and fell fifteen feet to the alley, bursting into pieces just behind the man Griffin was after.

Dunbar Waddy sprinted toward the street, dreadlocks splayed over his naked shoulders. His bare feet splashed through puddles, seemingly oblivious to shards of glass littering cracked macadam.

Griffin went over the side of the iron railing and dropped to the alley, landing on ankles and knees strengthened by weekend hikes in the mountains. He felt a slight twinge in his right leg as he gave chase.

Sprinting fast, Waddy reached the empty street and turned right. Griffin went by the same spot five seconds later.

Waddy bypassed another alley, choosing to stay on the

street even thought it was brightly lit. Maybe he felt safer in the open. But there were no witnesses—not in this section of the city this late at night. A zone even cops stayed out of. Most cops.

Griffin struggled to keep pace. His pulse pounded in his eyes. What kept him going was the memory of two bronze coffins. Mother and son. Draped in flowers on a rainy, cold June day that seemed like winter, with tent flaps whipped by a stiff wind. Less than two weeks ago, yet it seemed like a year.

It had taken Dunbar Waddy this long after the funeral to make a mistake, to use a hideout one of Griffin's snitches knew about. Now, Waddy was making another mistake. He had a hundred-yard lead; perhaps thinking he could increase that, outdistance Griffin up the incline, Waddy ran to the Marrow Street Bridge.

The two men, breathing hard, sprinted onto the aged mile-long span that crossed a narrow isthmus of black harbor. Poor design and corrupt city maintenance contracts kept the bridge closed more than it was open. Tonight, it was closed. A quarter mile up the steep rise, a tall chain fence was Waddy's dead end.

Waddy scaled halfway up before looking to the other side. There was a gaping hole in the bridge floor; between jagged support rods, building lights reflected off inky water. Waddy released his catlike hold on chain link and dropped back to the safe side of the fence.

He glanced back. Griffin closing in.

Waddy lurched to the bridge's side, braced both hands on the rail, and brought his feet up. Was perched like a gymnast about to vault the horse, when Griffin fired his weapon.

Waddy took hits in the right shoulder and cheekbone. The shot to his face was especially vicious, looking to have torn off the lower half of his jaw. The impact drove

Waddy over the edge. He tumbled toward the water in an awkward spiral.

Griffin leaned over the rail and chased him with nine more shots, emptying the gun's clip just before Waddy hit the water with a hard splash.

As the ripples of Dunbar Waddy's fall gradually quieted across raven water, Jimmy Griffin pulled off the ski mask. He used it to wipe the gun clean, then bundled both objects together, threw them into the harbor, and walked off the bridge.

God, but he was tired. It started to rain again. Leftover drizzle, no more storms. The storm had passed.

Griffin let the rain wash perspiration from his face. He anticipated the warm comfort of being in bed with his wife, touching Carla's smooth skin while she slept naked under the sheets. She always smelled wonderful, looked wonderful, felt wonderful.

It had taken so long to finally be with her, his worst fear was of not having her one day. . . .

1.

Four Years Later—

On an eighty-five-degree August Tuesday, Jimmy Griffin led four uniformed cops inside Pussycat Licks.

The porn shop reeked of powerful disinfectant, burn-skin-to-the-bone stuff used to wash down linoleum floors. Windows painted black were streaked with condensation as the air-conditioning groaned to keep up with the heat.

Griffin looked too stylish for a cop or the weather, wearing pleated slacks, shirt, blazer, and splash-print tie. Secretaries at the office talked about him, wished he wasn't married—some would have settled for him not being so faithful to his wife. He was six-one, solidly built, with a powerful angular jaw, clear eyes, and thick hair he let grow slightly longer than the current style.

Griffin rapped his knuckles on the glass counter and toppled a pile of tokens the gay change man had been stacking to see himself through the boredom. "Run-of-the-mill raid," Griffin announced. "Don't panic. Don't run."

A tired old man with a thin salty beard shut a blacks-on-whites magazine and stuffed it back on the rack. He was the only patron.

Pussycat Licks was unusually empty for a hot day, but Griffin had something to do with that. This wasn't exactly a surprise.

Later there would be a press conference. Griffin's boss, City Attorney Richard Marish, would display cartons of seized porn tapes and announce another blow against "moral-depravation." Which Griffin figured was fitting seeing as Marish was an expert on moral depravation if there ever was one.

TV news would cover the story and the mayor would be happy, because the mayor had been getting flack for keeping a white City Attorney on an otherwise strong black reelection ticket.

Of particular nuisance was the Urban League of Black Baptists. The ULBB directors—black and wealthy—didn't really have any dispute with the mayor, but the ULBB's 75,000-member congregation—black and poor—wanted Marish out. They claimed he'd been rubber stamping police brutality cases and letting sin run wild.

The ULBB board—who liked being wined and dined at official dinners—wanted desperately to be able to endorse the mayor for reelection (especially since he was a shoe-in). But they needed a foundation to justify an endorsement—or so they advised in a confidential and since shredded memo. Without that "hook to hang their hat on," the ULBB board members might just get booted out of cushy jobs—which, unbeknown to most of their congregation, involved hefty salaries and perks.

It was this scenario that had been laid out to Jimmy Griffin. His objective was to find the mayor a hat rack for the "goddamned Baptists."

Seeing as the ULBB were staunch antipornographers and not too free speech minded (unless it was their own 1st Amendment rights being restrained), Griffin figured a few pornography raids, while not exactly novel, were still good pulp for Sunday sermons.

Griffin had also suggested warning targeted shops

about the raid. God forbid a ULBB board member be snuggled in a peep-show booth with a $50 hooker.

This fine political thinking earned Griffin a heartfelt *attaboy* from Richard Marish and got a smile from his longtime friend, Mickey Blane, who was Marish's Number One.

Days like this made Griffin all the gladder he'd taken Blane up on that offer to leave the police department for an investigator's job in the City Attorney's office. It wasn't as good as being a prosecutor—which Griffin had always wanted—but since fate kept detouring him from law school at least he felt closer to the "law" angle of the term: law enforcement.

The uniformed officers assigned to Griffin for the Pussycat Licks's raid started down dark catacomb rows of peep booths. They took their time, knowing it was a puff assignment, perfect for "career" street cops looking for a way to put in a day without getting shot at.

Like Saunders. Thirty pounds overweight. Couldn't run a hundred yards on a bet. Wearing shiny new shoes that squeaked from a puddle he'd stepped in getting out of the car.

The queer change man with the tidy mustache hauled the first carton of videocassettes out of the storage room and surrendered it.

Griffin recognized some of the movies from raids he'd been on ten years ago, when Swedish-this or Swedish-that had to be in all the titles. Wedging the box under his arm, Griffin moved to the mouth of peep-show aisles. "Come on, let's go. Help me with these boxes."

His band of slackers had collected in a back corner. Somebody, probably Saunders, was breathing hard.

Griffin rapped the flimsy wall. "Let's go! We're done here." When they didn't answer, he started toward them, muttering.

Narrow aisles lined with cheap hinged doors were cramped like a rat's tunnel. There was barely enough light to see. Stapled to the walls were explicit glossy photos showing what a patron could expect for his quarters.

Saunders saw Griffin coming. "Someone in here, Jimmy."

Sure enough, a red bulb glowed above one of the booths, the sign that someone was inside.

"What the hell?" Griffin wondered aloud. Some people just couldn't handle a warning. "You knocked?"

"Five times." Saunders gasped from exertion.

"So what's the problem? All that weight you're carrying. Bust down the thing. It's a two-dollar latch."

"Somethin's against it. It ain't budgin'."

Griffin stuck the box of tapes into Saunders's gut. "Move."

They were all more than glad to get out of Griffin's way. Hell, break down a door, you could put out your shoulder. And it was softball season.

Griffin hit the door, splintering the frame, but it still caught. "Jesus! What's in there?"

"Told you."

The latch was already busted; something was wedged against the door along the floor. Griffin took a second hit, moving it enough to let hazy light into the booth. He yanked Saunders's flashlight from the big man's belt. Used the butt end to bang a hole through cheap paneling. He stuck the light in, worked the beam around, and saw the body.

"Christ! Call an ambulance. Hurry up!" Griffin shoved Saunders, grabbed two of the other uniforms by their jacket sleeves. "Get some lights turned on back here."

They went running.

Griffin shouldered his way into an adjoining booth and kicked the common wall until it splintered. He pushed through the damage and saw her sprawled against the door.

Stone naked. A young woman with blond hair. Her eyes were wide open and glazed, focused at a point far beyond the ceiling. A red hexagon had been painted across the front of her body, points at her shoulders, hips, throat, and just above the line of her pubic hair.

From its dark hue, Griffin first thought the crude symbol had been drawn in blood. Then he detected the smell of oil-based paint: a few ounces in a small glass jar left beneath the booth's wooden bench. Griffin located that, but nothing else: no clothes.

Griffin moved the woman carefully into the aisle. Overhead lights came on, cutting through blue darkness.

The woman's pulse was strong but arrhythmic. She was alive. But when Griffin saw her eyes in the light, his relief was short-lived. Her pupils looked to be a quarter inch in diameter, big enough to allow a thousand nightmares into her head.

Four years ago, Griffin had seen three other women with eyes like that; they'd called the symptom—and the killer—Bright Eyes. His real name had been Dunbar Waddy.

2.

Griffin thought he might not catch Mickey Blane before Blane left the City Attorney's office at his usual premature hour, but today his friend was not only still at work, but in court. A recent rash of prosecutors defecting to private practice left Blane shorthanded.

Instead of holding down the fort in his office with a view, waiting for a high-profile matter to litigate, Blane was almost unthinkably on a nothing case, hand-holding a new assistant prosecutor through an evidence-suppression hearing.

Two months out of University of Baltimore, the new lawyer looked like he should be surfing Cape Hatteras, not trying cases. Professor Warnken's criminal law hadn't even been one of his better grades, but a job was a job, especially with the world starting to realize lawyers were like gum balls, a dime a dozen and equally hard to swallow.

So far, the perp's lawyer was eating the kid up. A shark down to the dull sheen of a gray Armani suit, defense counsel had been making money at this racket since the new prosecutor was two. *Two.* At every opportunity, the shark shouted objections to rattle the rookie. And each time Judge Carter muttered, "Sustained," the surf-lawyer sweated a few more ice pellets.

On the witness stand, a prematurely bald cop couldn't remember his lines. In spite of the Supreme Court giving him *Leon* and *Gates,* et al., he was dangerously close to blowing this.

Blane had even prepped him: "Make sure you say it was an honest mistake. You went into the wrong apartment as result of misreading numbers."

COP: "The wrong number, right, got it."

BLANE: "You're sure?"

COP: "Yeah. I got it."

BLANE: "Because a simple hunch—even though it was a correct hunch—is not good probable cause."

COP: "No sweat."

Now, on the stand, the cop said everything *except* "honest mistake." And kept looking at Blane like he'd have cue cards for him.

Blane whispered to his young charge, "Honest mistake . . ."

Eyes blank with fear, the new prosecutor examined his witness: "So was it . . . ? So it was . . . ? Officer, was it the result of an honest mistake that you entered—?"

"Objection!" The shark leapt to his feet so fast he nearly knocked his chair over. "He's leading the witness *again.*"

"Sustained." Judge Carter never looked up from whatever he'd been scribbling the past ten minutes.

Shell-shocked, the kid turned toward Blane.

"Christ . . ." Blane surrendered. "Do the best you can." He tilted his chair back toward Griffin, who waited behind the rail separating trial tables from a near-vacant gallery. Over his shoulder, Blane asked, "What's up?"

Griffin's expression warned it wasn't good news. "Hang in there, buddy, but we might have a new Bright Eyes."

"What?" Blane abruptly put his chair down on all fours and pivoted toward Griffin, hunched forward to keep this private.

"It's not definite, but the girl had the look. Those real wide eyes. Heart beating wildly. I had to tell you because you gotta watch your ass until I find out for sure."

"Christ." Blane slapped the wooden rail with his palm, a sound that was picked up by trial table microphones.

The clerk waved for the judge to quiet Griffin and Blane, but Judge Carter was too busy scrolling notes for tonight's bar association speech—he'd just remembered one hell of an anecdote.

Griffin lowered his voice further. "They never did find a body, Mickey. Every day for the first month they started tearing down the Marrow Street Bridge we waited for them to find him."

Though trying not to show it, Blane looked vulnerable and didn't wear it well. He came from a money family. He used to kid—only half kidding, actually—he was too good-looking to be a public servant. Until four years ago, he'd seemed untouchable by tragedy; only it turned out fate had been holding back, waiting to deliver one big dose.

Griffin whispered, "You got your gun in your office? If not, I'll get one to—"

The clerk finally got Judge Carter's attention. He halted the surf lawyer's legal whipping just long enough to tell Blane and Griffin to take their conversation out in the hall.

Blane led the way to the door, walking quickly, leaving behind the surf lawyer who looked like a child dropped off for his first day of school. The defense attorney showed his teeth, all four rows of them.

Outside Courtroom #7, in the wide, empty corridor, aware of the building's reputation for strange acoustics, two old friends kept their exchange to a hush.

Blane, rigid with disbelief, said, "Who else knows about this?"

"The four cops on the raid. Ambulance crew. The hospital."

"Did you mention Bright Eyes to any of them?"

"No. Like I said, I'm not sure it's him. I'm going over to the hospital to—"

"Hospital?"

"Memorial. That's where they took the girl."

Blane shook his head and smacked the wall with his palm. "I don't fucking believe this. Shit." He started to hit the wall again, but stopped. "Get me some answers on this, Grif. Fast."

"I need an investigative team. A couple—"

Blane shook his head. "No way. We can't chance this leaking out. You run it alone. Have-to-know status. Don't tell anybody more than they absolutely have to know. And if the call's close, don't say anything. Okay? We in sync on this?"

Griffin hesitated.

"Okay, Grif? Are we together?"

Finally, Griffin nodded. The case was Blane's call. It had been from the start.

3.

An hour before dusk, Memorial Hospital was already hip deep in ambulances unloading gunshot victims. Hot days were the worst.

Today's drive-by shooting would have been the evening news lead a few years ago; now it probably wouldn't cover two paragraphs in the morning paper.

Just five inner-city blacks at the wrong place at the wrong time; ironically, two had been at a liquor store walk-up window buying Lotto tickets for Saturday's seven-million-dollar drawing. No one ever told them their chances of getting murdered in Baltimore were probably a thousand times greater than hitting the Pick-6.

Griffin made his way through the melee. There were so many people. The injured and their families. Screaming and crying. The terrible smell of antiseptic and adrenaline sweat.

The first drive-by victim was DOA. The doctor who'd worked on him still had blood up to his elbows when he told the man's wife. She collapsed hearing the news. The doctor caught her as she dropped to the floor and trails of her husband's blood soaked into her dress.

The cubicle in which Griffin's porn shop Jane Doe had been treated was now occupied by a car accident victim with a broken leg. He was being hurriedly bandaged to make room for the incoming.

"Over here, Jimmy." Trevor Bourbin had somehow

managed to find a plastic chair and empty corner. Bourbin was an overweight boxer's six-five who could only find clothes in big men's shops. It was ugly stuff, but the best his money could buy—as though people his size had no right to complain about style if something fit right off the rack. "They moved her upstairs. Still no ID, but Missing Persons hasn't done a check yet."

"You get a look at the paint on her?"

"Uh-huh." Bourbin was the city's supposed expert on cults and rituals, an assignment born of the police department's ethnocentric thinking. Somehow, Bourbin's Franco-Caribe heritage made him a natural for crimes related to the supernatural. His training was largely by way of FBI seminars and updates in the *Law Enforcement Bulletin*. "Painting don't necessarily mean nothing. Girl was probably along with the idea. Doctor said no signs of a struggle."

"Nothing you've seen before?"

"Nope." His size straining the chair, Bourbin rubbed large hands hypnotically over his thighs.

"You check the FBI for similars?" Griffin half hoped he hadn't.

Bourbin shook his head. "Been here the whole time waitin' on you."

"Don't mention belladonna to them, okay? Just the hexagon." Griffin's request was just that, not an order. Although he took charge of assignments by authority of the City Attorney's office, Griffin did not technically hold rank over any police officers.

Bourbin didn't say anything at first, then: "You think it's Bright Eyes again, don't you, Jimmy Grif? 'Cause she got that look in her eyes. I saw it." Bourbin contemplated Griffin, waiting for an answer he didn't get. "People in the department still wonder how you missed catching him last time. Seeing what he did. Case's still technically open. Somebody finds out I'm concealing information, gonna be my ass."

Griffin placed his hand against the pale green wall and leaned over Bourbin. His shadow barely covered the big man. Quietly, he said, "I'm not asking you to conceal anything . . . just not to volunteer it."

Still rubbing his thighs, Bourbin offered a faint nod. "Don' hang me out there too far, Jimmy Grif. I don't got no friend in the City Attorney's office to bail me out if things go down wrong."

For a couple years while he was a cop, Griffin's wife Carla used to hate it when he called to say he wasn't going to be home for dinner. She'd pout playfully and purr sexy little obscenities about what she'd do for him if he *would* come home.

Sometimes, Griffin managed to sneak off, even if it meant leaving his partner in the squad car to cover the radio while he and Carla went to bed. If a call happened to come in while Griffin and Carla were going wild, Griffin's partner would cue him with three quick blasts on the horn. Around the station, the term "three horner" became a catch phrase for emergencies, although few people understood—or appreciated—how the name originated.

It wasn't like that anymore. Tonight, when Griffin called to say he'd be late, Carla merely responded, "Okay."

Griffin had known ahead of time what her reaction would be, and it made him ache.

Shortly after Diana and Jeremy had been killed, Carla started suffering bouts of depression. She couldn't seem to shake the horror. Or maybe it was the fear that Dunbar Waddy—the one they called Bright Eyes—was still out there. That what had happened to Mickey Blane's wife and son could happen again to someone else.

Carla's reaction was something Griffin had never considered when planning Waddy's murder. There was no way he could tell her the truth. No way he could tell anyone except Blane; because Blane *had* to know.

Maybe Carla, like others, blamed Griffin for Dunbar Waddy having never been caught. Or maybe it was another reason—*reasons,* even. Who knew? Not Griffin. No one would tell him what was wrong with his wife. Not Carla. Not the therapist she was seeing.

All he knew was that little by little, Carla had withdrawn from him. A slow, painful process, like having a long needle stuck into his belly. In a way, it was like his father's alcoholism all over again. Griffin felt like he was forever waiting for someone he loved to get better.

Now, Griffin ate alone in the hospital cafeteria. A decent bowl of soup and lousy hamburger.

Every few minutes, he checked his watch, an expensive Baume and Mercier Carla had given him two birthdays ago. Dr. Finley, Jane Doe's attending physician, said he'd have time to talk around 9:30. It was now 9:20.

Griffin emptied his cafeteria tray in the trash can and headed for the elevator.

The man in the gray plant technician's shirt, jeans, and Orioles's cap considered the hospital a great place to kill someone. People died there all the time. In the emergency room, he'd seen two bodies on gurneys, sheets pulled over their heads. Nobody gave them as much consideration as an overflowing trash bag waiting for collection. Everyone was too busy.

Just like the doctors and nurses on the fifth-floor hall. They returned his bored nod, assuming he was another in a long line of maintenance men trying to figure out why the air-conditioning would have some sections of the fifth floor freezing cold while others were hot enough to grow orchids.

The tool belt strapped around his waist, like the gray uniform shirt, was stolen from an unlocked maintenance room in the basement. The syringe in his shirt pocket, though, that was his own.

Jane Doe shared a room with one other patient. Neither, however, was aware of the other. The woman in the bed nearest the window was terminal with cancer, and receiving pain relief via a morphine drip. She hadn't had visitors in five days; as far as her family was concerned, she was already dead.

As for Jane Doe, with the exception of a pale rose rash on her left torso (possible reaction to disinfectant scrub used unsuccessfully on the red paint), her symptoms had changed little from admission. Nonresponsive, pulse down from 135 to 110, echoing arrhythmic beeps on the heart monitor. A respirator controlled her breathing.

Although not certain of his diagnosis pending test results, Dr. Finley suspected she might remain in this incoherent state full time. Only two months out of medical school, he'd never treated a patient on belladonna, but was aware of its unforgiving effect. Permanent brain damage was a real possibility, leaving its user's mind as vacant as her eyes were starry.

The man in the gray uniform shirt would have concurred with the doctor's opinion had he been asked. But no one did, just like no one asked why he was going into Room 531, or why he closed the door behind him. Why he locked it.

Griffin stopped at the fifth-floor nurses' station and asked for Dr. Finley.

Kelly Harrel looked up from a mound of paperwork. Her white uniform was about out of starch. She was four hours from the end of her third twelve-hour shift in as many days.

She'd need every one of her upcoming four days off to recover. Then she'd be back on for three more. Sometimes the money didn't seem worth it. Her schedule was so far off the normal nine to five, her social life was nil.

"We sent Finley home," she told Griffin. "He was out on his feet. He'd been here two straight days. The young ones," she commented. Harrel, only thirty-two herself, envied the stamina and drive of those who thought they could make a difference.

"Did he leave any messages for me? I'm with the City Attorney's office." Griffin withdrew his investigator's shield and gestured toward the end of the hall. "About Jane Doe."

Harrel checked a scattered array of pink while-you-were-out slips. "Don't see any."

"What about her lab reports? It's urgent. I'd asked him to check her for belladonna."

"Belladonna? There's a rare bird." She looked through a short stack of pages just up from the lab and shook her head. "Not here. Maybe in her room."

"Can we look?"

Harrel managed an accommodating smile. "Sure." She had just pushed her chair back when the phone rang. "One minute?" she asked Griffin.

The man in the gray shirt wasn't arrogant about success. He knew he didn't have a lot of time. That was the trouble when fantasies became real. You could have endless, beautiful, uninterrupted daydreams, but as soon as those thoughts touched reality, you had to be efficient. Or else you got caught. And he had no intentions of being caught again.

He quickly pulled the sheet off the young woman he called Kay—the one the hospital knew only as Jane Doe.

He raised her white surgical gown to her throat, touching her body only incidentally in the process.

Standing back, he admired her in clear uninterrupted light. An exquisite body. Very young. Curvaceous. Smooth. A tan line that was quite erotic. She had been so willing, held so still while he'd painted the hexagon, even quivered with pleasure as the stroke of a wet camel-hair brush drew thick, oily color over her flesh.

The hospital had tried to wash off the hexagon; he would liked to have seen that. A pretty nurse wiping a soapy sponge over Kay's naked body, leaving watery trails along her sides. He wondered if, even unconscious, tripping on the drug, Kay's nipples had hardened and she'd quivered again with pleasure from being touched.

Aroused by that thought, he withdrew the syringe from the wadding in his shirt pocket, opened the shunt to the IV that dripped into Kay's arm, and injected belladonna.

He watched the liquid move slowly toward her vein and could almost feel the narcotic's heat surge into her body. The best part was coming up: brief convulsions followed by death and dreams as beautiful as her eyes.

"Private doctors." Kelly Harrel covered the phone and rolled her eyes at Griffin. "He's at the opera, calling in. Big shot. Only now *I'm* waiting for him while he dishes out money for his wife to buy a drink." Kelly removed her hand from the phone when the doctor came back on the line. "I'm still here." She used the sicky-sweet voice with which she mocked the pompous ones, only they never caught on.

It was pointless, really, going over vitals for the opera doc's five patients, because there was nothing wrong with any of them. Most were middle-aged women suffering a little ennui, probably in more need of a therapist or divorce than anything.

Dr. Dennison catered to the society crowd—people with money and good insurance. He'd wait until he had a handful of "lethargic" patients, then put them all in the hospital at once, kind of like a wholesale practice that charged retail rates. You couldn't make money doing hospital whistle stops for a single patient.

Dennison made Kelly Harrel repeat most of what she said, not because he was forgetful, but because lots of people he knew were walking by the pay phone in the Lyric and it made him look damned important to be engrossed in conversation.

By the time Dennison hung up, the curtain for Act Two was about to rise and he had to hustle back to his seat once everyone else had taken theirs. A few thousand people would see him and those who knew understood he'd likely been handling an emergency. Doc putting on a little show himself.

The only other meaningful event that transpired during the phone call was that Jane Doe's heart stopped beating. She was dead when Griffin and the nurse got to her room.

Against the cool concrete wall of the enclosed stairwell, the man opened his shirt and breathed deeply of stale, trapped air.

He was aroused, his penis swelling.

Kay would be dead now. He knew that. He regretted not being able to watch her die. To stare at her naked body as the convulsions took hold. It was his favorite part. Seeing them die.

He continued to draw deep breaths into his lungs until it quieted him. He had no other choice. There was no way he could go back and see her again. It was too risky. He had to fight that urge.

Control and discipline. That's what kept you from getting caught.

4.

In spite of Griffin's insistence, the on-call physician who took over Jane Doe's death in Dr. Finley's absence said there was no way a cause of death could be established tonight. No way, not tonight. Five people having died, Jane Doe making six.

Two victims of the drive-by were dead, as was another man brought in on an unrelated stabbing; a fourth had died by failing to "just say no" to an overdose of crack cocaine. Number five was a terminal leukemia patient who had finally wilted in the face of diminishing odds.

Griffin resigned himself to call it a night. Sometimes, you had to know when to stop pushing. Arguing with hospitals was one of those times. Hospitals were getting more and more like government all the time: big, sluggish, inefficient, and killing the people they were created to help.

It was twenty after eleven by the time Griffin got home.

Thirty-five years ago, the building in which Griffin and Carla owned the first floor was a single, three-story rowhouse—what they called a town house beyond Charm City. The area had been favored by a gentile class of upper-middle-class WASPs who also owned summer homes in spacious western and northern counties.

Every spring, when colorful dogwoods and azaleas

exploded in full blossom, there used to be a parade along the then-graceful street. Every city official rode in the procession, waving from the backseat of a Cadillac convertible until Kennedy was assassinated. After that, the city fathers, overestimating their own importance, grew paranoid of being shot and switched to covered sedans.

The street now only resembled antebellum days in the worn lines of its architecture. Once plentiful azaleas had become overgrown and were torn out, replaced by hardier hybrid evergreens more immune to toxic city air. When the dogwoods' roots had begun to crack the sidewalk, they'd been chopped down, their footprints covered in concrete.

The WASPs had air-conditioning installed in their summer houses and moved there full-time, selling off city properties to developers who swarmed in like greedy termites, gutting onetime elegant buildings and converting them to condos and apartments.

Griffin and Carla's building was sided in white wood with a steep red farmhouse roof and common front porch. Inside, it was quiet. Carla no doubt asleep or at least pretending to be. Griffin locked the deadbolt and crossed the living room, a modest area furnished primarily with a matching sofa and love seat of whitewashed planking fitted with cabana-stripe cushions.

The door to the second bedroom was left slightly ajar. A pale night-light cast a pleasing glow over the small room.

Griffin entered, slipped off his blazer and shoulder holster, and rolled up the sleeves to his dress shirt (the City Attorney's office, like silk-stocking law firms, imposed a dress code that strictly forbid short sleeves regardless of weather.) Griffin lifted his daughter from her crib and whispered, "I hope your day's been better than mine."

Cassie had been awake, idly considering a tropical fish mobile suspended above her crib. She was so clean and innocent in his hands, her flesh smooth and soft with powder. Seven months old, not all that small considering she'd been five weeks premature.

Griffin turned off the intercom that connected Cassie's room to Carla's. He settled into the oversized chair wedged into a corner by the window and propped Cassie on his knee. She smiled at him and made pleasant, wet sounds.

"So how've you been today? Taking care of your mommy?"

Cassie squirmed, but seemed mostly contented in Griffin's hold. Her little sounds showed no indication of turning to cries. She was a pleasant baby, seemingly unaffected by the world around her. Griffin often found that trait infectious and appreciated the relief. Especially tonight.

What bothered Griffin most was that he'd always known there would be a price to pay for his actions that night, hunting down Bright Eyes. For a while, he'd thought Carla's depression was that punishment, but maybe that wasn't enough. Maybe now, Bright Eyes himself had come to play shylock.

Griffin tried not to let his imagination carry him too far. He was good under pressure, always had been, because he was confident he could handle whatever was thrown at him. You hung in, you battled, and you won. If Cassie never learned anything else from him, he hoped she learned that.

Griffin reached for the phone. "Let's call Grandpa, whaddayou say? You wanna talk to Grandpa? Hear lies about his golf game?"

Cassie stuck an interested hand toward the phone. Griffin let her fingers play across buttons too difficult for her to push. He touched Memory-3 and the phone quickly dialed his parents' bungalow in Fort Myers, Florida. His relationship with his father was much different now than fifteen years ago.

Growing up, Griffin's trouble at home was public knowledge. His father's drunken rages often carried into the street. Wild Charlie Griffin waving his police revolver, threatening to shoot anyone who crossed him.

Griffin's sister couldn't handle it. She left when she was seventeen. Griffin not only stayed, but never said anything detrimental about his father. He'd hung in there, saw it through. His patience and understanding paid off.

His parents were now enjoying comfortable retirement in Florida. His father having been cold sober for seven years straight.

Now, Charlie Griffin answered his son's long-distance call on the second ring. A booming, gregarious hello for a man not quite six feet tall.

"How yah doing, Dad?"

"Any better I'd be dangerous. That my Cassie I hear?"

Her gurgling was more pronounced as she became entranced twisting the phone cord.

"Yeah, the one and only."

"She's a beaut. When are you going to bring her down here to see us? Mother said the other day she can't believe we move to Florida and you have a baby. All that time telling us you're not having kids, we're out of the state two years and, bingo, the grandchild we'd given up on ever having is born."

Charlie Griffin always referred to Cassie as his only grandchild even though Griffin's sister had three children. As far as Charlie was concerned, when Leslie left the family, it was as good as dying. Charlie's avoidance of alcohol didn't make him any less stubborn, just less violent about it—these days, you could disagree with him and not start a fistfight.

"Mother saw advertisements for cheap airfare the other day. You could come down and play a little golf. Mother could watch Cassie. We'd have a ball."

"We'll see."

"He says, 'We'll see,' " Charlie called away from the phone, maybe announcing this to Griffin's mom, maybe not; he had a habit of putting words in his wife's mouth. That way, it could look like she was complaining about something that was really troubling him. Whenever Charlie told Griffin, "Mother's worried about you," even though it may have been true, he really meant, *I'm* worried about you.

"Mother says, 'Uh-huh,' " his dad said after a pause.

Griffin had never known his mother to say *uh-huh* in his life. He smiled and whispered to Cassie, "Grandpa's up to his old tricks."

"Don't be telling my only granddaughter no lies." Charlie laughed. He didn't mind getting caught at his own game. An entirely different person away from alcohol. "So what's new in that old cesspool of a city you still live in?"

"New case."

"Yeah. Good one? Not just more niggers shootin' one another up like I saw in *USA Today*. Caption under this picture says Zulu warriors with spears in South Africa kill fifteen people at a funeral. I'm expecting to see jungle bunnies in war paint and loincloths, that kind of shit. Hell, picture looks like goddamned downtown Detroit, bunch of boons with T-shirts and baseball caps on sideways holding spears up in the air."

Griffin needed to move the conversation back to safer ground. No sense getting his father turfing up racial grounds. "We found a Jane Doe OD'ed in a peep-show place and no one knows who she is. There's only one entrance to the place and the guy who works there didn't see her come in."

"But the guy's a fag, right?"

"How'd you know that?"

"They're all fags running those places. Have been for years. You obviously don't hang out in the better parts of town." Charlie took a drink of something. Ice cubes rattled against glass. Years ago, Griffin's stomach would have knotted, waiting for the booze to take effect. Now, Charlie's favorite drink was powdered iced-tea mix. "So your fag working there's so busy watching the asses of all the men, he's not going to notice the last thing in the world he's interested in, which is a woman."

"Homosexual or not, he's going to notice a young woman in a porn shop."

"Probably figured she was a whore looking to do some quickies. How else's she gonna get in there unless she walks in?"

"I don't know."

"What else you got? What'd she OD on?"

"I'm still waiting for lab tests." Griffin wasn't going to mention suspicions of belladonna.

"She got needle marks?"

"None I saw. No tracks."

"Any blotter paper on her?"

"No, but someone could have taken that."

"Yeah, who?"

"Someone was with her."

"You said you didn't have any witnesses."

"When we found her she was naked . . ."

"What?" Like that was crazy.

". . . and there weren't any clothes in the booth, so I

think you'd agree even a homosexual would have seen her come in the place bare-assed."

Unwilling to lighten up on that topic, Charlie Griffin grunted, "Who knows with them pluggers."

Lose your sense of humor about the way he thinks, Griffin reminded himself, and you'll go insane.

Charlie said, "So she's in there with someone else, they do some downers, watch some video, she knocks herself out on the stuff, and the guy splits. That what you're telling me? Sounds like a B case. Why bother?" B cases were how they referred to pleasure crimes when Griffin's father was on the force. "It's an accident. Even if whoever was with her gave her the stuff, without motive you maybe get manslaughter. But probably not. Don't waste your time. Leave it to the cops. Buy a plane ticket and bring my granddaughter down here so I can see how big she's getting. All I can picture is that sweet little baby doll we saw in the hospital."

Griffin pulled Cassie to his chest. Her inconsequential weight still felt good against him. "I'll send some more pictures."

"Pictures, hell! I want the real thing."

"Say hi to Mom. I gotta go."

Charlie partially covered the phone and hollered, "Says he's gotta go." Then: "Mother says only place you gotta go is Fort Myers, Florida, to bring us our grandchild."

Griffin smiled. "Talk to you soon. Cassie says hello."

"All right. You take care, son." Charlie Griffin made sticky kissing sounds for Cassie before hanging up.

Griffin set down the phone and slouched deeper into the big chair.

After a while, with Cassie's head on his chest, soothed by his heartbeat, they were both asleep.

* * *

Half a mile away, a man in a gray uniform shirt and Orioles's cap drove west out of the city and started thinking back about the one he'd called Effie. A lithe little girl he'd done in Jamaica. How she'd been so charmed about his stories of the United States. Yeah, mon, how he was going to take her there one day. Sweet lies that encouraged her trust, and when she saw him shooting up a benign liquid he said was a new wonder drug brought down from the States, she wanted to try some.

What she got was a different syringe, one laced with belladonna. It brightened her eyes, made her stare at him so lovingly the whole time he drew the brush over her dark cinnamon flesh, layering glistening lines of oily paint that dried to a hard patina.

She'd been the first one he'd ever painted. But he'd known instantly he'd paint all the next ones as well. Little touches were powerful triggers like that. Sensory thrills. Like being back in this city, where it all started. He was very eager to reminisce and make new memories. Deciding he'd been gone too long.

5.

"I hope it's all right to call you here. Your service said you were out of town, but they didn't think it was a vacation."

The anxious voice, following the torturous ringing of the hotel phone, was more than Liz McKinley could handle at this hour of the morning—assuming it was still morning, and she couldn't swear to that.

The voice said, "I don't know if you remember me. We met about four years ago. My name's Kelly Harrel. I'm a nurse at Memorial Hospital."

Liz McKinley had no idea who this was, where Memorial Hospital was, and, until seeing the hotel logo on the memo pad beside the phone, hadn't been too damned sure where she was. Although she did now know the time: 7:27 A.M., according to the nightstand clock the Marriott kindly provided for charging outrageous rates.

"You said if I ever had a story for you there was a five-hundred-dollar finder's fee."

Liz kicked her mind into forward gear. Her publisher had upped the finder's fee to a grand—competition was tough in the tabloids—but if whoever this was would settle for five, Liz could pocket the other five for herself. Assuming there was a story.

"I was working last night—"

"Can you hold on a second, honey?" Liz asked, just

now realizing she was naked. Her inhibitions were few, but she had this thing about not being able to talk unless she was wearing bottoms. "Just a second, okay?" She set the phone down and felt below the sheet for her panties. Found them beneath whoever the guy was sleeping beside her. Liz got a good hold and gave a sharp pull; her panties came free like a tablecloth pulled out beneath dishes by a decent magician. She slipped into them and went back to the phone. "Sorry." Her usually raspy voice was further infected by sleep. "What did you say your name was again?"

"Kelly Harrel."

Liz scribbled her caller's name on the memo pad. "What've you got for me, Kelly?"

"The last time you were here, it was about three murders. Women who were killed by overdoses of belladonna."

Liz tried hard to remember. It was all a blur sometimes. So much sensationalism between then and now. "Give me a little more."

"The police found the guy who killed the women. He was Jamaican. He was convicted, but something happened after. He was out of jail and killed the prosecutor's wife and son."

Liz remembered. Baltimore Bright Eyes. Maybe only a six on the zero-to-ten gruesome scale, but a definite ten for wicked kinkiness. Very profitable. Sexual killers were a big draw in grocery store checkout lines. "Whatever happened to him?" Liz asked. "To Bright Eyes?"

"He disappeared," the nurse said, "but I think he might be back. We had a belladonna overdose last night."

"A woman?"

"Yes."

Liz became hyperactive with excitement. She had to

get to the airport, screw this story she was on. She'd buy the first available ticket on whatever would get her there fastest. "Do me a favor, Kelly, okay? Do you have a fax machine?"

"There's one I can use down the hall in—"

"I'm going to give you my editor's number. Fax him a copy of whatever coverage is in your local papers. I'll repay you for whatever the charges are."

"It's not in any of the papers."

"What?"

"The hospital's trying to cover it up."

My God, Liz thought. A scoop. She saw her headline now, bold black letters filling the front page down to the fold: OLD BRIGHT EYES IS BACK. "Where can I call you when I get into town?"

"Jimmy?" Carla Griffin rapped lightly on the door. "Jimmy, it's seven-forty-five." She didn't open the door. "Jimmy?"

Griffin pressed his forefinger and thumb into the corner of his eyes and rubbed until it stopped feeling good and started to hurt.

"Jimmy?"

"I'm awake. Thanks." Griffin was sprawled across the big chair in which he'd slept. His shirt was balled on the floor.

"Is Cassie up?"

She was in her crib, lying on her stomach, watching him.

Griffin waved at his daughter. "She's fine. Changed and fed around five-thirty. But I'll check her again."

"I got blueberry muffins at Sutton Place yesterday. Do you want one?"

"Thanks, two. And use butter—no slipping in that margarine."

As Carla turned from the door, her bare feet squeaked quietly on the hardwood floor.

Griffin stared at the door Carla hadn't opened, not even to peek in, not for a second. Some days he could almost believe it didn't bother him. Not today. It was too early in the morning to lie to himself, pretend he understood what was wrong with his wife and that the therapy was helping.

Carla was the same today as she'd been yesterday as she'd been last month as she'd been like what seemed like forever.

There had been a brief ray of hope last year. Not her old self, but Carla showed renewed affection for him. After months of being emotionally unable to have sex with him, Carla became intensely passionate. She and Griffin went to the mountains for a long weekend. Carla was tireless in bed, full of energy.

Even though Griffin suspected it was something her therapist had suggested, he'd been encouraged. Once they were home, the improvement stabilized, though he sensed it was a struggle for her.

Then Carla found out she was pregnant. One impulsive weekend after years of careful sex. Carla was devastated. They'd never wanted to have children, but had never really *done* anything about it, either.

The unthinkable word was *abortion*. The prospect hovered darkly, further clouding a strained relationship until her first trimester passed. Based on all they'd ever read about a safe time frame within which to have an abortion, the issue became moot.

Griffin was relieved, Carla, too, but he suspected for different reasons. Although she no longer attended church, Carla had been raised Catholic. Old-school Catholic, where abortion was murder. So while her unplanned pregnancy may have pitted her religion against her career, there was never really a choice.

For Griffin, he found as Carla's stomach grew, so did the idea of being a father. He'd hoped Carla would respond the same way, but by her fifth month, she was so despondent her therapist suggested she and Griffin separate for the sake of Carla's—and the baby's—health.

Griffin drew the line there. He exploded in the therapist's office. No way. No more conclusions being reached without his input and without explanation. He wanted to know what was going on. What the hell was wrong with his wife!

Carla's therapist remained as emotionless as a rag through Griffin's brief tirade. Finally telling him, "When Carla decides it's time to explain, it will be time to explain."

Nobody explained anything, but Carla hadn't moved out, either.

After he showered, there were two steam-warmed blueberry muffins waiting for Griffin on a decorative Mikasa plate. There was also a fresh cup of French Roast coffee.

The early years of their marriage had never featured such simple delicacies. Neither Carla nor Griffin came from families of "pomp and circumstance." Savoir faire was Carla's acquired taste, a postdepression phenomenon.

Griffin figured these continental breakfasts and the stylish clothes and gifts she bought him were attempts to compensate in material goods what she was unable to offer emotionally. It didn't work. Without Cassie, this would have been the loneliest time in his life, worse than all the years of his father's drinking. His only solace was maybe it was helping Carla and if she didn't get too elaborate they could afford it.

Griffin's salary with the City Attorney's office—thanks to Mickey Blane—was steps above the police department, and Carla almost matched that as a paralegal.

She'd started in a mega-lawyer firm and had been good enough to work freelance from home after Cassie's birth. In what used to be "their" bedroom, Carla set up an office, working on a computer that accessed the West-Law research database and ran a fax board to receive and send work without ever leaving the house.

Griffin was spreading a liberal pad of butter across his second muffin when Carla came into the room.

She was slender and beautiful, wearing a flower-print summer robe belted at her waist, an elegant item mail-ordered from the Victoria's Secrets catalog. The skin on her arms and legs was smooth and supple. She looked perfectly well, so desirable Griffin often had to remind himself that wasn't the case.

Today, however, there *was* a difference. Carla stood just inside the squared arch that led to the hall. She held a cup of tea securely in both hands. As she sipped her warm drink, heat steamed the thin lenses of Vittadini glasses resting on her delicate nose. She said, "You don't like it, do you?"

Griffin blinked and forced a smile. God, she'd cut her hair. Her long, glorious auburn hair. What he used to run his fingers through for hours was now a short, efficient crop of layers hugging her head like a cap. "No . . . it's fine. Really."

She retreated to her office, aware of his lie.

Griffin stared at his plate and wondered what the hell was he supposed to do.

6.

Griffin had been waiting in Mickey Blane's office for an hour by the time his friend arrived at 10:40 A.M.

As second in command, Blane had a spacious office with a good view of the city. Oak paneled walls were oiled twice yearly. The furnishings were expensive antique reproductions, uncomfortable as hell. Griffin would settle for the big cushy chair in Cassie's nursery any day.

Blane was without a briefcase; unlike the attorneys he supervised, his work didn't go home. Blane shut the door and hung his blazer on a brass hook mounted to the back of it.

Griffin was concerned to see Blane wasn't wearing his gun, but, didn't say anything. If Dunbar Waddy was back, Blane had to keep in mind there could be unfinished business on his sick mind. Bright Eyes hadn't just meant to kill Blane's wife and son; he'd wanted Blane, too.

Griffin said, "Jane Doe died last night."

"Shit." Blane rapped his desk, looked at his old friend. "Belladonna?"

"Apparently not."

"Apparently?"

"Something's wrong. I stopped by the hospital on the way in this morning. Picked up a note from Jane Doe's attending physician. Not a medical report like I'd asked for, but a note. Saying she'd died of a cerebral hemorrhage."

"But no belladonna."

"No. No belladonna."

Blane exhaled relief. "Well, that's good news, right? Something pops in her head? No belladonna so it's not him. We're okay."

"It doesn't make sense."

"Why not?"

"Because of this." Griffin flipped a copy of the crime scene team's report onto Blane's desk, their findings from the porno stall at Pussycat Licks where Jane Doe had been found. "No fingerprints."

Blane stared at the report, not reading it, but dreading it. "Goddamn it. God-Goddamn it."

Griffin sighed. "That's not the only bad news."

Blane slowly raised his eyes above the page.

"Carla cut her hair."

Blane didn't say anything until Griffin was halfway out the door. "Diana always used to fool with her hair, remember?" His stare became vacant, recalling his wife, murdered by Dunbar Waddy. "I think all women do that. They see a picture in a magazine, think if they get their hair styled to look like the model, their face and body will look like her, too."

Griffin said, "Tell me she's going to be okay. That this will all get better."

Blane hesitated just briefly enough so that when he said, "It will," Griffin knew he didn't believe it.

In another room at another Marriott, this one near Baltimore-Washington International, curtains opened to let in summer sunshine, Liz McKinley read the medical report Kelly Harrel had smuggled out of Memorial Hospi-

tal. A patient listed as "Jane Doe, pending positive identification."

Liz was going on four hours' sleep and countless cups
of USAir coffee; six hours ago, she'd been in Palm
Beach, Florida, working on a story about date rape
among the rich and famous, tentatively headlined WHEN
MONEY DOESN'T WANT TO HEAR NO. The piece had been
going absolutely nowhere; the only reason Liz had hung
with it was a hefty expense account and a variety of
available men who were pleasant reminders why she'd
never married.

Jane Doe's report was very brief. "Her heart blew,"
Liz concluded, speaking in the jargon her paper favored.
She jotted notes on hotel stationery.

"But belladonna caused the cardiac arrest." Kelly Harrel sat on a desk chair beside where Liz slouched across
the bed. She, too, was suffering from a lack of sleep.
Usually, after her third twelve-hour shift, Kelly zonked
for at least ten hours.

Leaning closer to Liz, she pointed to lab results
packed in eye-tiring lists of single-spaced lines. "This is
from blood drawn shortly after Jane Doe's admission.
Atropa belladonna: six hundred nanograms per milliliter. Now look at the postmortem. Twelve hours later.
Atropa belladonna: fifty-six-hundred nanograms per
milliliter. Eight times more." Kelly sat back. "Somebody
shot her up with a fresh dose."

Liz evaluated her source. Kelly Harrel was about Liz's
age—early thirties—old enough to shuck off youthful
naïveté and idealism and get down to life's basics before
it was too late. She kept herself well, managing the most
with a plain face and figure. Her general efficiency of
motion likely bade well on performance evaluations.

Kelly said, "But there's more to it than the overdose."

"What?"

"A couple things." Harrel folded her arms as though bracing herself. "First of all, last year, in three months, we had nine patients die from postoperative infections. That's very high. There was a panic. The media got wind of it." She shifted uncomfortably in the chair, posture tightening. "I know this is callous to say, but it was very bad for business. People were afraid to have surgery in our hospital. We were in the middle of a money crunch anyway, so it became a real problem."

Liz wondered what this had to do with Jane Doe.

"We went through everything," Harrel continued, "all our pre- and postoperative procedures. *Everything*. The hospital even hired outside consultants to review us, thinking we were missing something. Which we were, but it was a private detective working for relatives of one of the people who died that found the problem."

"Yeah . . . ?" Liz prompted.

"One of our volunteers murdered the patients. A retired nurse. And she knew how to do it. She injected bacteria into their IV tubes. There's a shunt, an access point in the line we use to inject other substances along with the drip to keep from making unnecessary skin punctures. She shot the bacteria into the IV line. There was no way to trace it and the deaths looked like normal postoperative infections. If she had only done one or two people, no one would have been suspicious. But nine?"

"You think she murdered Jane Doe?"

Kelly Harrel shook her head. "No. She's gone. That's not the point. The thing is, the private detective who found out about our volunteer last year? After settling a few lawsuits, the hospital hired him as director of security. Within an hour of Jane Doe's postmortem, he was on the hall asking questions. Wanting to know if anyone saw anything suspicious. He said his investigation was routine, but I knew why he was there. Dr. Finley assisted on the postmortem. He saw the belladonna level and reported it to security. That woman was killed in our hospital. Someone overdosed her on the same drug that caused her to be admitted."

"The same person?" Liz wondered aloud. "Bright Eyes? He hits her up once in the porn shop with belladonna, and when that doesn't kill her, comes to the hospital and whacks her with a second, monster shot."

"She got more belladonna in her somehow."

Liz was liking this large. "What about the police?"

"An investigator who was there last night came back this morning. I was still hanging around, waiting for this." Harrel held up the report. "Dr. Finley left a copy of his report for him, but the security man switched it for a note that said Jane Doe died of a cerebral hemorrhage. Natural causes."

Liz wasn't sure Bright Eyes was back for an encore—four years was a long time not to be crazy—but there was a slant she saw working into a good headline: a hospital covering up murder to keep its own skeletons from doing a telling two-step out of the closet.

Liz pointed toward the wet bar. "You want some coffee? They've got this special hot water faucet. It only does instant, but it beats popping caffeine pills."

Kelly passed.

Liz ran scalding water into a plain cup and dumped in a packet of coffee crystals. "Can belladonna be given the same way your volunteer lady injected the bacteria? Through the shunt?"

"I don't see why not. It's a liquid."

"And I assume Jane Doe was on an IV."

Harrel nodded.

Liz opened packets of sugar, lots of sugar, and stirred them into her cup.

"There was something else," Harrel said. "Jane Doe had been painted."

"Painted?"

"She had a red hexagon drawn on the front of her body. On her skin."

Oh, how sweet, Liz thought, *now* we're really getting somewhere. Even if this wasn't Bright Eyes, hexagons—devil worship stuff—really sold papers, especially in the Bible Belt. "When are you next on duty?"

"Sunday. I have four days off."

"Good. I've got a Friday deadline to make Monday's edition. So I'm probably going to have to stir the soup at the hospital to get things rolling. And I'm a really nasty cook. You might not want to watch."

7.

Griffin's office was a good place to think. The secretaries referred to it as Grif's tomb. Cozy and dimly lit. No windows. Subject to the incessant hum of an outmoded air-conditioning system the city's low bidder had bastardized to specs during a renovation fifteen years ago.

Griffin never turned on the overhead fluorescents, opting instead for a green-globe banker's lamp Carla had given him. His desk and small credenza were free of clutter, symbols of his knack for organization. On a fan-back chair he used as an informal shelf were recent copies of *The Daily Record*, the city's "lawyer's daily" that included advance sheets on recent court decisions.

Griffin stayed more current on case law than most of the prosecutors; a habit started when he was a cop, back when going to law school had seemed a real possibility, not an elusive dream.

His office personal effects were limited to a framed college diploma (B.S. in criminology from U of B) and a few pictures. Only Cassie's photo was recent. The picture of him repelling the slick face of a state park cliff was six years old. Carla's portrait, a semicheesecake glossy, had been a predepression Valentine's gift. The group snapshot was from a vacation in Aruba; everyone smiling so happily, arm in arm, a row of them: Griffin, Carla, Mickey Blane, Blane's wife, Diana, and their two-year-old, Jeremy. Carla said it was morbid for him to keep it. Griffin couldn't put it away. It meant more to him than he could ever admit.

An hour after leaving Blane's office, Griffin reviewed the Jane Doe outline he'd begun last night. What bothered him most wasn't that Missing Persons hadn't come up with her ID, or the hexagon painted on her body, but the damned lack of fingerprints.

The crime scene technicians reported no prints in certain areas of the porn stall while other sections were smeared with so many prints that identifying a single exemplar was difficult.

Wiping fingerprints clean implied criminal intent. And while it was far from a rare trick used to avoid detection, it had been part of Bright Eyes's M.O.

Before Bright Eyes's true identity had been discovered, the FBI had been called in to create a profile based on crime scene evidence. Their theory was that Bright Eyes was a peculiar hybrid: very organized, but also very emotional.

That his victims were left in areas cleaned of fingerprints led them to the hypothesis that Waddy didn't use gloves. His attraction to his victims created a compulsion to feel them with his bare hands while his analytical side provided the patience to thoroughly wipe the scene after he was finished.

In any event, in Jane Doe's case, the deliberate erasure of fingerprints didn't jibe with her dying from a brain hemorrhage. It was an accidental death in a purposeful setting. Didn't make sense at all. Maybe Dr. Finley could better explain it in person.

"Girlie, the last thing I need is some scum rag reporter running loose in this hospital."

Liz thought, Girlie? Did he actually call me *girlie*?

This overblown pile of muscle gone to flab in a brown
polyester sack of suit?

Memorial Hospital's chief of security trying to be
tough, but looking at Liz's breasts the whole time. "You
print one word of what you've just told me and your
douche bag newspaper is gonna be buried to its crossed
eyes in lawsuits."

Liz clasped her hands together. "Great. We love being
sued. It gets us on the national news. That would cost
millions in advertising. Millions. Even if you won—
which you wouldn't—it's still cheaper for us to pay
damages than buy all that airtime. So why not be a little
cooperative? I'm not trying to bust you on the Arsenic
and Old Nurse thing." Liz already had a headline for that
story: NURSE VOLUNTEER MURDERS PATIENTS. "I just want
to know about Jane Doe. That's all. You get me medical
reports and pictures, I'll go away and forget the other
story entirely." Seated comfortably in the security man's
office, behind closed doors, Liz smiled amicably. Beside
her chair, her oversized handbag contained the usual ne-
cessities: a 35mm camera and miniature tape recorder;
the recorder was on.

Rawley Jenkins glared at her. His dark eyes appeared
like slits above full cheeks and meaty jowls. He was a
big man whose presence was easily intimidating.

But Liz McKinley was not intimidated. She had an
old trick. If someone tried to muscle her, she pictured
them on the toilet straining to have a bowel movement.
An admittedly scatological thought, but it worked. The
moment she'd laid eyes on Rawley Jenkins, this six-six
hulk of age fifty or so machismo rumbling across the
threshold of his office, she'd imagined him on the john,
face red and sweating, a vein in his forehead about to
bust, that sweep of hair he combed across a bald spot
hanging over one eye. She'd almost busted out laughing.

Now, Jenkins didn't look especially happy contemplating her offer.

Liz said, "Come on, how about it, Raw?" Figuring someone had surely nicknamed him that before now, the guys he'd played high school football with, growling and spitting mud on a wet November day.

"I don't make deals, girl. You got no right to any medical records. No how, no way. And you come back on hospital property again, I'm having you arrested for trespassing. Unless, of course," Jenkins scowl deepened, "an ambulance brings you in. Then we'd be glad to have you."

If it had been Monday, even Tuesday, Liz wouldn't have minded being arrested, because ending up in jail was another good way to get free publicity. Not that she thought Jenkins would do it knowing what she had on the hospital, but Liz couldn't take the chance.

Today was Wednesday. She had a deadline coming up in less than forty-eight hours. Writing for a weekly was tough like that. Getting a scoop was all timing; if she missed Monday's edition with BRIGHT EYES IS BACK, it would be another seven days before her story hit.

To make sure Jenkins couldn't call the cops on her, Liz retreated to her rented Lincoln Continental parked across the street from Memorial's main entrance. She kept the air conditioner going and waited for Jane Doe's intern to come out.

Before her confrontation with Jenkins, Liz had talked to the head nurse on the fifth floor. She said Dr. Finley lived a few blocks from the hospital and walked home every day for lunch. She said look for a tall, young man, balding, who favored Dockers pants and walking shoes.

At quarter past one, someone fitting that description came down the wide marble steps. Liz zoomed her Canon auto-focus in on him and snapped a few shots, motor drive whirling.

Finley walked at an aerobic pace, earpieces to a stethoscope bouncing over the pocket of his lab coat. Despite warnings about addicts hoping for drugs who liked to waylay doctors, Finley always forgot to change out of hospital garb before leaving work.

Traffic was light along the tree-lined street. Liz stowed her camera and coasted the Continental along-side Finley, matching his pace. She lowered the passenger window. "Want a ride, sailor?"

Figuring only someone who knew him would make such an offer, Dr. Finley stopped and leaned down to see inside the bronze luxury car.

"Doc Finley?" Liz confirmed.

He looked puzzled, but not the least on guard, the brilliant scattered sort. No more than twenty-six and already absorbed in his own intellectual world.

"My name's Liz McKinley. I'm a reporter and I need some help on a story."

"Uh, well . . ." Finley seemed unsure how to answer. He pointed up the street. "I'm on my way home for lunch."

"I could drive you." Liz noticed Finley didn't wear a wedding band, just a Casio watch.

"It's only two blocks."

"I won't take much of your time. Five minutes?"

Finley looked up the street again.

"Three minutes?"

Finley looked her over in an unoffensive way, as though about to begin her annual physical, then conceded, "All right."

Liz was about to open the passenger door when Finley let himself in. When he leaned toward her, Liz drew back, thinking he was about to touch her, but Finley merely nodded and returned to his seat. "Air bag," he commented, having checked.

"Good."

8.

Griffin waited until Trevor Bourbin was finished in court before checking with him about Jane Doe. There was still no ID on the girl, but the National Center for Missing Children was being contacted.

As for the hexagon painted on her body, the symbol was so common to devil worship it was difficult to narrow down the possibilities. But Bourbin had talked to someone at the FBI—not mentioning belladonna, he assured Griffin—and they were going to check it out, do a little database dancing for cross references.

From his brief meeting with Bourbin, Griffin drove to Memorial Hospital. Shortly after 2:30 P.M., he was halfway up the marble entrance steps when a woman called his name.

From the street behind him, half wisecracking, "Hey, Griffin. Detective Griffin." Giving him a title he hadn't held since leaving the police department. With the City Attorney's office he was an investigator.

Griffin turned and saw her at the curb, hip leaning against a Lincoln Continental. A face and voice that presented a sense of attraction and experience. Dressed in a slinky blouse and pants.

"Come 'ere, Griffin." Something familiar about her as she waved him toward her. "But hustle it up. Bad news travels fast."

Proceeding down the stairs, shielding sun from his

eyes, Griffin tried to remember where the hell he knew her from. He had a feeling he was going to be sorry when he did.

Liz McKinley said, "I'd meet you halfway, but I'm *persona non grata* around here." Blond bangs fell into her eyes as she tilted her head toward the hospital. Liz ran a hand through her hair, mussing it. "Used to be short and auburn—thought I'd see if it was possible to have any more fun as a blonde. Jury's still out."

Griffin wondered if she'd seen a hairstyling article in a fashion magazine. Regardless, he still couldn't place her.

Liz motioned for him to get in the car. The seat was still warm from Dr. Finley; they'd only finished lunch ten minutes ago. Liz had been going over her notes when Griffin had shown. She'd snapped a few photos before alerting him. "I'm just dangerous, not armed," she said when he didn't appear eager to accept her invitation.

Griffin looked inside the car, saw a big pocketbook resting on photocopied tearsheets, the banner *America Exposed* printed atop each page. Four-year-old articles about Bright Eyes. He stared at her and, like trying to ID defendants at trial who'd changed their appearance, imagined her with different color hair, four years younger. "You're the reporter . . ." He made her sound criminal.

Liz nodded. "You want a drink? 'Cause I sure do." She got in behind the wheel and waited. After a five count, Griffin joined her, but didn't close the door until Liz said, "This's likely gonna take a while."

"It's your town," Liz said, driving south toward downtown, "you pick the bar."

Griffin didn't speak. He was reading the hospital report on Jane Doe. Seeing about the belladonna. Seeing red about being duped, but controlling it. Although he couldn't really say he was surprised. Wasn't that why he'd gone back to the hospital? Because it hadn't made sense: Jane Doe supposedly dying of natural causes in a place wiped free of fingerprints?

"It wasn't the doctor," Liz said. "I just finished talking to him. Nice kid, a little out there, but honest. Finley left a copy of the report for you. It was the security chief. Rawley Jenkins. He's the one who switched it."

Griffin muttered a quick expletive.

"I take it you know him."

"Uh-huh." Griffin sounded none too happy. "Although it's a little extreme for him to foul up a police investigation because of an old grudge. I don't even know how he found out I'm working the case . . . Then again, you do."

Liz understood that was a question, but didn't answer. "I don't think Jenkins did it because of you. But I can't say why—at least not right now."

"How come?"

"I'd compromise my source."

"But you'd tell me if it was relevant."

"Yes."

Griffin believed her, but how Liz behaved four years ago had laid a foundation for that trust.

She'd come in late on the Bright Eyes case, her rag tabloid not having been interested until they were sure they had a good serial killer on their hands. She'd dug as hard, been as aggressive as those writing for the "established" press, which was expected, but when it came time to show a little restraint, it was Liz McKinley who outshone the rest.

While the local papers and wire services had cameras pressed to Mickey Blane's face at the funeral of his wife and son, Liz McKinley held back, showing surprising respect and compassion. She stuck to the story, not the tragedy. She still got enough weepy pictures to sell papers, but her cover shot from the funeral, instead of being a close-up of a pained Mickey Blane, had been a wide angle of the two coffins just after graveside services.

Everyone was walking away, Mickey Blane in the back of the group, between Griffin and Carla, his arm around both friends for support.

Behind them, side-by-side graves, one hole so small.

About fifty yards away, Blane looked back over his shoulder, to say good-bye one last time, and *that* was the shot Liz McKinley had taken. It was haunting, empty, and cold. Blane against a background of mourners dressed in black. An image partially obscured by the same rain that cast rivulets of water over the coffins. The sorrow on Blane's face making it clear that even though he was walking away, part of him was always going to be in that field.

If Liz McKinley had been working for a "real" newspaper, she'd have won an award for that shot.

It was bright, yet cool in the atrium bar of the Hyatt Regency.

The fifteenth-floor view through bronzed glass walls was of Baltimore's famed "Rousian" Inner Harbor, a gemstone locale constantly polished by a city as its crowning image; a desperately needed revenue source to combat the budget restraints and social nightmares that threatened to throw every modern city into the abyss of bankruptcy and social melee.

This clear summer day, the harbor's calm waters were dotted with two-person paddleboats manned by tourists and AWOL office workers pretending it wasn't hot. A trio of water taxis dodged the small plastic craft, ferrying riders between points of interest.

Liz McKinley leaned back in a tub chair, separated from Griffin by a round cocktail table. Manhandling a vodka tonic, she waited until Griffin had time to review the entire hospital report before asking, "So . . . you think it's him? You think Bright Eyes did this girl?"

"I don't know. But I'd like it not to get out until I know for sure."

Liz toasted him with her quickly disappearing vodka. "That's a diplomatic way to ask me not to do a story."

Griffin sat forward, forearms resting on his thighs. He reached for his beer. "I guess that's what I am asking, isn't it? Just that you hold off until I know one way or the other."

"It's asking too much." She cut right to it, leaning closer because even empty bars had ears. "I've got one helluva scoop. Your local papers didn't get this. Which I can only interpret as the sign of a really sick society, that a naked girl in a porn shop with a hexagon painted on her isn't news. The end of civilization *is* near." Liz finished her vodka and held up the empty glass so the cocktail waitress would get the idea.

Grif said, "If you run a story, he might take off on us. If he's here, I've got a chance to get him." Appealing to her sensibilities.

"He didn't run last time and the papers were splashed with it. Lots of terror and front-page news. A couple false arrests as I recall."

"News creates that kind of pressure."

"It also makes people aware."

"It makes them panic. Every call we got about Waddy last time—and there were thousands—was a dead end. It was luck we caught him."

"So maybe this time, maybe right now, as we sit here waiting for this no-brain-in-a-short-skirt waitress to bring me another drink, some other no-brain girl's being shot up with belladonna and having Bright Eyes do his Rembrandt on her tits. And maybe she might read a newspaper and realize Mister Goodtimes is a killer."

"Then we should call the TV stations right now and let them know. Why wait for your story?"

Liz smiled. "Mmm, a man with a quick mind, how unusual." She spoke as though reporting to a third person. "Unlike the gruff and slovenly Rawley Jenkins threatening to arrest her or cause physical harm, the intrepid Detective Griffin strikes a more subtle blow, letting the reporter of a weekly grocery store sheet know if she doesn't agree to hold her story, he'll undermine her scoop by giving it to TV. The question is: is he bluffing?"

"No," Griffin assured. "As soon as your story breaks, the local media's all over it anyway, so why not give it to them now. You ruin my investigation, I'll ruin your story."

Liz sucked an ice chunk from her empty glass. "He looks like a gentleman in that spiffy suit, but behind that handsome style is the heart of an assassin."

The waitress arrived with Liz's refill.

Liz took it, winked, said, "Thanks, toots." Then, to Griffin once the girl had gone: "Always wanted to say that."

Griffin considered Liz. A pretty woman who other men would refer to as ballsy. He wondered briefly what her life was like, her work, but within seconds idle curiosity receded. "What about it? Do we have a deal?"

"Mmm, a deal, he asks." She drank less hungrily on her fresh vodka. "Usually, a deal involves an exchange of some sort. What you've proposed so far is only that *I* hold off on my story. What're *you* offering in return?"

"Not to go to the TV stations."

"Not enough. You wouldn't do that anyway. I need something from you, Griffin. I need something good."

He had something good for her all right, too good. A story about a cop chasing a Jamaican through the streets four years ago, shooting him in cold blood. "What about police records? All the notes from the old case."

"What's in there I don't already have?"

"I don't know. Neither will you unless you look."

Liz considered this. She glanced at her watch. "That buys you until noon Friday. Not quite forty-eight hours."

Griffin sighed. "It's a start."

Liz figured he didn't have to know she didn't need to file her story until Friday anyway. Besides, the police reports might not contain anything new for her, and she'd made enough deals in her time to know you only traded for a sure thing, you didn't want Monty Hall's Door Number One or the box beside Carol Merrill.

Griffin finished off his beer. "Where are you staying? I'll drop the reports off."

Liz looked around the atrium bar, appraising its ambiance. "My stuff's at the Marriott out by the airport, but I think I'll move here. Be a little closer to the action."

"Ten o'clock tonight okay?"

"Sure. Bring it up to my room. We'll have more drinks."

Griffin pushed out of the tub chair and stood. "I'll leave it at the desk. I know too many people in this town."

Liz looked up at him, innocence with sweet vodka breath. "Meaning?"

"Somebody sees me going into a woman's hotel room, they figure something's going on."

"Fine. We'll leave the door open. Let them see for themselves . . . I don't mind being watched."

Not unappreciative of the offer, Griffin said, "I'll

leave the stuff at the desk." He set one of his City Attorney cards on the table. "If you need to get in touch, try the office first, then the beeper, then home."

As he walked away, Liz said, "You know it's just a wedding ring, Griffin, not an anchor." She tried to remember the last faithful married man she'd known. Couldn't do it. So maybe Griffin had somebody else on the side. That was the strange thing about men: they'd be loyal to their girlfriends, to hell with their wives. One of many reasons Liz preferred being the girlfriend.

9.

On the street, not to his face, they called Jack Karupka "The Kroop." His office *was* the thirty-fifth—and top— floor of The Harbor Tower, a modern beauty designed to inspire the city skyline; which made it ironic The Kroop had his office there. Triangular architectural lines sent the upper seven floors jutting into the sky like a spike atop a base twenty-eight levels of strong chrome and glass.

The Kroop was a lawyer, but he didn't go to court, didn't file pleadings, hadn't cracked a law book in ten years. The Kroop was the kind of lawyer you saw if you wanted to get something done, and you understood and appreciated that *really* getting something done rarely had anything to do with the court system.

Still, Michelle Aronson thought $50,000 was a lot of money to pay a man she'd never met before. Especially since he didn't look like she'd expected.

Karupka was fifty-two, articulate, and well mannered with a lean strong build inherited from maternal Austrian heritage. Someone who'd look perfectly at home with front-row orchestra seats. The Kroop's appearance was very distinctive, with his intelligent facial bones, and coarse salt-and-pepper hair trimmed to a uniform half inch over his entire scalp.

"Frankly, Miss Aronson," Karupka said softly, calling her Miss even though she was married—he'd never got-

ten into the *Ms.* business, "you can have it done for fifty
dollars. I'm not kidding. You can walk out of this office,
turn two corners, and—you know the right person—
hand them the money, you've got yourself a deal."

Karupka shrugged, an easy, genuine motion. There
was still enough StreetSpeak in him to show he hadn't
always been this flush. "Who knows, they pull it off,
you've got a winner. But you don't approach the right
individual—you approach a cop or someone who knows
your husband—I think you see the picture. And, maybe
again, somebody just takes your fifty dollars and you
never see them again. Unless they call you on the phone
or stop by your house to demand another fifty—maybe a
hundred this time—to keep from telling the police, or
your husband, what you asked them to do."

Michelle Aronson sat across from Karupka wearing a
Dolce & Gabbana blouse and skirt, and Manolo Blahnik
heels. A stunning thirty-two-year-old woman who didn't
need five strings of Japanese pearls dipping into her
cleavage, a pricy coiffure and makeup application, or
wrist of gold bracelets to look good. Those were just
bold accessories to make what was already enviable
even more so.

Being here with Karupka, after months of waiting,
Michelle found herself surprisingly at ease. She thought
this would be difficult—that she would at least be nervous.
Maybe her mind was more made up than she thought. She
did want the bastard dead, didn't she? Wasn't that what
she'd spent hundreds of hours telling her friends, her
mother, anyone who would listen, even the people who'd
warned her not to marry Greg in the first place?

A divorce would have been okay; Michelle had tried
that first, but Greg had a superslick lawyer. Michelle's
first lawyer had been a wimp who, it turned out, hated
women and was maybe even a closet homosexual; her

second lawyer wasn't much better. Seeing she was about to get royally screwed on the divorce settlement, Michelle had seen no alternative than to move back in with Greg. Which she'd done. In separate bedrooms now, but Greg had the key to her door and came in whenever he liked, *did* whatever he wanted, and told her not to scream.

Greg also had two million in assets he'd successfully hidden from Michelle's other lawyers, making it look like he and Michelle were living a grand lifestyle on credit. He claimed they didn't own anything, and if she wanted to split, that was fine, she could have half the bills.

"The problem, Mr. Karupka," Michelle said, "is that I don't have fifty thousand dollars to pay you right now. My husband does, but I—"

The Kroop held up his hand. "Sometimes there are simple procedures; sometimes they are more complex. I know how much money your husband has, Miss Aronson. I know where he keeps it."

That surprised the hell out of Michelle.

"I also know he's abused you and should pay for it. We can worry about the money after. Right now, you want to make sure your husband is not only out of the picture, but taken out in the right way. Given the heat your divorce generated, reconciliation notwithstanding, you obviously have motive. The police will come to you, which is why it has to be done carefully, in a way you will never be suspected." The Kroop let the importance of that point linger. "For example, maybe you should take a vacation. Alone. A monthlong cruise. Do you like the Caribbean? Jamaica? It's one of my favorite places."

In dim office light, Michelle detected a thin smile across Karupka's lips. "And when I get back from this vacation . . . ?"

"Before then, you may get a call, perhaps while in

Ocho Rios, that something terrible has happened to your husband."

Michelle Aronson felt as though the deed had already been done.

"The one thing you remember," Karupka advised. "Murders mean business. It's not something that happens and you get over it. You live with it. That means, no matter how it happens, what happens, you have to be prepared for the worst."

She didn't understand. "You said I wouldn't get caught."

"You won't. You'll be away clean with three-point-five million dollars. *That's* how much your husband is really worth, Miss Aronson. But to make that kind of money, there is always a price. You have to be willing to pay that price."

She hesitated, but only briefly, not long enough to be considered evidence of doubt. "Whatever happens to him, I can live with it."

Karupka leaned back in his leather seat. The chair's mechanism didn't make a sound. "I'm not talking about what happens to him."

Jack Karupka's beginnings in the legal profession had not been celebrated. He took a year off after college for a shoestring tour of Europe, then began law school courtesy of a low-interest student loan. His academic career was middle of the road, but back then you didn't have to be *Law Review* to get a decent job.

Karupka started with a small downtown firm where everybody did a little bit of everything, no specializing like today. He got his feet wet on criminal trials before moving into personal injury work.

Most of his cases were straightforward. If Karupka sensed a client was trying to play a little Whiplash

Willie, he dumped them. For a couple years, other lawyers made decent fees on the frauds Karupka threw away. They said Jack Karupka didn't know how to "work" a PI case, didn't know how to sweat insurance companies. Sure, you'd get beat on a couple losers that ended up in front of a jury, but most times if you hung tough, like playing a bad poker hand, the insurance company would fold right before trial.

Karupka didn't want that kind of reputation. The head of the firm, Gerry Zimmerman, believed that, too. A lawyer was nothing more than his name with judges, other lawyers, clients, the media if you were lucky enough to get some ink. "Don't be associated with losers," Zimmerman lectured, so he didn't mind Karupka dumping whiplash cases some shyster was going to end up settling for four or five grand.

Insurance adjusters, tightfisted folks assigned to settle claims out of court, also knew Karupka's reputation. That he wasn't a bullshitter. So most of Karupka's cases settled within a few months of final medicals instead of two or three years after haggling, lying, and going to trial with a dog.

But then along came Samuel Edmonds, a city bus driver who got broadsided by a drunk driver back before it was socially unacceptable to be tanked up behind the wheel. It was a nasty crash, no question about liability: Edmonds had been in the right, it was the drunk's fault.

For all the busted glass and bent metal in the wreck, Edmonds didn't seem that badly hurt. Wasn't even admitted to the hospital the night of the accident. Was treated for bumps and bruises and released.

Two weeks later, feeling a little better, but nagged by increasing pressure in his back, Edmonds was driving to work. It would have been his first day back. His wife, who Edmonds was going to drop at her department store job, was in the passenger seat.

On the interstate, Edmonds, without any history of medical problems, suffered a vicious back spasm. His entire right side locked. He lost control of the car and smashed into a concrete dividing wall at fifty miles per hour.

His wife died in the crash. Edmonds lost a leg and his right eye. His own insurance was only the state required minimum, so once they paid him off—then canceled him— Samuel Edmonds was looking at the rest of his life on one leg, with one eye, only a tenth of his medical bills paid, and nothing left for rehabilitation.

That wasn't what ticked Karupka. It saddened him, but beyond cursing fate, the second accident was a closed chapter. It was the first accident.

When the drunk's insurance company learned of Edmond's second accident, they denied that injuries suffered by Edmonds at the hands of their client could have contributed to the second accident in any way. How could it? they pretended to believe. Because after being hit by their insured, Edmonds had been okay. Who knew why his back went into a spasm. Maybe he'd done something around the house. It could have been anything.

Could have been, Karupka thought, but wasn't. The insurance company knew that, too. So did their adjuster, a smart ass named Levrebre. Only Levrebre was leading the office's annual pool to see who could settle their cases for the least money and wasn't about to have his lead ruined by Samuel Edmonds.

Karupka found out Levrebre lived in town, went to a certain strip bar every Wednesday—amateur night—to watch women from the audience get up on stage. A weasel, Karupka thought as soon as he saw Levrebre that night in the club.

Levrebre sat up front, drank cheap beer, yelled and screamed too much. When Levrebre went to the bathroom, Karupka followed him. There was one other guy in the john. Levrebre stepped up to the urinal, made a big production about unzipping his pants, how it was hard to get his "big boy" out once the ladies had him riled up.

Karupka relieved himself two stalls away.

The other guy in the john flushed the toilet and left.

Levrebre had a little trouble peeing, finally got a stream started when Karupka moved behind him, said, "I'm Jack Karupka. Samuel Edmonds's lawyer."

Levrebre got nervous, pretended he didn't know what Karupka was talking about. A real tough guy on the phone, but not so tough in person.

"Six months," Karupka said. "You've been jerking me around six months. And I don't appreciate it."

"Hey, man, hey." Levrebre didn't have *any* trouble getting his johnson back behind his zipper, even dribbled a little on the front of his pants. He turned to face Karupka with both hands up, palms exposed in a gesture of surrender. "It's a job, you know. Don't take it personal." He glanced anxiously toward the door, hoping someone would come in.

"Yeah, you see, that's where you're wrong. It's not a job. It's this guy's life." Karupka grabbed Levrebre's collar, surprising him with his strength. "Samuel Edmonds got no money, no job, no insurance. He's lost his house, living on food stamps—"

"Maybe we can do something." The guy started trembling.

"You could've done something five months ago, schmuck."

"Hey, I didn't know, okay. Now we'll do something. Tomorrow morning—"

Karupka shoved him against the urinal, smacking him against hard porcelain.

Levrebre grimaced as ribs cracked, but was too scared to feel the pain just yet. "Please, man, please."

"Tomorrow morning you might think this was just a fluke, maybe I'm a little drunk, had a bad day. You might take the chance and jerk me off some more, figure our paths will never cross again. Which is why I'm telling you I know you live at four-five-seven Arcada Avenue. That your wife drives a green Buick four-door and your daughter goes to kindergarten at—"

"Please, man, please, don't hurt my family." Levrebre shook violently. The front of his pants became sopping wet as urine he hadn't been able to spend into the toilet trembled from his bladder.

"I'm not gonna hurt your family," Karupka promised. "I'm gonna hurt you." He hit Levrebre square in the face, snapping his head back against the tile wall. Let him drop unconscious to the floor, losing three teeth Karupka had loosened with his fist when he landed face-down.

Karupka wiped the man's blood off his hand on a paper towel and left the club.

A week later, when Levrebre returned to work, the first call he made was to Jack Karupka, settling Samuel Edmonds's case for the policy limits. A half of a million dollars.

That was the day Jack Karupka realized what it took to be a successful lawyer. He'd been getting better ever since.

10.

Mickey Blane had left the office for the day. Griffin, using a lobby payphone in the Hyatt, should have known better. For Blane to be at work two days in a row past four o'clock would have been a record.

Griffin tried Blane's car phone, struck out there, and managed no better than an answering machine at his friend's condo. He would have rather delivered the bad tidings about Jane Doe in person, but there was too much else to do. "The news I got this morning from the hospital . . ." he told Blane's machine, ". . . scratch it. Call me when you get in. Beeper until eleven. Home after that."

Outside in the heat, Griffin started walking until he spotted a squad car parked near Water Street. He showed his City Attorney's badge and had a patrolman with whiskey on his breath take him up to Memorial Hospital.

The cop, Corporal Mackey, was about Griffin's age, with a rubber face and potbelly, no doubt beginning to look like his father years ahead of schedule. Exchanging small talk, Mackey spoke cautiously toward his window as though aware of the alcohol on his tongue.

Griffin sat up front to better observe Mackey's driving, wanting to make sure the street cop had only helped himself to one shot from a flask, not two or three. He seemed fine.

At Memorial's side entrance, Griffin thanked Mackey

for the ride, said, "Take it easy on the Jack Daniel's, okay?"

Thankful there wasn't going to be anything more to it, Mackey apologized. Said it was just a miniature a store owner slipped him as thanks for keeping an eye on his place.

Griffin didn't really think about how he'd just had a beer himself until he was inside the hospital. Funny how it was always the other guy's drinking that was a problem.

Memorial Hospital's Security Chief, Rawley Jenkins stood at the fifth-floor nurses' station looking over a computer printout of yesterday's duty roster.

"Anybody see who did it?"

Jenkins turned abruptly. Seeing Griffin, he was about to say something nasty, but realized where he was. Lots of people bustling around, but no one too busy to miss an argument. And Jenkins *was* trying to low-profile this mess. He gestured Griffin to the elevator, and Griffin nodded.

Jenkins exchanged hellos with two suited women on the elevator, not speaking to Griffin until they were alone. "Looks like I can't fucking get away from the Griffin family no matter how hard I try. Your old man almost gets me killed fifteen years ago. Makes me wonder what I can expect from you."

"I got a copy of the report you tried to keep from me."

Jenkins's jaw tightened so hard it looked like his molars might explode. When the elevator opened to the first floor, Jenkins exited abruptly between doctors and visitors.

Griffin was half a step behind, their conversation once again on hold. They proceeded to Jenkins's office, passing Jenkins's secretary without so much as a nod.

Jenkins closed his inner-office door. Arms crossed, he leaned against the front corner of his desk. "Sit down." He nodded to the chair in front of him, wanting Griffin positioned where he could loom over him. Body language intimidation.

Griffin remained standing. He rested his hands on the back of the chair Jenkins wanted him sitting in.

Wide venetian blinds kept out late afternoon sun. A lack of accessories and style made Jenkins's office little better than an interrogation room.

Griffin said, "Somebody murdered Jane Doe in her bed."

"You don't know that for a —"

"Your intern *thinks* she was murdered."

Jenkins muttered, "That little prick."

"He's not going to do anything to cross you. Apparently the kid knows his politics."

Jenkins grunted approval.

"Can't say the same for me. I need to talk to your staff."

Jenkins shook his head. "Nobody saw anything."

Griffin pinpointed his interest. "I want to know if they saw a particular person."

Jenkins stopped for a moment. "You've got a suspect?"

"Maybe."

"Somebody who works here?"

"I don't know, but I wouldn't think so."

Jenkins's shoulders relaxed with a tinge of relief. "So who is it?"

Griffin shook his head. "I can't afford a leak to the media. The fewer people who know, the better my chances are."

"Well, I think that chance is already pissed. A reporter was in here. From one of those rumor rags full of dead

Elvis sightings and self-motivational bullcrap for ugly broads."

"I've talked to her," Griffin assured. "We've got a deal."

"Hell, a deal." Jenkins moved behind his desk. He pushed open slats of venetian blinds and peered out into the sun. "That's what makes this town go around, isn't it? Deals?"

"Maybe it used to." Griffin thinking back to the days his father and Jenkins hoofed a beat, busting heads, doing God knows what else. Retired guys now who thought their way had been better—crime had been lower, hadn't it? Missing the big picture how the world was changing.

Still looking outside, Jenkins said, "So whaddayou want?"

"To talk to the staff. Check your visitor records. Show a picture around."

"And I can't do that?" Jenkins was clearly uncomfortable with the prospect of the police—albeit a City Attorney investigator—in his domain. "Or," he closed the blinds, "is it that you don't trust me? Because of your old man?"

"I got no personal gripe with you, Rawley. What happened between you and my father is old news."

Jenkins sat down with some effort, showing age. "Not to me it's not. It's my news every day. I got a bullet that far from my spine," he measured off an inch with his fingers, "because your old man was supposed to be backing me up but didn't. I didn't fucking walk right for almost a year. Department outted me on disability an ant couldn't live on. I ended up doing PI work, trying to catch husbands and wives cheating on one another. Fuckin' dog work. Sleeping in cars while two people so ugly no one should've married 'em in the first place are shaking the sheets in some twenty-dollar motel. Now this." He opened his arms as though preparing to catch a huge beach ball, the gesture indicating the close walls of his office. "Thirty-five-nine, plus benefits. On the force I'd've had closer to sixty as a captain by now."

"I'm sorry."

Jenkins dropped a thick hand wearily on his desk. Feeling sorry for himself was an old tune he'd long grown tired of singing. "Ah, fuck it." He rotated his head slightly, grimacing as his neck loosened. "At least you don't look like your old man. You're lucky."

Griffin suppressed the urge to defend his father. There was another side to the story Jenkins had just told, but now was not the time to raise it. Not when Griffin felt close to getting what he wanted from a man who was, by history, a supposed enemy.

Jenkins said, "So who's this suspect you got? Why the big secret?" When Griffin didn't reply, Jenkins grumbled. "Hmph. Must be good." Then he laughed. "Not your boss, is it? That yutz Dickie Marish. Talk about wackos."

Griffin wondered if Jenkins's need to keep Jane Doe's murder quiet was on par with his own orders to keep the case under wraps. Maybe letting Jenkins in was the only way to be sure nothing was held back. He decided to take the chance. If nothing else, Jenkins could save Griffin a day's worth of investigation. Questioning the staff would be a time-consuming process. And Mickey Blane had told him to be quick about this investigation.

Griffin now sat in the chair Jenkins had originally pointed him toward. "You remember the guy who killed Mickey Blane's family?"

Jenkins rubbed the back of his neck. "Yeah. Some spook. On trial for killing those women. Did 'em with drugs and . . . Christ." He started looking through Jane

Doe's records on his desk. "He did 'em with—what's it called?"

"Belladonna."

"Belladonna," Jenkins confirmed quietly. He exhaled and sat back. "Goddamn, I knew it sounded familiar, but all these fucking medical terms, they all tend to get mixed up . . ." His sentence trailed off, replaced by new understanding. "That guy was the biggest crime and trial in a decade. Your case."

Griffin nodded.

"People in the department think you fucked up. Word was you had an informant tell you where the guy was but you never followed up."

Griffin didn't flinch.

Jenkins considered Griffin for a long time, taking an interrogator's pause. "Something happened, didn't it? Your father was a pissass cop, but you were a good one. Something went down and you got the blame." When Griffin didn't respond, Jenkins smiled for the first time all day. "Christ, you are cold when you want to be, aren't you, boy?"

Griffin remained stoic. Another reason he wanted Rawley Jenkins's help was, in spite of the guy's impudent personality, he'd been a streetwise cop.

Jenkins nodded. "Whaddayou want me to do?"

11.

Griffin let the phone ring in case Carla was busy with Cassie. It was almost five forty-five P.M., when he usually called if he was going to be late or miss dinner, which he was about to tell her now if she'd only pick up the—

"Hello." Carla was breathless.

"Hey. It's me."

"Jimmy, hi. I'm sorry, I just got in the door."

"Everything okay?"

"Fine."

She resented him asking that, Griffin could tell. She didn't like questions about how her day was going, as though it was pressuring her to get better. But, hell, he didn't mean it that way. It was more a rhetorical how-yah-doing? How come every question had to be such a loaded issue?

Carla asked, "Did you try to call earlier? I thought I heard it ringing."

"No. I waited because there was a chance I could sneak home for dinner." Which he'd still do if she showed any enthusiasm for the idea. No chance.

Carla sounded relieved. "That's okay, I understand."

Cops he still kept in touch with on the force asked him how long he was going to put up with his wife acting this way, that if *their* wife did this to them she'd be out on her ass. Griffin telling them he was good at putting up with trouble, a damned professional.

Griffin said, "If Mickey calls before I get home, tell him to beep me. I left a message on his machine, but you know how he is with returning messages."

"I was going to call him anyway. What would you think about having him over for dinner tomorrow night?"

"Good. Yeah, real good. Just tell him to leave his damn baby boomer Trivial Pursuit at home. Tell him we all didn't have so much time to watch TV growing up. He's murder on those *Leave It to Beaver* questions."

Carla laughed. A sign of life Griffin cherished. Sometimes when they got together with Mickey it was like old times, the three of them carrying on in high school. Blane the rich kid with the snazzy car. Cheerleader Carla. Griffin the semistar jock. A strange chemistry that had improved with age.

"Tomorrow," Griffin said, "I'll make sure I get work finished in time. No excuses."

"You won't surprise us being late."

Jack Karupka, a/k/a The Kroop, didn't keep regular office hours, but had a tendency to work well into the night. His secretary—who spent most of her nine-hour day alone in an office nearly as plush as Karupka's—headed home promptly at five-thirty. Which meant Karupka had the thirty-fifth floor all to himself.

Only fifteen hundred square feet was finished office space. The remainder was Karupka's gym, spa, and running track; There was also a gourmet kitchen, where The Kroop sometimes cooked for himself, other times he had a chef he'd met in the islands come in and fix dinner for them both.

Since his divorce, Karupka's relationship with the chef, Connie Davis, was as domesticated as he cared to be.

Wednesday night, however, Karupka didn't eat dinner. He was intent on several pending "cases," giving extensive thought to what was always the most difficult issue: finding dependable talent to do the work.

In the beginning, it had been easy. Karupka represented a wide assortment of criminal clients, a pool of prospective players who owed him money and would be glad to work off their debt in trade. In fact, establishing this type of relationship with his clients—becoming one of their own—increased Karupka's already strong stature among them. Especially when Karupka started his own one-man firm. There was a sense of family, defendants figuring Karupka wouldn't want them to go to jail because he needed them on the outside.

Over time, however, as the world grew more complicated, what needed to be done became equally complex. Finding that right twist of intelligence and savagery was a real chore. It also cost more money.

About the time the Berlin Wall came down, Karupka had a run of success with former East bloc intelligence officers, soldiers on the run, afraid of being sold out as their home country flirted with democracy. But, God, those commies loved the vodka; some of them dove into the bottle so deeply, Karupka had become a near expert at alcohol rehabilitation. He even kept an apartment in the city to dry them out.

Karupka was still mentally reviewing his inventory of talent for new jobs as he packed up for the day. Got into the private elevator that wasn't supposed to be private, but Karupka had a passkey that brought it straight up to his floor and took him to the underground garage.

He needed someone for Michelle Aronson's husband. That was going to be easy money. Because Greg Aronson had assets of five million, not three and a half. Judging from Michelle's expression when he'd told her about the three and a half, and that the hack lawyers she had before hadn't been able to find that much, Karupka was going to end up with his fifty thousand fee, *plus* the one and a half mil he wasn't going to tell her about. What they called a "silent fee" in the old days, rerouting clients' money they never knew they had.

Karupka envisioned some kind of accident for Greg Aronson. A quirk of fate. Aronson's habit was to stop at a particular convenience store for coffee in the morning. Karupka could have his man waiting there, make it look like a botched robbery, blow Aronson away.

He'd almost settled on that when the elevator doors opened to the lower garage level, most of the other cars already gone for the day. And there he was, leaning against the hood of Karupka's big Mercedes.

Karupka remained by the elevator.

The man smiled; an expression that was often captivating.

The Kroop didn't blink. "You're not supposed to be here."

"It's a quick trip. In and out. Limited purposes."

"It's not good. Not good at all."

When the man shrugged in reply, Karupka knew there was no reasoning with him. The calm, psychotic ones were the worst. So damned impertinent.

"Well," Karupka replied as though accepting the situation, "we may as well have a drink. Let's go up." He withdrew the elevator passkey from his pocket. An accomplished sailor, Karupka knew sometimes the only way to handle the wind was to go with it.

In the wood-paneled elevator, Karupka could smell the man's sweat, and it was tinged with a killer's adrenaline. Evidence of arousal driven by murder long after the deed was done. "Was she anyone that'll make the news?" Karupka asked, sensing he'd already killed another one.

The man watched the floor indicator rise quickly toward thirty-five. Around the twenty-first floor, he said, "No. Just a runaway."

The city stored its police records in the musty basement of the Central District Building. After years of budgetary battles, back cases were finally being placed on microfiche. It wasn't that someone had seen the light about the benefits of film and rapid retrieval over paper and disorganization, but that the microfilm company had agreed to kick back enough money to a city manager to make the deal happen.

Equipment purchased, the process continued to be a race against time. Now the city didn't have funds to hire a clerk to put the old criminal records on microfilm. Because it was either a new clerk *or* a new judge—not both. And since the judge had taken five years of indecisive cocktail parties for the Court of Appeals to approve, it was a judge the city was going to get.

Pending a "microfilm technician," tens of thousands of dollars' worth of equipment and film rapidly approaching expiration sat in the same mildewing basement as the court records they were meant to document.

Griffin used the entrance to Central District marked PERSONNEL ONLY, signed the after-hours log, and went down to the records basement.

The area was an OSHA violation waiting for an inspector intrepid enough to venture into the building's claustrophobic bowels. The ceiling was low and packed with fluorescent lights, the exposed tubes of which flickered weakly. Narrow rows of metal standing shelves ran the length of the room without interruption. The air was hot and tasted as wet and old as the building itself.

Griffin removed his suit jacket, but not finding a clean place to hang it, put it back on.

He already had a case number—obtained from the City Attorney's office—so he bypassed crusty index books and proceeded directly to R-Kive boxes stacked two deep and not necessarily in precise numerical order (counting wasn't a prerequisite to work in the court system).

After a few misses, he found the right box, figured there was a fifty-fifty chance the Dunbar Waddy file would be inside. He removed the dusty top and saw he was in luck. He stared for a few beats at the label, WADDY, DUNBAR W., then took a breath and withdrew the thick folder, placed it inside a fresh accordion file, and smuggled it out of the building.

Like an asymptomatic patient diagnosed with a disease, Griffin found himself anticipating the onset of pain.

Griffin ran pages of Dunbar Waddy's police file through the photocopying machine in the darkened City Attorney's office. Reviewing his old notes for the first time in four years affected him like seeing family pictures taken months before a tragedy struck; perfectly innocent snapshots made haunting by subsequent events.

Into the photocopier's sheet feeder went crime scene pictures he'd tried to forget—Mickey Blane's Diana and Jeremy.

Four years ago, Griffin's own eyes had seen what these pictures captured; it was what made him decide to kill a man. To cleanse the horror.

Since then, he'd lived with the guilt of having done it.

A man with a conscience living in a savage world. At times, maybe more often than he could honestly say, he regretted what he'd done.

Now, looking at these photographs, he wondered if he'd do it again.

12.

The Hyatt had a small lobby bar in case any of its guests couldn't wait out a two-minute elevator ride to the larger atrium lounge. For the convenience, the cost of sucking down a vodka tonic at ground level was no more exorbitant than fifteen floors up.

Luckily for Liz, her expense account considered alcohol a reporter's necessity. Although Liz didn't drink in order to work; she drank because she liked it, had from the first time she'd sipped the stuff at a high school party.

By the time she was seventeen, she could pick the most sophisticated of locks to friends' parents' liquor cabinets. And, in the process, discovered an early interest for nosing into other people's business.

A party in someone's house when their parents were gone was like Christmas to Liz. She'd steal off with her drink, wander into Mom and Dad's bedroom, and skillfully go through drawers and closets to see what kind of neat stuff was stashed away.

Her favorite discoveries were drugs—marijuana and quaaludes back then—and pornography, usually pre-video 8mm, Polaroids, and mail-order magazines. But it wasn't only her prurient interests that enjoyed being fed; her natural curiosity ran high. She wanted to know what kind of clothes someone wore or what kind of books they read. Jewelry was fun. Diaries like gold.

Liz always liked the side of a person you didn't see in public much more than the "face" they put on to address the real world.

Maybe this made her a natural reporter, maybe a natural snoop. Either way, she loved her job, didn't mind writing for a paper that was admittedly trashy, in fact, felt more honest about it.

All newspapers had sleaze running through their blood; some were just less covert about it. Hell, everyone knew what really sold. What was so wrong with that? Liz would rather read something that was fun as opposed to squinting at that damned tiny print in the *Washington Post,* pretending to be interested in news articles duller than medieval history. Face it, poll one hundred people and all would rather know what really happened the night Teddy Kennedy thought his car was a boat instead of the Democrats' latest position on Medicare.

Tonight, drinking in the lobby bar with a view of the front door, Liz waited for Jimmy Griffin to arrive with his part of the deal: the police reports. She watched other hotel guests come and go in the meantime, played mental games with herself, making up stories about where they were from, who they were staying in the hotel with, and was it someone they happened to be married to.

She wondered how many times she was right guessing from looks. Probably more often than not; amazing how many times you *could* judge books from their covers.

Griffin finally arrived a little after ten, a look of purpose about him, a substantial folder tucked under his arm. Liz hadn't planned on talking to him, just watching, doing her voyeur game. But as Griffin turned toward the front desk, Liz found herself drawn to him.

Griffin was a tough "cover" to call, more intriguing today than four years ago.

Telling the bartender she was going for her friend—not skipping on her tab—Liz started across the lobby. Wearing a tight top and leather pants; her cheap bar-girl look. Liz came up behind Griffin.

He turned just as she was upon him. A much different look in his eyes than earlier. A quiet rage burning, borderline out of control. Yet still so contained on the outside. Liz's favorite kind of man, the kind who held it all in; they were so much fun to watch explode.

"Drink?" she invited, motioning toward the bar. "I've already got one going."

"Don't do that here," Griffin said.

Liz started unwrapping the elastic strap that held tight the accordion folder. "My room then?"

"As soon as I leave."

The bartender came over to Liz and Griffin. They sat at one of five cocktail tables nestled inside a court formed by faux marble planters stocked with ferns. Save a businessman at the bar who'd made eyes at Liz before Griffin's arrival, they were the only patrons.

"Beer?" Liz asked Griffin. "It's on me."

"Seven-Up, Sprite," Griffin said, "whichever you've got."

"How'm I going to get you drunk on that?" Liz saw from Griffin's expression that had been the wrong thing to say.

The bartender, waiting to see if Griffin was going to change his order, nodded and withdrew when he didn't.

Diverting the conversation from her apparent opening glitch, Liz referred to the folder as she set it by her feet. "Anything good?"

"Depends on what you already know." Griffin appeared uncomfortable in the small upholstered chair, restless and distracted.

Liz sensed something had happened, maybe something new with the case. "So how was your afternoon?" An innocent probe, hoping he'd volunteer something good.

"My afternoon?"

"Did you see 'Raw' Jenkins?"

Griffin nodded.

"And?"

"We're working it out."

Liz smiled sarcastically. "Do you want to talk about this later, or is this the kind of conversation we're going to have from here on in?"

Griffin was surprised by her accusatory tone, which confirmed to Liz he wasn't entirely "here." It would be natural for him to be tired after working all day, but he seemed alert, intense even, far from fatigued. He just wasn't paying attention to *her* and that was annoying, as though by giving her the file, he was brushing her off.

"Did something happen today?" Liz pressed. "A new lead? Another body?" Wondering if she could be that lucky.

"No."

"Are you being straight with me? I don't want . . ." Liz stopped when Griffin grabbed the folder beside her feet. She thought he was taking it back, but he roughly opened it, pulled out one of the stacks of clipped pages, copies of crime scene photographs.

Flipping to one taken in a living room. A woman tied to a chair, her neck slumped forward, blood all over the front of her blouse from where her throat had been slit. On the floor in front of her, the body of a small boy in another pile of blood. Her son. His head five feet from his neck, positioned peculiarly on its side, which was how it had stopped rolling.

Liz was shocked. These pictures had never been released to the public.

"They were my friends." Griffin's words were harsh,
spoken quietly. "My best friend's wife and son."

Liz was still staring in horror as Griffin abruptly
stuffed the papers back into the file. Her voice was so
tightly squeezed in her throat, Griffin never heard her
apology.

He was already on his feet, heading for the door.

When the bartender brought over Griffin's drink, Liz
slugged it down, thinking—hoping—it was a triple
vodka. The sugary soda choked her. She coughed and
spit it out over the front of her. By the time she'd cleared
her throat, there was intense pain in her chest.

The man who'd been watching her from the bar came
over and asked if she was all right. Liz thanked him,
then saw all he was really interested in was if the spilled
soda had gotten her top wet enough to make it stick to
her breasts. She told him to go screw himself, grabbed
the folder, and went up to her room.

A bottle of Tanqueray with two bottles of mixer was
fifty-four dollars from room service. She told them to
hurry it up.

He quietly opened the door to the bedroom.

Carla Griffin was asleep beneath a thin sheet that lay
along the curves of her body. Her bare arm and shoulders, one slender ankle, and a gracefully shaped foot
protruded from the bedcover.

Streetlights shone in through uncovered transom windows inset above the French doors. Indirect light cast the
entire room in an even pale glow.

When Carla had redesigned the bedroom, planning to
work out of the house, the back wall had been bowed out
to create space for her workstation. Griffin hadn't liked

the idea of so many windows and the French doors—glass wasn't secure—but Carla wanted a view of the brick-walled garden she tended outside. She refused to be made a prisoner of the city.

She wasn't as cautious now as she had been before Diana and Jeremy were murdered. Griffin worried about that. Part of his amateur psychoanalysis wondered if Carla was *trying* to subject herself to the type of violence Diana and Jeremy had suffered. Punishing herself.

Or was that Griffin's imagination torturing him? Another manifestation of *his* guilt. How could what happened to Mickey Blane's family have had anything to do with Carla?

Besides, such self-endangerment would surely have come out in her therapy. Her counselor wouldn't let her do anything that subjected her to harm.

Griffin watched his wife sleep peacefully. Wished he could crawl into bed with her like he used to.

How long you gonna put up with that, Grif? he heard his cop friends asking.

As long as it takes.

Griffin quietly closed the door and went to Cassie's room. She was awake as she always seemed to be this time of night, when Griffin usually came to bed.

He lifted her easily into his arms, settled into the comfortable chair, and stroked her head awhile. Gradually, he was calmed by her presence, anxieties of his day being pushed away by his daughter as they once had been by his wife.

Griffin rocked her, exchanging smiles and a meaningless sound now and then. After a while, when he sat forward, Cassie reached for the phone along with him. Griffin marveled how her instincts sometimes seemed so attuned to his habits. "Time to call Grandpa," he said, figuring she already knew that.

Cassie cried loudly, almost a scream. Carla was calling his name, but sounded distant as though not really there.

Griffin was back on the Marrow Street Bridge. Dunbar Waddy standing in front of him, staring at him. Griffin realizing he'd forgotten to wear a mask this time. His face was uncovered. Waddy now knew who he was.

Cassie wailing horribly as Griffin raised the gun to Waddy's head. A live round in the chamber of the 9mm weapon. Warm metal in his cold hand. Carla yelling his name again, terrified, but Griffin couldn't say for sure she was trying to stop him.

Griffin expecting Waddy to dive over the side of the bridge like last time. But he didn't. Waddy kept staring Griffin down, daring him to shoot. So he did. Pulling the trigger. Bullets striking Waddy just as they had the last time, tearing up his face and shoulder. Waddy thrown to the ground by the impact.

Cassie screaming terribly. Griffin turning to look for her. Couldn't find her. And when he turned back to where Waddy had gone down, the Jamaican was gone. No sign of him. No blood. Nothing.

Then a rapping sound, firm, determined. Someone trying to alert him. "Jimmy. Jimmy!" Carla's voice.

Griffin snapped awake in the big chair. Heard Cassie crying. Carla knocking on the door.

"Jimmy?"

He sat up quickly, immediately going to Cassie's crib. "I'm awake." He picked up Cassie. Her diaper was soaked. She wailed against his ear, making his head ring. Griffin carried her to the door. Spoke to Carla over their daughter's crying. "I got her. Sorry." He opened the door and was surprised by the sight of Carla, the short haircut.

Carla drew her robe closed tightly and averted her

eyes. He was breaking one of the rules. "Are you all right with her?" she asked.

Griffin braced his crying daughter to his chest. "She just needs to be changed."

Carla retreated to her room.

Griffin found it ironic he was far less upset by his dream than the fact his wife couldn't emotionally handle the sight of him holding Cassie.

13.

Thursday morning, Michelle Aronson's husband, Greg, pulled his shiny-red Mercedes 450SEL into the 7-Eleven parking lot. It was eight-twenty A.M. The Kroop had said he'd be there at eight-fifteen. Close enough.

The man was waiting for Aronson, standing in the closet-size area the convenience store stocked with three video games. Early in the morning and already the place smelled like hot dogs.

The man plunked in a new quarter and worked keypad buttons, manipulating a martial arts expert's kicks, punches, and jumps against a variety of mutated attackers.

They'd go nuts over this game in Jamaica. They craved technology, anything fast and computerized and loud. Would pump quarters into a machine like this for hours.

Playing the game, the man watched the reflection on the screen's glass cover. Without having to turn around, he could watch Greg Aronson.

Aronson picked a *Wall Street Journal* from the news-stand. Went to the coffee machine and fixed his own gigantic cup of black, caffeinated, three sugars no cream. Stirred it. Snapped on a plastic cap. Got in line at the counter.

Aronson looked like a pretty boy. Not big or athletic, especially not in comparison to the hoss beside him: a sweaty trucker hauling a sunrise six-pack under a beefy arm.

Aronson wasn't going to be a problem. It was the location. The convenience store was busy.

Witnesses weren't necessarily bad; sometimes the more people saw you, the more varied the description they'd give the cops. Having a man point a gun at you made him look lots bigger and demented once it was over. Lots of people robbed by a guy five-ten would swear he was at least six-two and add thirty pounds when talking to the cops.

This was too many people, though. In and out. That much motion made the scene uncontrollable.

Some of the hacks he'd known, they wouldn't care. They'd do it just to get it done. Take their money and their chances. Those were your two-hundred-dollar killers, maybe worth a grand if you were desperate.

The man at the video game wasn't desperate. He was careful, he planned. He was inventive. Especially for getting ten grand for the job, what he'd negotiated The Kroop up to as a figure last night. For ten grand, he was going to deliver a classic, something everyone would remember and talk about for years.

And while he'd never killed anyone for money before, he didn't see where it would make much difference. Only that Aronson wasn't a victim he'd have picked on his own. The others—all women except one—had attracted him in a very deep physical sense.

His fulfillment came not only from killing them, but from the experience leading up to their death. Letting daydreams spawn fantasies that became plans, which became real. An entire cycle of pleasure.

It might take a little while to get the feel for Aronson. A few days to see what kind of fantasies he could conjure up. Just because he was getting paid for it didn't mean he couldn't enjoy it.

14.

Carla placed Griffin's breakfast of croissants and market-made jam on the table and walked down the hall to the bathroom. Her gait was carefree this morning, a mannerism Griffin used to interpret as a positive sign, except it always faded. As though she'd fool herself into "being well" for a couple hours. Like she'd fooled him last summer on their getaway to the mountains, raising his hopes.

Over her shoulder Carla said, "Don't forget Mickey's coming for dinner tonight. Don't be late." Her short hair, already washed and brushed, bounced against her neck. Griffin hated it.

"Did you tell him I need to talk to him?"

"Uh-huh," she replied, which could have as easily meant she'd forgotten he'd asked her to do that yesterday.

Griffin ate half of one croissant and left for work.

"This the best picture you got?" Rawley Jenkins looked at the photocopied shot of Dunbar Waddy taken from the police file. Everything else had been cleared from his desk. Jenkins grunted. "Looks like ten thousand other boogers we got in this city, except for the snarled-up hair. Whaddathey call that shit?"

"Dreadlocks."

Jenkins's disgust was obvious. If it wasn't white,

Anglo-Saxon, and male, chances were he didn't like it. Jenkins was a lot like Griffin's father that way. "Wasn't he part of some gang the Jamaicans had going?"

Griffin sat across from Jenkins. Elbow on the worn arm of a generic office chair, two fingers supporting his chin. "Waddy wasn't part of it, but hung with a posse called Terra-Raj. Drug runners mostly. They tried extortion for a little while, did a couple of botched hit jobs. Eventually they either got killed, deported, broke off on their own, or graduated up to New York."

"This country's gonna have to do something with our fucking immigration laws before these third world banana suckers drag us under by our ankles." Jenkins considered the heft of pages in his hand, Griffin having given him a copy of the entire police department file. "I'm gonna need a day to digest this."

"Have you interviewed the hospital staff?"

"I've been through everyone who's here. Judging from this guy's nasty mug, he'd've been noticed. Although a couple nurses went off duty before I got to them. They won't be back until Sunday. Three-on four-off's the shift change."

"I don't have until Sunday. My deal with the reporter buys me a gag on her story until tomorrow noon."

"Jesus, Jimmy, how the hell you gonna turn a four-year-old case in twenty-four hours?"

"Don't expect to. I just need something else I can feed her to buy more time."

Jenkins slapped down the folder. Morning sun didn't reach his office windows, making the room artificially bright under fluorescents. "Don't trust her. You give her much, she's gonna end up screwing you. Screwin' us both."

"She's not after you."

Jenkins grunt was accompanied by half a laugh this

time. "Don't be sure. She knows about a problem we had around here last year. Now I'm not saying it was a problem . . ." Jenkins stopped himself, looked at the folder Griffin had entrusted him with, and reconsidered his lie. "Yeah, hell, we had a security mess last year. A staffer mercy-killing terminal patients. Before they hired me. That's why I tried to keep you from knowing Jane Doe was murdered in the hospital. It wasn't personal. You should know that . . . because of what happened between me and your father."

Griffin nodded. Jenkins's candor was reassuring, his alliance even more so. As though some good parts of the past could be revived. "Help me get this guy, Rawley. I don't think I've got a lot of time."

"This may sound a little strange, Jimmy Grif, but here it comes shootin' at you."

"Go." Nine forty-five A.M., Griffin was in his office, Waddy's police file spread across his desk covered in a halo of light from the gooseneck lamp. He wedged the phone against his shoulder.

On the other end of the line, Trevor Bourbin said, "This hexagon painting on a nude woman? Woman I talked to at the FBI says it's something one of their agents has seen before, but not at a crime scene. At a dinner theater."

"What?"

"Yeah. Down in Jamaica? One of those hedonist resorts? Those one price buys all the beer, wine, and cigarettes you could ever want places?"

"Yeah?"

"They put on these shows a couple nights a week. Some gets pretty outrageous. This one night they got this play supposed to be some kind of sacrifice ritual. Virgins to the Gods, that oldie but goodie. There's lots of drums beating, people chanting, and the girl who's gonna be sacrificed? They strip her down naked, lay her on the stage, and this guy paints a big red hexagon on her body before they give her to the Gods."

"So what is it, some kind of Jamaican ritual? Voodoo?"

"FBI's checking with Kingston. Said they'd let me know. You get any information out of Jane Doe yet?"

"No." Griffin hadn't told Bourbin she was dead. He didn't have the luxury of giving Bourbin the truth just yet. Bourbin would get appreciably edgy about not turning a murder case over to homicide. If Bourbin asked, Griffin was backing the hospital's official version: cerebral hemorrhage, no belladonna—subject to rediagnosis at a later date. "Let me know as soon as you hear from the feds. I'll catch you later."

Griffin hung up as though in a hurry. In case Bourbin was inspired to call back, Griffin buzzed the receptionist, told her no calls except for Mickey Blane, "Whenever his majesty manages to make it in this morning."

With his door closed, the building's air-conditioning system humming on the other side of his wall, Griffin went back to the old police file. For the most part, ghosts raised in the form of dust off each page last night had been absorbed into problems of the present.

The Bright Eyes case had developed quickly and ended on a bizarre stroke of luck. As a result, the investigation had been underdeveloped. A rush to get Waddy to court hadn't helped.

Mickey Blane had a weak case to prosecute ten days before trial. It was only Blane's plea negotiations that saved it. But the plea backfired.

Waddy, notwithstanding claims of innocence on all charges *including* the count of rape the police had walked in on, entered a nolo contendere plea to one count of felony murder. His overworked public defender said as an illegal immigrant, Waddy would likely be deported, not jailed. Only the judge saw it differently. Banged Waddy for fifty years.

Waddy appealed on numerous grounds. The one that looked good was ineffective counsel. His new lawyer, someone he suddenly had money for, filed a writ of habeas corpus. At a motions hearing, flaws in the state's case began to unravel like cheap stitching.

Waddy was granted bail pending appeal. The public, which had been force-fed Bright Eyes's horror in the media for months, was outraged. There was panic that a known killer had been released. The judge who'd writted him out was picketed and threatened. The City Attorney's office came under fire for being ineffective.

Seventy-two hours later it got worse: on a sticky summer night, Dunbar Waddy broke into Mickey Blane's suburban house and slaughtered Blane's wife and son, would have likely killed Blane, too, only he hadn't been home.

The media had a field day. There was a call for City Attorney Richard Marish's resignation, which only his adroit political skills managed to avoid.

Marish went on the counteroffensive with his "Asking the World" speech, in which he repeated the phrase, "I ask the world . . ." and then offered countless questions.

One was: "I ask the world if in the eyes of reasonable men, I wouldn't have done everything in my power to keep jailed the murderer who throughout these proceedings threatened my righthand man and his family. A savage who immediately upon being released by Judge Schuman made good on that threat and butchered a beautiful woman and her young son."

Under bright television lights in the City Attorney's conference room, Richard Marish gave that speech with his arm around Mickey Blane. Blane had sobbed horribly, his distress so bitterly apparent no one ever stopped to consider there had been no previous mention of threats against Blane or his family; that Marish had conveniently invented the angle for the press conference. Nor did anyone mention—or maybe realize—that Marish's arm wasn't around Blane as an act of solace, but because Blane was so drunk he'd have fallen over without support.

What had been problematic then for the city—and Griffin—remained today. There was little understanding not only why Waddy had killed the three women with belladonna, but how he had managed it. There was no motive. Waddy didn't appear to have any substantial prior history with the women before killing them.

Even the FBI had been fooled. A team of investigators had reviewed the crime scenes and victims in intricate detail and constructed a psychological profile of Waddy. Their theory: Waddy was a white male; mid-to-late twenties; average build; physically attractive; most likely sexually inexperienced; average to slightly above average IQ; raised in a single parent home; likely moved from place to place with frequency during childhood; was either an only child or the older of two or three siblings; thought to be Catholic or influenced by Catholicism.

Yet when Waddy was captured, he turned out to be black, five-nine, reed thin, with narrow-set eyes that appeared maniacal, wore his hair in shoulder-length dreadlocks, was twenty-two, and had never finished the third grade.

He'd been in the U.S. illegally via Miami for six months to the day he was found with his pants around his ankles, on top of Leslie Connors—victim number three—a thirty-five-year-old white housewife, mother of

two, who worked part-time in a trendy clothing store.
Leslie Connors having been in the midst of a fatal
seizure resulting from an overdose of belladonna as
Waddy held her down, and thrust his erection inside her
full bore.

That's what he'd been doing when the police broke
down the door and caught him.

Waddy screaming he was innocent as they hauled him
angrily to jail.

15.

"Hi. Mrs. Griffin?" Liz McKinley sat on a painted wood rail of the front porch to the Griffins' home. A very cozy setting with hanging pots of impatiens and fuchsia, some containers still dripping from a recent watering.

Carla's expression, which had been quite happy walking toward home, tightened with suspicion.

Liz, despite her hangover, moved off the railing with a playful hop, wanting to appear lighthearted and casual to put Griffin's wife at ease. "I'm sorry to drop by unannounced. My name's Liz. I'm a freelance writer. I'm working on a piece about police wives and I thought maybe you'd let me interview you."

"Why me?" Carla remained at the porch's top step, cautious.

Liz thought, Honey, relax, do you think every smiling face is a con artist—even though in this case it's true. "To be perfectly honest, I had a captain's wife lined up, but she backed out on me. She thought I was from *Redbook,* didn't really understand what it meant for me to be a freelancer, that I might have to reangle my story depending on who I can sell it to. She said if she ended up in *Cosmo* her husband would kill her. Apparently he thinks it's a fascist publication." Liz laughed. "Go figure, huh."

Carla relaxed just enough for Liz to feel hopeful.

"I won't take much of your time, or if you want to

clear it with your husband first, I could come back some—"

"No. I won't have to ask."

Ow, Liz, you are so smart, she thought to herself. Score another hit for the pat lines she used to get people talking. The implications of having to get permission from a husband was an odds-on winner. No matter how good a marriage was, how much of a feminist a wife claimed *not* to be, inferring that kind of servility—needing approval just to have a conversation—usually struck a nerve.

Carla moved toward the front door, taking keys from her purse. "My daughter's upstairs—a woman watches her for me. I'll get her and be right back down."

"Sure." Liz retook her seat on the railing.

She found Carla Griffin to be quite attractive. Her makeup expertly applied, the scent of her perfume flush from body heat. Maybe she'd had a lunch date. Carla was certainly dressed for it, wearing a flowery sundress with an above-the-knee hem and shoulder straps—one twisted—that crossed and buttoned midway down her back. An outfit for meeting girlfriends at an outdoor cafe.

Liz overheard Carla and the woman upstairs. Carla, in baby talk, prompting her child to say "Bye-byes." Liz thinking, please, spare me. She was a cold heart about kids until one was in her lap, at which point she wondered how she was ever going to live without one—but she was; doctors had assured her of that.

Carla descended the stairs, long legs coming into view, Liz wondering enviously if those legs were ever going to meet a torso. A definite catch for Griffin. Liz remembered Carla from the funeral of the prosecutor's wife and son, how she'd looked beautiful even in mourning. Now, she didn't look a single pound heavier after having a child. Wasn't much different at all except her hair was much shorter.

Liz asked, "What's her name?"

"Cassie." Carla had her daughter wrapped proudly in both arms.

"She looks like you."

She kissed Cassie's forehead. "I'm gone two hours and I miss her."

When Carla struggled briefly with her keys, Liz offered to help. Carla shook her head and unlocked the door, readjusting Cassie onto her hip once inside.

Liz followed. "This is a nice place. Nice decor. Kind of Scandinavian/country."

The Griffins' taste ran toward comfortable style on a medium budget. A high ceiling, pale hardwood floors, and tall windows created the illusion of space in the small living room. The proper placement of furniture had been influenced by decorating magazines. Fifteen feet from the front door, a wide archway led to a dining room and bedroom hall.

Carla put Cassie in a playpen that sat back against the living-room wall, shaded from the front windows by a silk fichus tree. "How did you get my name?" Carla wasn't being defensive, but not receptive either. "I'm not really a police wife anymore."

"Oh?"

"My husband left the department a few years ago. He works in the City Attorney's office now."

Liz hadn't known that; she'd assumed Griffin was still a detective.

"Good thing I told you before you wasted a lot of tape."

"How's that?"

Carla gestured to Liz's big pocketbook. Aggression seeping through a mild-mannered front as though having been lying in wait. "I assume you have a cassette recorder. No sense burning up any more tape. I mean it is on, isn't it?"

Liz reached into her bag and withdrew her recorder, holding it to show the cassette wasn't turning. "Not guilty," she pled amicably. Sensing a tremor of coldness from Carla, Liz gestured toward the door. "I've caught you at a bad time. I'll show myself out."

"Wait, I'm sorry." Carla's apology was sincere. "I have bad memories of reporters, that's all."

"That's okay," Liz grasped the doorknob. The sun's heat radiated through glass panes and made the warm apartment seem more so. "You were in a good mood until you saw me. I should have called. We'll do it some other time."

"Do you like iced tea? I have some raspberry tea already chilled. Let me fix a glass and we can sit out back in the garden."

Liz pretended to hesitate. "You're sure?"

Carla nodded. "I could use a little more contact with the outside world. My work's a little solitary."

"Being a mom?"

"No. I'm a paralegal, but I work out of the house. Come on back, I'll show you my office." There was notable pride in Carla's voice.

On the way through the condo, voyeur Liz inventoried everything, trying to get a feel what it was like for Griffin and his wife to live here.

What struck her immediately was a sense of tidiness. The condo was medium-size, yet not in the disarray one would expect dropping in unannounced on a family with an infant. There was no clutter, nor penchant for knickknacks. Tabletops, walls, and the fireplace mantel failed to boast the prerequisite family photographs and memorabilia. A glance into the kitchen uncovered not a single dirty dish.

"This is it," Carla said.

Her office was an unsectioned half of the master bedroom. An elaborate computer desk fit precisely into a bayed window wall; obviously custom built. Carla opened decorator shutters to reveal a serene view of a shady garden encircled by a high brick wall.

Liz had always wanted a workroom like this; she thought about it whenever she was sprawled across a hotel bed pecking away on the keys of her laptop, expecting the screen to go kafluey on her—like they all did—any minute.

Carla unlocked and opened French doors into the private garden. "Make yourself comfortable outside. I'll get the tea and move Cassie in here."

"Need any help?"

"Nope. Do you like sugar? Sweetener in your tea?"

"Pounds of sugar." Liz started toward the garden, but remained in the bedroom once Carla was out of sight. She kept an ear toward the kitchen. While Carla opened the refrigerator, Liz peeked around the workstation.

Files were so neatly stacked it was difficult to read more than the top couple pages without disturbing their order. An inordinate number of documents were faxes. The top file's cover page was from a law firm, references to an antitrust matter. Pretty heady.

Hearing ice cubes dropped into glasses, Liz moved closer to the garden door and scanned the "living" part of the bedroom.

The wallpaper was pretty and new: long repeats of Jamaican roses against a pale mauve background. Very soothing. The bedspread was covered in a coordinating duveau. Ruffle-edge pillows in yet another companion fabric were tossed against a French colonial headboard.

There were two nightstands, but only one had anything on it: a reading lamp and popular fashion magazines.

A single dresser sported a hand-carved jewelry box and the only photograph Liz had seen so far: an old black-and-white, three people in it, but from across the room, Liz couldn't make out their faces.

When Carla shut the refrigerator door, Liz snuck out to the garden, sat her pocketbook on a wrought-iron chair, and was considering rows of sweet-smelling lavender when Carla came out with the tea.

"Let me make a quick stop in the bathroom and move Cassie; then we can talk. I'll tell you *all* about myself." Carla's offer was clear with friendly sarcasm.

"Take your time. This's a great garden."

"It soothes the soul." Carla set two iced teas on the table before retreating inside.

As far as Carla telling Liz all about her life was concerned, Liz felt like she already knew more than Carla would ever confess. That's why she'd needed to get inside the house. Getting inside the bedroom, hell, it didn't get any better than that.

Liz waited in the garden fifteen minutes for Carla to rejoin her. Carla spent most of that time in the bathroom; getting Cassie settled in the bedroom only took a couple of minutes.

When Liz's initial questions proved unthreatening, Carla became relaxed to the point of enjoying herself. Going on for quite a while with Liz about the perils and perks of working freelance, picking your own hours, but unsure when the next paycheck was coming and for how much.

Talking about how she'd started as a paralegal, Carla said, "We all wanted to be lawyers, ever since high school."

"All?" Liz asked.

"Jimmy, Mickey, and I."

"Mickey Blane?" Liz guessed, Carla having referred to him twice already.

"We met in ninth grade. A lifetime ago, *two* lifetimes maybe. So much has happened since." Carla shook her head, saddened for a moment, but pushing on. "We were a real group. On the surface, it looked like we'd have nothing in common, but we were inseparable.

"Jimmy was a gung-ho jock, always trying to lose himself in sports. His family life was horrible. His father was a violent drunk. They've made up since, but I still can't stand the man. Not after all he's done.

"I was from the same 'side of the tracks,' shall we say, as Jimmy. My parents were working class. My mom died when I was eleven. My dad remarried a younger woman who was divorced and had two kids. I was supposed to blend in, but I didn't. I started raising hell in school. Supposedly I was mad at the world for taking my mom, and mad at my father for finding someone to take her place when I couldn't.

"Anyway, in high school, I started to get my act together. Jimmy and Mickey had a lot to do with that. Mickey especially. He was the rich kid. His father was a make-it-from-scratch almost millionaire. He'd worked his way up to president of an equipment rental company. He bought the owner out and tripled business by the time Mickey was halfway through law school."

Carla sounded impressed, telling the story. "He just sold the business two years ago for fifteen million, not including the land that he's leasing to the new company owners. He's a very shrewd man. The kind who demands loyalty, but pays for it. The thing is, he was never crazy about Mickey hanging around with Jimmy and me. I think he was afraid we'd be a bad influence."

"So why didn't Mickey follow, his father's foot-steps?"

"Mr. Blane—listen to me, I still call him that, but he's always been 'Mister' to me. Anyway, he didn't want Mickey to work a business job. He wanted him to be a doctor or lawyer. Not for the money, but the prestige. Mickey doesn't have to worry about money. Mr. Blane has seen to it he has plenty of that. Trust funds out the wazoo. Mr. Blane's determined that Mickey make a name for himself."

"So the City Attorney's office is his stepping-stone."

Carla sipped her tea. "He hopes so. You know, he's coming over for dinner tonight. Maybe you'd want to in-terview him for another story. Young power profes-sional, something like that."

This much hospitality Liz wasn't expecting. "Can't tonight. Maybe another time." Liz checked how much tape she had left on the first side of the cassette, the recorder sitting on the wrought-iron table as benign ob-server. "You started talking about *all* of you going to law school?"

Carla nodded, more animated now. Having come a long way from suspicion in the last forty minutes. "Mid-way through college, I was running out of money and patience. Back then, I didn't have what it took to do all the reading. The law interested me, but not the school-ing. I concentrated on paralegal courses and figured if the bug really bit me, I could always try night school. That's the route Jimmy took.

"He went to community college after high school and got an AA degree. He joined the police force and I guess was twenty-five—no, twenty-six—when he finished col-lege at night. He got accepted into law school and was going to start when his father had a stroke. That was about . . . I guess eight years ago, seven maybe.

"The police department health plan covered his father's medical bills, but he'd run up such bad debt, lots of it with bookies, Jimmy had to help out his mom. He worked a lot of overtime on the force and part-time as a security guard in a shopping mall. It was really getting to him, all the hours and . . ." Carla looked away. ". . . some other rough times . . . for all of us a few years ago. Two of our friends were killed."

"I'm sorry."

Carla folded her hand around a napkin made wet by her tea glass. "It was Mickey's wife and son who were killed. This maniac Mickey prosecuted for murder got out of jail and killed them. It was horrible."

Carla successfully fought back tears. "After that, Jimmy wasn't acting right. None of us were. But Jimmy especially. That's when Mickey moved him into the CA's office as an investigator. About a year later, Jimmy got reaccepted into law school. Mickey even had it set up for the CA's office to cover part of the tuition. Jimmy went one year and then we got a little unplanned surprise named Cassie."

Carla nodded toward the bedroom, where Cassie, bored with toys in her playpen, had fallen asleep. "I told Jimmy to stay in school—we'd make out fine on his salary until I got back on my feet. He didn't want to chance it. He's very conservative with money. I guess after what his father had done.

"Jimmy took a leave of absence from law school. I know it killed him. But he'll go back. Maybe this January. He's thinking about it." Carla made herself smile. "But that's not what you wanted to talk about, was it?"

"I think," Liz said, "life is too hard sometimes." She folded her hands across her lap, truly enjoying this garden, a block of peace nestled away from the city's bane. Clematis with palm-size blossoms climbingtrellis work.

Fragrant nursery-bred honeysuckle with purple-crimson flowers. "Sometimes it makes me lose my incentive to work. Who knows, I'll probably never even write this article. I think it's just an excuse to talk with new people. Take a peek at their to see what I'm missing."

"Are you married?" Carla asked, becoming the questioner.

"No." Liz sat up and reached for her tea, wishing there was some nice Russian vodka in it. "I'm determinedly single. I like men too much to be married."

"That could get you in trouble," Carla warned knowingly, then: "You don't live around here, do you?"

"Columbus, Ohio to Pittsburgh to Orlando to Phoenix to Las Vegas—Vegas was great, lots of trouble in Las Vegas." Liz's throaty voice made merely naming cities sound lewd. "Now I'm in Atlanta. It's got a good airport, so I can travel around on stories."

"Isn't that expensive?"

"Mmm-hmm. I get audited every three years. The IRS hates letting you deduct plane fare, but magazines want national coverage. I can't make a living interviewing people in Atlanta."

"Well, then," Carla proposed, becoming a career motivator, "let's talk about something that will give you a good story to sell."

Liz reached for her recorder, which had just run out of tape. Turning the cassette over, she asked innocently, "How about let's look around your house. With this garden, I bet I could sell a piece on the decorating ideas of the work-at-home professional-slash-wife-slash-mother."

16.

Mickey Blane looked like hell. Twenty minutes ago, Griffin had told him about belladonna killing Jane Doe after all, not a cerebral hemorrhage. Blane, who'd arrived to work at twelve forty-five P.M. in a fine mood, had kicked over a chair, ranted about reaming out the hospital, expelling so much anxiety in the process it appeared to have numbed him.

Now, City Attorney Richard Marish closed the door to Mickey Blane's office to keep private whatever urgent matter Blane needed to talk about. "What's the problem?" When Blane didn't respond immediately, the City Attorney looked to Griffin.

"There was a murder at Memorial Hospital two nights ago. An overdose of belladonna."

"And . . . ?" For a classic politician, Marish was not one for subtleties around the office. He wanted matters laid out for him, point-blank, all the details; don't throw him a piece of meat, he wanted the whole damned cow. Besides which, his memory for particulars—as it was for case law—proved no better than elusive. Only names of people who'd tried to screw him were remembered without fail, and perhaps since that list was so long there wasn't room for other data.

Griffin didn't like Marish. He considered him slippery as they came; no need to open a door for Marish to enter a room when he could slide through a crack. And while

Griffin tried to keep his opinion of his boss concealed, he suspected Marish knew. Good thing Marish didn't care about personalities—he cared about someone doing a job.

"Belladonna," Griffin explained, "is what Bright Eyes used to kill his victims. It's possible we've got him again."

Like water heated slowly to a roiling boil, the news took a few seconds to ignite Marish's ire. "Jesus, fucking Christ, boys." He put his fists against Blane's desk and leaned forward. "My ass is on the line for every shittin' little thing that goes wrong in this city. Crack dealers hiring nine-year-old pushers and users gunning them down outside elementary schools, getting fucking blood all over my drug-free-zone signs. Christ, remember that front-page picture in the newspaper? It made the fucking national syndicates. AP assholes.

"Then I do something good, the TV people at the goddamned six o'clock news bump my press conference about the porno raid to eleven o'clock when all those prissy Baptists are asleep, and now you're telling me a serial killer we should have put away years ago is back?"

Though outraged, Marish kept his voice down—words that traveled through walls traveled through halls. He wasn't a big man, but fiery, known to throw himself into fistfights. One former courthouse reporter once compared Marish to the late baseball manager Billy Martin, saying he expected to find Marish in the halls of circuit court, hauling a box of dirt to kick over a defense attorney's loafers.

"How'd it happen?" Marish looked directly at Griffin, who supplied the details, including how Memorial Hospital tried to conceal the incident.

"Just like a bunch of fucking doctors to cover their

ass." Marish half flung himself into a chair like an over-grown infant having a fit. He slumped miserably, rubbed his hand so high up his forehead he knocked the hair spray hold off sideswept black hair. "Makes me wish I was a malpractice attorney every time I see a hospital. Those quacks."

Griffin didn't bother to point out the obvious: that if Rawley Jenkins hadn't kept the death quiet, the newspapers—not just one reporter—would have been all over them by now.

"I think," Griffin offered, breaking a short, mean silence, "the reporter will stay quiet if we can offer her some exclusive angle to the story once it breaks."

"Once it breaks!" Marish sat up so abruptly, he appeared to have leapt from the chair even as he remained seated. He gripped wooden armrests. "This story *doesn't* break. It breaks, *we* break. You know how many people I got out there are looking to bust my ass?" Marish's arm pointed like a ramrod for Blane's window, accusing the city outside as a whole. "This may come as a big shock to some people, but this city's sixty-five-percent black, another twenty-percent ethnic, less than fifteen-percent white, and they got themselves a black mayor, black attorney general, comptroller, council president, school superintendent, police chief, assistant police chief, half the circuit bench . . ." Marish's tirade slowed with intensity. "But they got themselves a white City Attorney." He poked his own chest hard. "They got a white nothing else, but City Attorney. And they don't like it." Enunciating each word of that sentence with another jab at his chest. .

"I'm here because I'm good. I got a good office. You boys are good. But that doesn't matter because I'm not the right fucking color for the job no more, but I hang on because the mayor knows I do a good job, he knows I save his ass on crime. That that lip-service foul-up he *had* to promote to chief of police would have him up to his eyeballs in crack houses if I wasn't here riding the fat chief's fat ass. That doesn't matter to *them*."

Marish's arm shot toward the window again. "They want to fucking hang me. And all they need's a noose." Marish straightened the front of his suit coat, which had become twisted. "You tell me this sicko killer's back, my friends, you just gave them the rope and instructions how to tie it around my neck."

Griffin hated Marish's Napoleonic spats. They accomplished nothing. So he didn't wait so long as for Marish to take a breath before coming back at him, albeit diplomatically, sidestepping, like shadowboxing a tornado. "If Dunbar Waddy—Bright Eyes," Griffin clarified when Marish's expression revealed he didn't know anyone named Waddy. "If he's back—and I'm not positive he is—but if it is him, or if it's a copycat that could resurrect memories of Bright Eyes—which would be damaging as well—and he goes on a spree and someone, like this reporter for example, lets it out that we helped the hospital cover up the first murder . . . I think we're going to lose more than jobs."

"So what're you saying?" Marish demanded.

"The reporter is a problem. A potential killer is a separate problem. We deal with each separately. The reporter we guarantee some exclusive information once the story breaks."

Marish flinched at the idea of the story breaking, but let Griffin finish.

"The killer—again *if* there is a killer—we need to find in a hurry. I've been going over the old case file and—"

"Our file?" Blane interrupted sharply.

"The police file."

"Christ," Marish said, "don't let anybody see you with

it. Somebody starts talking, rumors fucking fly like pigeons and seagulls, a whole flock of them over us ready to take a ceremonious dump on our heads."

"I know," Griffin assured. "I took it out last night, nobody saw me. And what I've found, going over it, are lots of problems. We had a bad case at trial."

"What are you saying?" Mickey Blane's voice pitched an octave higher with stress.

Marish held out his hand. "Let him finish, goddamn it." It was highly unusual for Marish to call down his number one like that. To Griffin, he demanded, "Get to it. Bottom line."

"We should consider calling the FBI to go over—"

Marish threw up his hands. "Hell no!"

"They were way off base last time, Grif," Blane complained loudly, quieting when Marish waved for him to keep it down. "What're you thinking about? And how are we going to keep it quiet with feds all over the place?"

"They'd be consultants. We're going to them for help. It's not a federal case. And they've got good security," Griffin defended. "Damned little leaks out of their office. And it's a long shot better than turning it over to homicide."

"Homicide!" Marish and Blane practically screamed the word in unison, both continuing to talk at once until Marish took charge.

"Look, you said this might not be the same killer. It's only one victim, right? So what's the problem—public relationswise—if it does come out we suspected, *suspected,* I say, a possible copycat or even the same maniac. We didn't ignore it. We conducted our own investigation. You are investigating it, right?"

Griffin nodded.

"Vigorously?"

"Not like I could with a team of investigators."

"Out of the question. *You're* on it, *you* carry the ball. Our ass is covered for the time being. No sense causing a public panic or detouring police manpower unnecessarily, right? On a hunch. A maybe." Marish checked his theory by looking at Blane, who showed immediate agreement. "And if there is another killing, one we can't keep quiet, then we rethink FBI." Marish pointed to Griffin. "How many days between killings the last time?"

"It varied. About ten between one and two, less between two and three."

"Sounds like you got some time. *If* it is him again. For now, you and Mickey get together, reassign all your present cases to that fucking Gerremo, who'd I'd goddamned fire if his uncle wasn't connected to about ten thousand wop votes. And you," he pointed to Blane, "make it look like you're being cautious the guy might be back for you. Remember I made it sound like Waddy had threatened you. If he's back, you should be scared."

Griffin thought, leave it to Marish to point out the obvious. "What about the reporter?" he asked his boss.

"Yeah, right, okay? What's her name again?"

"Liz McKinley. Writes for *America Exposed*."

"Tell her she gets exclusive photo rights to every crime scene and victim and we'll throw in all our interrogation tapes with the maniac once we catch him. Hell, she can sit in on the interrogation if she wants."

Griffin knew the offer was strictly bluff. Worst of it was, Griffin knew he'd sell Liz McKinley on the deal. He was good at selling Marish's deals. It was a large part of what they paid him for. Team effort.

*   *   *

Twenty minutes after their meeting, City Attorney Richard Marish called Mickey Blane to his office. The door was, out of habit, closed.

Marish had a wide window, a beautiful view of the city, but kept solarized pleated shades lowered to the sill. He didn't want to be reminded of all the people out there who, he was convinced, desperately wanted him out of a job. The only time he raised the shades was if he'd sneak some young date into his office at night, show her the city's amber lights, hoping to seduce her with the panorama so he could mount her on his desk. Marish thought the city was romantic at night. During the day it was ugly.

"I don't think I have to remind you," Marish said, "that when you wanted me to hire Griffin, I asked if he was going to be a public relations problem. Since he *was* the cop who blew the Bright Eyes case, let that fucker out from under our nose when we had him. And you said, I believe the exact quote was, 'No way.' You assured me Bright Eyes wasn't going to come back to haunt us. It was put to rest. That *is* what you told me."

Blane nodded, but pointed out, "We both know it's not Griffin's fault."

"*We* know. Yeah, that's true. But *they* don't know." Marish gestured to the window behind him without turning to look at the indistinct-though-ubiquitous "theys" who roamed, lived, and voted in the city. "So if it turns out this matter doesn't go away like it should, we're going to have to make the right moves. And I'm not just saying this for me. We've talked about this. Next year, we win the election with the mayor, it's my last term. Five years from now, this's your office. We've done all the right things to keep you in line. The mayor's happy with the idea, hell, probably happier than with me. You're younger, better looking, got a liberal background, positive civil rights record." Marish paused to let Blane absorb that. "But you're going to always have to consider your relationship with Griffin. He's a cloud. A fucking storm if Bright Eyes hits us."

"I've known him for twenty years, Dick. He's my best friend."

Marish tried his best sympathetic delivery, though he and Blane both understood he didn't have it in him. "If Bright Eyes wanders around doing a little encore, you know the fucking papers are going to latch on to Griffin, hound him like horny dogs. How does he feel the killer he couldn't catch, the one who murdered his friend's family—*your family*—is back? They're going to hit you with the same questions. Hard as hell. How you stand up, how you show leadership is going to play a long way in people's minds when it comes time to vote for you in five years."

Blane wasn't a political neophyte, but sometimes had to force his mind to think like Marish. It wasn't natural.

"You see what I'm talking about?" Marish waited for an answer.

17.

Maria Jenni was nineteen years old. Her beautiful dark hair bespoke pure Sicilian heritage. She was a mediocre art student whose two-year stay at a local art institute was more involved with the consumption of narcotics than creating oil paintings she claimed would one day make her famous.

Two in-patient stays at drug rehab centers failed to diminish her taste for the stuff. She liked being high, the way it made her feel, how her painting seemed stunning under the influence.

Four years ago, the city police found Maria Jenni naked and dead in a second-floor room in a cheap motel off Caton Avenue. Facedown, her arms spread above her head as though reaching for bedposts that weren't there. Her midsection had been raised by a pillow, her legs spread as though positioned for someone to have intercourse with her from behind. Yet there was no indication of sexual activity. No semen. No signs of struggle.

Needle tattoos between her toes pointed to an OD, except there were no needles found in the room, no drug paraphernalia of any kind. Her clothes were missing and the clerk assured police that when Miss Jenni had checked in late the previous night, paying cash, she'd been clothed. She'd also been alone.

An autopsy was ordered, and when initial drug screens came back negative, save insignificant traces of marijuana, additional tests were ordered. There had to be an explanation as to why her pupils were so wide open, a more exaggerated response than associated with cocaine, PCP, or LSD.

That was when they found belladonna, a clearly murderous dose. Given the rare occurrence of the drug and the assumption your average street user probably had no idea as to what was a safe hit of the stuff, the case was considered suspicious, though likely accidental.

That the girl's clothes and any drug paraphernalia were gone implied that Maria had not been alone, but more likely than not, whoever had been with her probably got scared and took off once Maria started having the seizures that preceded her death.

Surprisingly, that portions of the motel room were free of fingerprints didn't receive much police attention. The homicide detective who'd breezed through the scene already had twenty-nine open cases, didn't like the sounds of thirty, and attributed the absence of prints to the room being cleaned thoroughly between occupants. After all, most of the motel's "guests" only stayed for a few hours before going home to spouses with a good excuse for where they'd spent their time.

Ten nights later, Susanna Doran-Michaels was found in a downtown hotel of adulterous repute. Doran-Michaels was a striking twenty-year-old blonde who'd found limited success as a fashion model, but even greater prosperity in wedlock. At the time of her death, she'd been married three months to a prominent banker twice her age.

Like Jenni, Doran-Michaels was found naked, positioned suggestively on a double bed stripped of its sheets. She had two pillows bolstered under her hips, raising her ass a little higher than Jenni had been found. Her long legs made for a provocative view from behind, spread as far as the muscles along her inner thighs would allow.

Her clothes were missing from the room, as was the gold chain she always wore around her neck: a long snake-pattern necklace that dipped between her breasts, dangling a gold cross against her cleavage.

Doran-Michaels's room was free of fingerprints, but only in certain areas; other sections were covered with prints. Those exemplars resulted in some embarrassing moments for a few cheating wives and husbands unlucky enough to have fingerprints on record and also to have recently been in that room. Three such interviews netted zero suspects.

Other similarities between Jenni and Doran-Michaels included a lack of evidence of a struggle; no sign of sexual activity—no semen, no pubic hairs—and belladonna, although not apparently by injection as in the Doran-Michaels case, had caused death.

Doran-Michaels had been Griffin's introduction to Bright Eyes. Griffin had been the city's youngest homicide detective at the time. A hotshot with a great record. He was tireless and patient, listening to hours of witness statements, able to sift through the rubble for useful information.

Doran-Michaels's husband, Harry, was a suspect. His short marriage to Susanna Doran had been volatile. Griffin discovered Harry Michaels had put a private investigator after his wife who'd twice caught her in adulterous situations; the night of her death, however, the PI had inconveniently been on another case.

What ultimately cleared Harry Michaels was a solid alibi. Continuously, for two days before and after Susanna's death, Harry had been out of town on business.

As a result of Doran-Michaels, the media grabbed the case and had a bonanza. A sexual serial killer on the prowl. Big news. A longtime police-blotter reporter coined the term Bright Eyes for the wide-open stare shared by both dead women.

The city went into a frenzy. Lots of pressure on the police, extra man hours threatening to put a weak budget even deeper in the red.

Seven days after Doran-Michaels there was a major breakthrough. Pure chance captured Bright Eyes.

Nine-seventeen P.M., a warm June evening, the eastern district police received a 911. A struggle, a woman's scream, coming from an apartment in a building quickly becoming famous for domestic disputes between the Jamaicans who inhabited most of the block.

Two cars were dispatched at 9:23 P.M. Both took their time getting there. Domestic spats were lousy calls. Husband and wife beating each other up. For some reason usually brawling in the kitchen, where knives and rolling pins and corkscrews, bottle openers, any of a dozen things could do serious bodily harm.

It never seemed to fail that the cops would go in, try to break the fight up, one of the two combatants would turn the fight on *them*. The cops would get rough with the resister, and then the spouse who'd been getting mauled, probably bloodied in the process, would start beating on the cops. Yelling they were hurting their husband, wife, boyfriend, whatever.

Then the rest of the family, who'd been hiding behind closed doors to stay out of the melee, would come in screaming police brutality. Pretty soon, you had neighbors joining the fun with their rolling pins, knives, and guns. By which time you were borderline riot.

Lots of cops got hurt that way, which was why dispatch sent two cars, four cops.

When they'd arrived at the address—a brick building with colorful curtains flapping at opened windows—

they were pleasantly surprised to hear it was quiet. No screaming, just the predictable reggae music blaring somewhere on the third floor.

Quiet, however, could be good news or bad. They might walk in and find the fighting had stopped and turned to screwing. More than one domestic call had been answered to find a couple who had just been punching each other going wild in the bedroom. Then again, sometimes one of them was dead.

On the call that night, the cops found Leslie Connors. A white, thirty-five-year-old housewife, mother of two, naked in a vacant apartment. A rough piece of duct tape strapped tightly over her mouth. Her face turning blue from lack of oxygen. Suffering violent convulsions as she was being viciously raped by a thin Jamaican with long dreadlocks.

Her assailant was Dunbar Waddy. He'd already climaxed in her once, was doing it again—so into his act he never heard the police until they were pulling him off her.

While Waddy was subdued, the duct tape was removed from Leslie's mouth, but she didn't breathe. Mouth to mouth failed. The ambulance was too late. She died at the scene.

"What I want to know," Rawley Jenkins told Griffin over kosher hot dogs at Lexington Market, "is how that booger got 'em to go along with it. He was a pretty ugly-lookin' guy. A little crazy in the eyes, too, the way they were all yellowed over from smoking dope. Long dirty fingernails. Or am I that out of touch? That white girls could go for somebody like Waddy? Three of them?"

"Different world today, Rawley."

"I know I'm a bigot—ain't apologizing for that to no one—but come on, it doesn't make sense."

"We considered it, and the only thing we came up with was that he either lured them with drugs or, at least in the third victim's case, the housewife, might have doped her unknowingly, then took her to the apartment once she was out of it. The night she was killed, she was at a dance club, partying with a bunch of the college kids she worked with in a clothing store. There was a reggae band there, so Waddy could have blended in. Then again, the kids she worked with said the woman was wilder than she looked."

"But not so wild she's going to want to take a ride with Dunbar Waddy for a tour of Little Kingston."

"Probably not that wild," Griffin admitted.

Jenkins took a big bite of kosher dog, talked with his mouth full. "But who knows, huh, Jimmy? Maybe Waddy had a big one." Jenkins waggled what was left of his dog. "One of them foot longs. All these porn shops got special movies and magazines about blacks and whites, so it's turning somebody on."

At three thirty P.M., Lexington Market was on the slow side of lunch hour, primarily catering to grocery shoppers prowling individual stalls stocked with fruits and vegetables, meats, poultry, seafood, and bakery items. An intoxicating mix of aromas.

The building was approximately the size of a football field. There was no air-conditioning, circulation being provided by huge caged fans set high in tall cinder block walls. The floors were concrete and routinely hosed down, squirting dirt into drain tiles, then covered with straw.

All the merchants' signs were either hand-painted or neon. The atmosphere more exotic than when Griffin's mother took him there as a kid.

The grocers were primarily Italian and Jewish then, as much numbers running going on as food sales. Most of the old guard had sold out to the new immigrants, Koreans, Vietnamese, and Indians. Stir-fry, curry, cayenne pepper, fish served whole with black bean sauce, bok choy, and sesame noodles were slowly overtaking pastas, tomato sauce, and pastrami. The garlic was better now, though, big, fist-sized heads of it hanging from wooden rafters, cloves the size of little fingers.

One reason Rawley Jenkins had taken the hospital job was to be close to the market. "And this way, once these hot dogs clog my arteries, I'll be close to the emergency room for my heart attack."

His kosher dog done for, Jenkins led Griffin to the market center where a Cantonese family had bought a business name along with the stall. "Hello, Mrs. Serio." Jenkins called the short Asian woman the same name as the former owner. Kidding her about it. She didn't get it, didn't care. Jenkins bought lots of food from her.

Behind the low refrigerator case, "Mrs. Serio" offered a thickly accented greeting.

Jenkins pointed to the menu suspended above the stall, held up four fingers. "Number four, Mrs. Serio."

"One or two?"

"Cold noodles over cucumber with peanut sauce," Jenkins told Griffin. "You in or out?"

"In."

Jenkins showed two fingers to the Chinese woman. "Two number fours."

She repeated the order, hurrying off to get it.

"You gotta love it," Jenkins told Griffin, leaning his weight against the counter. "That's the only English she speaks. Numbers. Number of what you want and how much it costs. Probably gross a million bucks out of this place a year. Cash. Gotta give it to the Asians, Jimmy. They work their asses off. Families get together, pool finances, everybody helps one another out, they all get ahead. You don't see them lining up for fucking welfare, sitting on their asses whining about handouts like a bunch of boogers."

Griffin, as when hearing his father's "editorials," instinctively looked around to see who within earshot Jenkins might be offending—and if they were looking to start a fight. It wouldn't be the first time Griffin had been in such a brawl. That had been one of the first times his father ever congratulated him for anything: Griffin managed to pull his dad out of a bar riot he'd started by calling someone a lazy-assed nigger. Thankfully, this afternoon, Griffin and Jenkins were pretty much to themselves.

"Christ, no," Jenkins ran on, "give those boogers an SBA loan, minority enterprise, they run out and lease a fucking Cadillac, buy VCRs and gold jewelry, then get some shifty bankruptcy lawyer to pull them out from under the loan, jump into a new corporate name, take out another loan." Jenkins grunted under his breath. "This country sometimes, I fucking swear."

The Cantonese Mrs. Serio returned promptly with their plates, counted out change faster than turning mah-jongg tiles.

Jenkins paid for Griffin's lunch. "My way of thanking you for an excuse to get out of the damned hospital for a change."

Eating distracted Jenkins from his bigotry. They ate at counter-height tables without chairs. Jenkins adding two beers to the party, homemade ale courtesy of a ruddy, stubborn Irishman.

Jenkins said, "I went through your witness list in the file. People Waddy used to hang with."

"I went over that, too. Figure if Waddy's back in town, he might look up his old friends. I'm going to check for current addresses when we're done here."

Jenkins pulled a folded sheet of legal pad from his pocket, snapped it open with one hand while trawling noodles with the other. "Saved you the trouble. A buddy of mine's nailed behind a desk over in western. He located two of the guys on the outside. One's inside."

Griffin hadn't expected Jenkins to be this interested. With Marish and Blane having nixed FBI involvement, Jenkins might be all the assistance he got.

Jenkins jammed a plastic fork of noodles into his mouth, slurping strands that stuck between his lips. Chewing like a Miss Manners nightmare, he said, "You take the one on the inside: Devon Simpson, nicknamed Bunny, as in fucks like a bunny. He's down in City doing five years for agg assault. I'll take the other two." Jenkins adeptly refolded his notes and shoved them into an inside pocket of his plaid suit coat. In the process, Griffin saw the silver-plated revolver, a short-barrel Colt Python, .357 magnum, holstered under Jenkins's arm.

"You got a license for that, Rawley, right?"

Jenkins's reply was a quick tilt of eyebrows. "Devon Simpson's only doin' five years, Jimmy. You better get down to City Jail fast before they parole him."

Griffin didn't like the mean spirit crawling over Jenkins's expression. The big man looking hungrier than for just the food he was scarfing down. "Let's check them out together. Good guy, bad guy. You play the bad guy." Hoping that would appeal to Jenkins.

The big man shook his head. "It's why I'm not even telling you right now who I'm gonna see. 'Cause you don't need to know what I'm gonna do." He chomped down on a fork of noodles. "Besides, there's not time. Noon tomorrow for the reporter, right? We need something for her. We cover twice the territory going separate."

"We'll be okay with her. Marish authorized me to cut her a pretty liberal deal, lots of access. She'll go for it."

"Fucking Dickie Marish." Jenkins wiped his mouth.

"Sorry, Jimmy, can't depend on him. I got my own concerns with this lady. Her story costs me my job."

Griffin wondered if Marish would okay the FBI if he knew Jenkins was "unofficially" on the investigation. "Just don't go crazy out there, all right?"

"Sure, no problem."

Griffin thinking, right, no problems at all, like when Jenkins and his father had been on the force together: beating confessions out of suspects for money as the dawn of civil rights tried to lift a shining sun onto a new day and Jenkins and Charlie Griffin tried to smack it back with their nightsticks. Griffin told Jenkins, "Don't do anything . . ."

Jenkins smiled at him.

Griffin said, "Call me if you need backup."

Jenkins appeared perfectly happy at the prospect of the afternoon and evening he'd planned for himself. "Call me if *you* need backup."

18.

Concrete walls don't breathe. That's what a veteran guard told Griffin the first time he was taken inside City Jail. That's why it smelled the way it did. Sour and old. Like the same air was inside now as when the final course of block had been laid in 1951.

Griffin didn't think that was it—stale air—in fact, he *knew* it wasn't. Because there were windows open all the time. Lots of air going through the place. The problem, the smell, came from the inside.

It came from pure fear. A unique terrified essence hanging in hot air like violent steam. And every time Griffin got a nose of it, he knew where he was. Like being in the jungle, where vines and leaves and insect-eaten wood bubbled in still ponds left from monsoon rains—a jailhouse's fear, like a jungle's decay, was everywhere.

In jail, the smell even took visible form. It covered wire-safety glass like a sweaty fog. Right in front of him, Griffin could see fear's imprint. He could smear it with his knuckles as he rapped on the glass, showing his detective's badge for the security officer.

The iron door buzzed and Griffin crossed the threshold. The line between inside and out. How many times had he made this trip—five hundred, a thousand?—it never mattered. Each time he crossed "the line," he thought about what it would feel like to know you weren't coming back out. The intense helplessness. Impossible futility.

Yet inside these walls were lots of bad fuckers who'd taken that step. Hadn't freaked, hadn't come apart—they were here. *Still* here. Doing the time. *Tha's right, man, jus' doin' it.*

Griffin left his gun at the security officer's desk. Another guard, one Griffin didn't know, escorted him to the interrogation room.

Two years after he joined the force, Griffin knew nearly every cop and guard in the city. Now he didn't know a third. The attrition rate was incredible. It had become a no-respect, no-honor job. How had that happened? It used to be a title: policeman. It *was* the law. Not anymore. By the time he'd left the force, being a cop was a bad joke—just keep the lid on the pot to keep it from blowing off, don't worry about what's inside.

It got so bad some guys went through their whole shift with their heads down. Avoiding other cops like it was some dirty job they were ashamed of. The sense of camaraderie and teamwork that once held the whole process together now oozed apart at the seams. The way it came down was like being on the losing team.

In the interrogation room, the guard said, "Devon Simpson, right?" He had wide, Germanic lips that didn't match his trace of Southern accent.

Griffin nodded, but the guard didn't respond to that. He wasn't looking at Griffin. He had his head down. "Yeah. Devon Simpson," Griffin said.

The guard left.

Griffin pulled one of three pine chairs from beneath the metal table, propped a foot on the seat, and braced an arm across his knee.

Ten minutes later, Devon Simpson walked in. Shoulders thrust back, feet dragging as though moving jelly legs. Near ninety degrees in the block and Devon had on a big wool cap—red, green, and black—into which was stuffed the length of his dreadlocks. As soon as he saw Griffin, Devon's mouth slowly formed hip protest in his distinctive Caribbean lilt. "Til mah lawyah here . . . I ain't sayin' nothin'."

Griffin nodded it was okay for the guard to leave.

The guard locked the door from the outside.

Griffin set the rules: "This isn't about you, Devon."

The Jamaican dropped listlessly into one of the chairs.

"You're clean, you're doing your time. No hassles."

Simpson angled his head back, looked down his wide nose at Griffin across the table. His skin was jet black, shiny with sweat.

"But," Griffin suggested, "maybe you'd like to cut some time off your stay here."

"No, mon . . ." Devon's head waved slowly back and forth.

"No . . . no . . . dis some kinna bullshit. I and I tell dat already. You wan' talk some kinna deal, sometin' mabbe I can do for you, it gotta go t'rouh my lawyah." He pressed two fingers to his lips, toking an imaginary joint. His fingernails were long and split.

"Yeah, well, the lawyer's out and time's short, so looks like we got no deal." Griffin rapped on the door for the guard, and suddenly Devon had some life in him.

"Hey, mon, wait a minute. Das it? Like dat?" His voice upped in pitch, sounding incredulous.

"That's it." Griffin rapped the door again, louder.

"Well, wait-wait-wait-wait-wait," Devon sang. "Don' be in such a rush." He slid his chair back and stood, started sauntering toward Griffin.

"Sit fucking down," Griffin demanded, pointing to the chair.

"H'okay. I and I can do dat, mon." Devon walked

backward, jail slippers skimming the floor, doing as Griffin ordered. "But le's talk, h'okay. You obviously come a long, long way to see Devon, mon. On dis terribly 'ot day." Devon talking as though reading a fairy tale.

The guard peered through the wire mesh glass. Griffin said, "Five more minutes, all right?"

The guard withdrew.

Griffin leaned against painted cinder block. Perspiration glued his shirt to his back.

Devon smiled, "H'okay. See, we'll talk. I'll tell you somet'ing and you'll get me out of 'ere, seen?"

"Depends on what you've got for me. If it's close, we'll call in your lawyer, get a judge, try to work it out."

"And a City Attorney, too, gotta have a prosecutor attorney go 'long wit' it."

Griffin showed his badge. "I am the City Attorney."

Devon nodded exaggerated approval as Griffin put away his shield.

Only then Griffin said, "Dunbar Waddy."

"Dunbah?" Devon jerked his head back as though Griffin's question had punched him. "What you want to ask me about 'im for? Dunbah a dead mon."

"How do you know?"

"Mon, everybody know dat. Deh police, deh knew where he was. He been ratted out. Police made it look like Dunbar slip away. *Oh, we can't find 'im. Where can dat niggah be?* Bullsheet, mon. Deh find 'im and kill 'im. Nobody kills a policeman's lady in dis town and lives, mon. Blam-blam-blam," Devon barked loudly. "It's all over for you. Not even the best lawyah in town can save you. Not even The Kroop."

"The Kroop?"

"Yah, seen, Karupka. Deh bad-ass lawyah, not even he can save you."

"Karupka wasn't Waddy's lawyer."

" 'Course not, mon, dat is what I'm tellin' you: *nobody could save a man done killed a policeman's lady.*

Can't be done by *nobody.* Not *even* somebody like deh Kroop."

"You know Karupka? He your lawyer?"

"Not my lawyah. How'm I gonna afford somebody like 'im? But other people in here, they known him. Everybody *known* 'im. Don't you? Must've been he's paid you, eh? Big mistah City Attorney you mus' get rich from 'im. He pays everybody."

Unbelievable, Griffin thought, where else but prison could a corrupt weasel like Jack Karupka be a legend. "You still haven't told me how you know Waddy's dead?"

"Mon, we back to dat again? I tell you, mon. Deh mon is dead. *Dead."*

"So where's his body?"

"Where his body! What are you, mon? Deh police gonna kill 'im, den bury 'im. You ain't gonna ever see dat boy's irie body. Nobody gonna see dat body ever again. Police kill you, dey take your soul wit' dem."

"You did used to hang out with him, right?"

"Yeah, mon, all deh time. Knew him in Jamaica, down Florida, and up 'ere."

"What if I told you, you tell me where Waddy is, help me find him, I can get two years cut off your sentence?"

"Oh, fuck, mon." Devon slid down in his chair and spread his arms like a grounded bird. "See? Fuckin' see? I knew I don' talk without a lawyah. I 'ave a lawyah in 'ere, he'd've worked me some kind of plea bahgain, jerk you along for a little while, get my ass outta here. Lawyah always tells me don' talk to no cop, no prosecutor attorney, it can't never help you. Don' say nothin'. Seen, if you'd've talked to my lawyah first, I'd have known what you lookin' for and would've had a nice lie all set up, somet'in to credit me some time. Tell you, yeah, I know where Dunbah is, lemme outta 'ere so I can take you to 'im. Now, you fuckin' tricked me into tellin' you what you want to know and what I gonna get for it? Nothin'." Devon slapped the table. "Fuck you, mon. Fuck your wife, too. Never talk wit'out a lawyah!"

19.

Griffin left City Jail with plenty of time to get his office-issued Ford Taurus across town and parked fairly close to home by five-forty-five P.M.

Walking down the block, he wondered if Devon Simpson's being so positive Dunbar Waddy was dead was good news. If Griffin could only prove that, maybe he could convince Marish to let him call in the FBI for a consult about Jane Doe, maybe even turn the case over to homicide.

Griffin would sneak this information to Blane during dinner when Carla was out of earshot, not wanting his wife to hear any references to Bright Eyes. She'd never been the same since Waddy had killed Blane's wife and son.

Unlocking the front door, Griffin expected his City Attorney friend would be there ahead of him. But Carla was alone in the living room, seated in a corner of the sofa. Looking fantastic in a long summer skirt; it buttoned high on one hip and was slit the rest of the way down, revealing luxurious legs. Her top was a loose-fitting dressy T-shirt. Her short hair styled with casual waves that had Griffin thinking he could grow to like this new look.

But something was wrong. Carla crossed her arms, angled one shoulder away from him, a very defensive pose even with her legs crossed sexily. "Mickey's not coming." As though it was Griffin's fault. "He said it had something to do with the office." She peered at him from beneath her bangs. "What happened today?"

Griffin froze momentarily. How could Blane hang him out like this? He knew Carla's sensitivities. "Nothing."

"Don't lie to me, Jimmy. Mickey said you had a big argument."

What the hell? Griffin wondered. "It was nothing. The usual politics. Marish going crazy."

"About what?"

Griffin tried to brush it off. "His press conference on that porn shop raid got buried by news people."

"That's it?" Carla was doubtful.

"No . . . that's not everything. But it was lots of little stuff like that."

"Mickey said you were mad at him. He said you'd start an argument if he came over."

"No. He's got it all wrong." Griffin took off his blazer and shoulder holster. The drive home in air-conditioning hadn't lessened the skinlike grip of his clothes after hot hours in Lexington Market and City Jail.

"Well, Mickey thinks you're mad at him."

"Here, look, I'll call him. Okay?" Griffin wondering what the hell Blane was thinking. An argument? It had been a discussion, that's all. Griffin wanting to call the FBI, and Blane and Marish telling him no. Blane had never taken an incident like that personally before. Griffin picked up the living-room extension and dialed Blane's condo. "Really," he assured Carla as the line rang, "it's nothing." He smiled. "You look great." Gazing at her legs.

It had been a very long time in between. Sex was always on Carla's terms, and generally out of obligation on her part, not interest. It made adultery tempting, but Griffin forced himself through it. Came close in weaker moments, but hadn't faltered. He worked hard at keeping himself away from temptation.

Griffin covered the mouthpiece, said, "Answering machine," when he got Blane's recorder.

Carla was perturbed. As though if everything couldn't be perfect tonight—three old friends having a simple dinner—she was going to go stir crazy.

"Mickey . . . Grif." He spoke cheerfully to the machine, as though showing Carla, see, how could I be mad at him and sound like this. "Hey, you should be here for dinner. Call when you get in." Griffin disconnected and redialed. "I'll try his car." He wanted Carla to calm down.

Not looking good, though. She got up from the sofa, arms still crossed, and headed back to the bedroom. The soles of her shoes smacked rigid steps to the hardwood.

Under his breath, Griffin urged, "Answer the phone, Mickey, goddamn it." All he got was a computer telling him the cell number he was trying to reach was not in service. He hung up and went down the hall.

Carla was in the bathroom, water running. He heard her close the medicine cabinet.

"Carla?" Griffin tapped the door gently with his knuckles, tried the knob. Locked. "Carla?"

The water snapped off. She opened the door and stormed past him, pocketbook slung over her shoulder. "I've got to get out for a while." As though trapped by her own psyche. "There's some zucchini lasagna from Sutton Place in the refrigerator. I was going to have it for lunch tomorrow, but help yourself."

Griffin followed her back down the hall. "Hon, come on, you're getting upset over nothing."

She started to cry. Grasping the side of her dress, she hurried for the front door, slender legs opening the fabric's long slit.

"Carla?" Griffin stopped at the archway to the dining room. Watched her through the front windows as she crossed the porch, went down the steps onto the sidewalk. He squeezed his hands into fists, then released them. "Damn it."

When these moods hit, she'd disappear for hours at a time, would go out driving, Griffin never knew where.

How long you gonna put up with that, Grif? Hell, man, that was my wife—

Yeah, yeah, yeah, he answered the voices in his head.

He gave himself a few minutes to cool off, then opened the door to Cassie's room.

She was awake on her back, reaching for rubber figures of tropical fish dangling hypnotically from the mobile over her crib. Far too innocent to have any concept of her parents' troubles, at least for now. But Griffin worried what effect Carla's illness would have on Cassie as she grew older, if Cassie would understand the situation better than he did. He hoped so for her sake.

"Looks like it's you and me for a while," Griffin whispered. He undressed, putting his clothes in the bag for the cleaners. "Give me five minutes to take a shower." He held up his hand, one finger at a time, and counted to five. "And then we'll have dinner and read a book. Something with a happy ending."

Liz McKinley knew she'd be taking a chance, but her afternoon with Carla Griffin had intensified her curiosity. She just had to see what the three of them were like—Griffin, Carla, and Mickey Blane—having dinner together. She only hoped they'd keep the front shades open so she could look in from where she parked across the street. If not, what the hell, maybe she'd knock on the door, tell Carla she'd decided to accept her offer to interview Blane, then catch the look on Griffin's face wondering what she was doing there.

Liz wasn't nearly as interested in that three-pound police file as she was in Griffin and his wife. There probably wasn't a story in either of them, but at least this was a fun way to wait for Bright Eyes to notch another victim.

Across the street from Griffin's apartment, Liz sat in her new rental car, a Thunderbird with six hundred miles and a car phone. Not wanting Griffin to recognize the Lincoln.

Liz was just getting comfortable, glad she was in the shade, when Carla Griffin came running out. Carla not looking back over her shoulder like she was being chased, just in a hurry.

Adjusting her side mirror, Liz followed Carla down the block, saw her get into her car, the Honda rumbling briefly as it came to life.

Liz debated whether to follow Carla or go inside and talk with Griffin. She opted for Carla. True, Carla could have been on a deadline for work, rushing to deliver or pick up papers. Or maybe any of a hundred other little boring household emergencies. But Liz's hunch was otherwise; she'd seen enough clues in the house today to guess what Mrs. Griffin did when she wasn't working as a paralegal or playing mom.

The motel was a series of single-level cottages set inside a horseshoe cutout of forest backing to State Park. Fifteen miles outside the city, directly on a main highway that ran straight to The Kroop's office within twenty minutes, forty during rush hour.

The farmhouse cottages were old, built thirty-five years ago when the area was considered the sticks. Frequented by migrant construction workers and adulterers, the license plates of cars parked recklessly on a gravel lot were half and half in-state or foreign.

The accommodations were cramped, but clean, $39 a night for singles, which was how everybody checked in. For ten extra bucks, you could get a waterbed room. Soft-X porn films brought in by satellite dish were $9.95 a run. Or you could rent a VCR and rougher tapes: ten bucks for the player, three dollars per tape.

All he was interested in was the room. Although a big fan of pornography, it was risky to have dealings with sex books or videos where records were kept. The police could get information like that and make it look bad against you. In front of a jury, everything was incriminating.

That's why he restricted himself to peep shows where you walked in anonymously, put in your tokens, saw what you wanted, *did* what you wanted, and left as facelessly as you entered.

Not being noticed, that was paramount.

Like the other day, taking the one he called Kay to Pussycat Licks. He'd had her stuff her hair inside a panama hat and wear a man's suit. Making her wait to come in until he was at the counter, diverting the attendant's attention.

She'd breezed by, head down, like any other embarrassed businessman. Picked a booth and waited for him.

Luscious Kay, an adventuresome college dropout, free-spirit runaway who hated her parents, loved dancing and getting stoned. Said the first night he'd gotten her off on belladonna she thought he was gorgeous and would like to take pictures of him naked.

In Pussycat Licks, they'd watched some mild S&M movies. He striped her naked, stood her against the wall, and painted on the hexagon with red oil-base enamel. Feeding her tiny doses of belladonna to get her flying. It

had been very intense, watching the seizures take hold,
rocking her like powerful orgasms that left her limp and
spent, so completely satisfied without ever having him
inside her. The come of her life.

Now, in the motel room, he opened his small suitcase.
All his clothes were in there, most of them lightweight,
suitable for the tropics where he'd been living. T-shirts,
shorts, running shoes, that was his "uniform"—very casual and showed off his body.

He was proud of the way he looked, a damn long way
from the rawboned kid who used to get kicked around
by his mother's boyfriends, older men who might have
been worried when his mother said she had a son until
they got a look at him.

He'd seen their eyes discounting him on sight, knowing they could push him out of the way like brushing off
a gnat. Do whatever they wanted to his mother without
having to worry about him. Not that she didn't want
them to do it, wouldn't make a lot of noise in the room
next to his, getting screwed all night by men she'd only
met a few hours ago.

It wasn't until he was older that he began to think the
men might be paying her, because while his mom had
been good-looking, more than willing, the men never
seemed to hang around too long. They sent gifts, sometimes little crap toys for him, like shoving money in a
parking meter, buying time.

Years had passed like that, moving from city to city,
staying with people who were supposed to be relatives,
except they never looked like him or talked like him.
Most thought he was odd, how he stayed to himself,
frightened and frail. Until he got older and started working out. He changed so fast, became powerful, and soon
nobody could control him. They still couldn't.

Standing before the small room's only mirror, he

dressed methodically, slipping on the tight dancer's leotard, a one-piece unit of black nylon that covered him from throat to wrist and ankle. Without underwear, his cock made a distinct bulge. He liked the pressure his swelling shaft stretched against the elastic; it reminded him of other times he'd worn this same garment. And the things he'd done while dressed this way.

Soon, maybe tonight, he was going to do some of those things again.

Carla Griffin drove like a city girl. Fast, aggressive, bordering on suicidal, treating red lights as optional.

Liz McKinley had a tough time keeping up. The Thunderbird's size kept her from squeezing through the same needle-eye gaps into which Carla shot the Prelude.

Twice, pinned back in traffic, Liz feared she'd lost Carla, only to catch up at a gridlocked intersection.

Less than fifteen minutes from home, Carla parked on the street in a residential section of upscale homes and renovated apartments.

Keeping low in her seat, Liz drove by and stopped fifty yards away. She noted a street sign as a landmark; after many turns and close calls during the reckless drive, she wasn't exactly sure where she was.

Grabbing her camera, window down, Liz turned in her seat and snapped off a series of pictures: Carla crossing the street against traffic; going through the decorative entrance gate into a brick courtyard, a small cluster of new midrise apartments called The Patios At Knollwood; Carla following the walkway to the building marked "A."

Liz smiled, having a good time.

She rewound her film and stuck in a roll of Kodak Tri-X black and white, upped the ASA to 1000. With the sun going down, lights around the Patios courtyard would be just enough to give her 1/15th-second exposures. The images would be blurry, but they'd be good enough.

"Get ready, boys and girls," Liz offered like a sarcastic kindergarten teacher, "because everybody going in and out of Building A is going to get his or her picture taken."

Camera ready, Liz waited for something to happen. She had a hunch it was going to be good.

20.

He drove a four-year-old Dodge Dynasty, a poor man's luxury car rented from a U-Save Auto franchise on the outskirts of town. The perfect nondescript car. Extremely unsuspicious. Cops rarely gave four-door sedans like that a second look, knowing they were driven by people as practical as the lines of the car itself: middle-management types who wanted a lesser-priced big car, retirees needing a large trunk to haul luggage on driving trips.

The Dynasty had a pretty big engine, but was still a piece of shit. He figured Chrysler could run all the ads they wanted about building better cars than the Japanese, but until the board of directors stopped giving themselves million-dollar raises and put more money in their workers' pockets they were going to keep getting junk that started falling apart at fifty thousand miles.

At least the air-conditioning worked. Dressed for adventure, wearing long sleeves and pants over the one-piece leotard made these dog days feel hotter still.

The sky was darkening, mean clouds rolling in with an evening thunderstorm, and it was humid as hell.

He took the main highway east, careful to follow the speed limit. Thinking how it was funny you could tell how close you were to the city by the number of barred shopping-center windows. Then the housing projects, demeaning places with industrial-strength wire-cage mesh thrown over open balconies as though keeping in the same people the merchants' bars were trying to keep out. Because if you were poor, you were surely a criminal.

He'd been treated like that growing up. His father gone, his mother hardly had any money. His clothes were all ripped hand-me-downs. Getting looked at like he was worthless, using up air and space meant for people with money, and believing that was true for a long time. But not anymore.

Near the heart of the city, what he knew people referred to as the vanilla cream center of a chocolate-ringed donut, he waved passing The Kroop's building as though Jack Karupka was standing on the corner. Knowing Karupka was likely up in his penthouse spire office, maybe worried about an old client who was back in the city and wasn't supposed to be. Perhaps Jack was even having second thoughts about hiring him for the Aronson job.

Karupka never looked worried, though. That was something he'd admired about his lawyer a long time ago: that even-keel expression, the ability to suppress panic and think under pressure. Which also allowed you to enjoy what you were doing.

And wasn't that what life was really all about? Enjoying yourself? He thought so. Which was why he had his red paint, camel-hair brushes, and syringes of belladonna along for the ride. Paint the town. Paint it, drug it, and watch it die. But slowly.

Gunpowder clouds tumbled across the city so quickly from her blind side, Liz McKinley didn't realize it was going to storm until the first huge drop of rain hit her windshield like a liquid stone. It startled her, as did the loud clap of thunder that followed.

The sky opened as though slashed by a butcher's

knife. Sheets of rain poured from a black sky, pelting the roof of the rented Thunderbird. Coming down so hard Liz could barely make out the entrance gate to the Patios At Knollwood. Her view of the apartment building Carla Griffin had entered became completely obliterated.

Street sounds changed instantly. Horns and engines were muffled under the rain. Tires rolled slowly through puddles formed at storm drains clogged by garbage. Pedestrians caught in the deluge ran with newspapers or briefcases over their heads, some screaming like overgrown children as their shoes splashed into potholes.

Slowly, the air became clean and pure as though charged by bolts of lightning that cracked behind a skyscraper horizon.

After twenty intense minutes, the storm moved on, leaving behind steaming streets and a mosaic sky of patchy clouds, spotless blue, and rays of purple-gold sunlight.

A slight drizzle remained as Liz got out of her car and crossed the street. She was unimpressed by the beauty nature trailed behind her thunderstorms. She wanted to know what the hell Carla Griffin was doing in Building A.

The ornate entrance gate was for looks, not security. Liz pushed open the heavy iron entry and walked into a bricked patio garden; on a much smaller scale, Carla Griffin's garden seemed modeled after this one. There was the same feeling of having found a safe harbor from city ugliness.

Elegant low-level apartment homes joined together by tall brick walls formed a three-sided cluster around the garden while the front entrance wall and gate closed the square.

Numerous benches and a screened gazebo were arranged around splendid planted areas into which a great deal of thought, expertise, and money had been dedicated. Far from a county exchange expert, Liz still would have sworn many of the shrubs and perennials were the same as in Carla's garden, definitely the packed rows of lavender if nothing else.

Liz went quickly to Building A's entrance, hoping Carla didn't happen to be looking out a front window. She no sooner had her handle on the door pull than it was opened from inside.

A suited concierge, briskly efficient, held the door for Liz. "Who are you here to visit?" A damned polite question, not at all as snooty as the marble foyer and high ceilings might look, but establishing quickly he knew Liz wasn't a resident.

"I don't think I should say." An adept liar, Liz let her voice flow a little raspier, shifting into the sexy clandestine tone she'd had lots of practice with. "Because this is a surprise visit and—who knows—you might tell his wife."

The concierge immediately appreciated the predicament Liz's deception created. If he adhered to strict security rules and told this pretty woman she would have to leave, that might anger one of the wealthy men who lived here, maybe a big tipper who'd leave a thin envelope this Christmas because his mistress had been snubbed. On the other hand, if she was lying . . .

She had already climaxed once, but knew she would again. So when his hard shaft withdrew from her slick vagina, Carla Griffin rolled onto her stomach. She reached for sturdy headboard posts and held on, raised her ass as he settled against her from behind.

His hands felt strong on her hips, holding her in position as his cock thrust powerfully into her, a much deeper sense of penetration than being taken face-to-face.

Clean sheets stuck to her moist flesh. It was cool in the big apartment, but she felt so hot. Her heart pounded furiously. Everything else was blocked out. There was nothing except the swell of his erection and pleasing tension of her pussy.

He took a long time. Minutes passed off the clock. At times she felt completely outside of herself with him. She always had. As though able to watch him make love to her, how their bodies came together, wondering how he could make her react the way he did when no one else could. The pace so frantic, his body tireless.

Prohibited passions were always best. Like the first time making love, how it was awkward and uncomfortable, a sense of disbelief it was happening, only he'd been experienced even then, had made her come three times the night he'd taken her virginity.

He'd likely make her come three times tonight as well. Carla just holding onto the bedposts, feeling the thrill of him, gasping, "Fuck me, Mickey. Fuck me."

Liz McKinley said, "Don't look," having convinced the doorman to walk a few steps ahead of her, escorting her through the halls of the three-story apartment house.

There were six units on each floor. Liz paused at each one, claiming she was going to slip a surreptitious note to her married lover. So as not to compromise "her man" she told the doorman she didn't *not* trust him, but still didn't want him to know under which door she was going to slip her nonexistent note. Which was why they were stopping at every door.

Still on the first floor, near the end of the hall, Liz listened desperately to hear Carla Griffin's voice, to get some hint as to which of the eighteen apartments she might be visiting. And having a pretty good idea just what it was she was doing.

Because earlier in the day, while Liz waited in the garden before the interview, Carla had been in the bathroom for a long time. Later, Liz helped herself to Carla's bathroom, checked the medicine cabinet and vanity, found some interesting prescription drugs—most notably Prozac—along with a very recently cleaned diaphragm.

What Carla liked most about the building was the quiet. The walls and windows were so well insulated, blocking out neighbors and the city like the walls of a tomb.

"You're quiet tonight." Sharing the big red bathtub and a bottle of champagne, Carla traced her toe softly along Mickey Blane's bare thigh.

"Work." He smiled.

"Mmm," she hummed thoughtfully. "Try not to think about it. That's why we're here. To not think about it. Not think about anything." Carla ran a hand through the new cut of her hair, liking the feel of it: kicky and free.

The oversized master bathroom smelled sweetly of lavender, Carla having squirted in lots of Crabtree & Evelyn bath gel while running the water. It was her favorite scent, like the inexpensive perfume she'd been wearing in twelfth grade when Blane first made love to her in his parents' bedroom. The night she'd lost her virginity to him.

Fifteen years later, the surroundings in which they snuck away were equally remarkable. A massive Jacuzzi tub in a room walled in shiny black tile. Gold-plated fixtures included a mini waterfall faucet that fed the bath. Very nice of Blane's friend to let them use it while he was out of the country; he seemed to travel frequently,

given the number of times Blane was able to meet her
here.

Carla sipped ticklish pink champagne, enjoying its
taste while watching Blane's flaccid shaft underwater.
Liking his soft size as much as when he was hard. Especially appreciative of the transition, very fond of taking
him into her mouth and holding him between her lips,
wrapping his member with her tongue until he began to
get large, not letting him go until his size was too much
to keep down.

"You're still thinking about work," she scolded playfully.

"I know," he admitted.

"Is it bad?"

"It's not . . ." He let the sentence go and slid around
the tub so they were side by side instead of face-to-face.
"Let's not talk about it," he suggested. "After all, it is
our anniversary."

Carla set down her champagne glass, kissed him,
whispered, "I want to leave him. It's too hard being with
him and loving you."

"I told you not to marry him."

"I was mad . . . because you married Diana."

"My father," Blane replied, suppressing a groan.

"We don't have to get married, or live together. It'll
work out better that way. Awhile after I get divorced,
we'll make it public. No one will suspect anything."

Blane considered her plan. "My father might even
croak by then . . . hopefully."

Liz McKinley was beginning to think everyone in the
Patios At Knollwood was dead. She couldn't remember
the last time she'd been in an apartment house that was
so quiet. But that was one thing you could count on
about the rich: they loved their quiet, as though the

slightest hint of someone else's existence was an adulteration of their own life.

Liz and her aiding-and-abetting concierge were on the third floor, sixteen doors into her search. No leads for Liz and the concierge getting jittery, maybe worrying Liz was slipping letter bombs under everyone's door. Working for rich people could make you as paranoid as they were.

At the final apartment door, Liz finally heard something. A blaring TV screaming a syndicated episode of *Murder She Wrote* toward deaf ears. Terrific. Big scoop, she thought sarcastically.

"Okay?" The concierge wanted to get back to his post.

No, Liz thought, not okay, but couldn't tell him that. Carla Griffin was in here somewhere, probably getting wonderfully screwed. Liz wanted to know all about it. If the guy Carla was seeing wasn't too gorgeous, maybe Liz wouldn't be too jealous. After all, for Carla to have a husband like Griffin *and* someone on the side—it just wasn't fair.

But for now, she was out of options. Liz thanked the concierge and went back to her car, too obsessed with her own thoughts to notice what had become a perfect sunset.

Liz dug into her pocketbook, found Jimmy Griffin's card, and called his home number on her cell phone. He answered on the third ring. A rather anxious hello. No, Liz thought, this isn't Carla calling. "It's me, Liz," she said, getting a perverse sense of satisfaction talking to Griffin while watching the building where she was sure his wife was getting it on with another man. "You haven't forgotten about me, have you?" Openly flirting with him. Another perverse pleasure; Liz was full of them.

"Of course not." Griffin was all business.

Cassie was jabbering somewhere nearby. Liz pictured Griffin, Mister Modern Father, cradling his daughter while doing serious work on the phone. "About eighteen hours till my deadline, lover. And that police file was a real yawn." Liz thinking wouldn't it be incredible if Carla came out right now, and Liz waved her over, said, "Come 'ere, honey. Someone on the line wants to talk to you."

"Here's the deal," Griffin said.

In the rental car, Liz made a face, as though saying, whoa, cut right to it why don't we. But all she let him hear was, "Okay . . . ?" Waiting for his offer.

"You keep the story dead until your next edition, not the one coming up. You're weekly, right?"

"Uh-huh."

"Okay. Something breaks in the meantime so that another paper beats you to press, we still save goodies for you."

"Like?"

Griffin ran through what Marish had authorized, finishing up with morgue pictures of any victims as though that was his trump card. When Liz didn't respond right away, Griffin asked, "Deal?"

"Interesting . . . but I've got to think about it."

"I don't have anything else to offer. You've been around, you know what I'm giving is a lot."

"Don't make me sound so old."

"You know what I mean." Griffin remained serious.

Liz couldn't lighten him up. My God, she thought, you really do love this woman. She's run out for the night and it's eating you up. Griffin had always struck her as a pretty tough guy, none of that macho bullshit, opening beer bottle caps with his teeth, but steely and determined. Ironic that what would hurt him the most wasn't physical pain.

"Okay, Detective Griffin," Liz said, "you got a deal. But as soon as something new breaks, you call me, right?"

"Good."

"All right. Listen . . ." Liz picked up her camera, held as steady as she could to photograph a guy coming out of Building A, passing under the bright light *now*. She hit the shutter. ". . . You want to—?"

"What was that sound?"

"I'm playing with my camera. Don't interrupt. I'm in the process of asking you out on a date and I'm very sensitive." Liz set down the camera. "Meet me for a drink later?"

"Thanks anyway."

"You could leave your doll baby I hear cooing in your lap with a sitter, couldn't you? Just hop out and meet me for a little while."

"Thanks anyway."

"Your wife's lucky you're so faithful. You are faithful, aren't you, Griffin? It's not just me?"

"It's not just you."

"Yeah, well, I figured. You take care. Keep in touch. I got this handy car phone now. Here's the number." She gave it to him, then hung up.

For Griffin's sake, Liz hoped Carla wasn't seeing another man. "But I know you are," Liz said out loud. "I just *know* that you are."

21

The first house he remembered living in as a child had been torn down. He stared at what was now an empty lot—stone, dirt, and broken bottles—in a pretty rough neighborhood. Lots of activity in and out of the place three doors down, probably dealing crack. Homeboys on the street checking out his Dodge Dynasty stopped at the curb, maybe thinking him a cop or some suburban rube in town looking to score some of that new heroin everyone was hot for.

He shifted into drive and headed down the block. This used to be a decent area. He'd lived here until he was five. That's when his father left. His mother was twenty-three at the time. At first, she said his father had been killed, but about a week later she got mad about something and said the old man had just left them. That he was a no-good bastard! His mother had screamed that at *him*, as though *he* was the no-good bastard, not his father. And he'd believed her. He wasn't any good. He couldn't have been. His father didn't want him.

He was scared of everything back then, everyone. All the moving from place to place didn't help. People who seemed so big and angry to him always showing up at their door, demanding money from his mother. He could still picture them over twenty years later.

The men would argue with his mother and she'd yell back, tell them they weren't going to get their god-

damned money because she couldn't pay them what she
didn't have. He never understood why his mother didn't
have money, he didn't understand anything, but whenever those people would come, he'd cry.

His mother would scream at him to stop being a baby.
She'd hit him hard, on the face and buttocks, sometimes
not stopping until his skin burned. That was how he
learned to count.

His mother would say he was going to get twenty
smackings and she'd grab him by his arm, hold him still
as he struggled uselessly to get away. She'd yell out each
number as she beat him. Soon he could count along so
he'd know how long it would be until she'd stop.

Sometimes he was undressed when she slapped him.
Hitting all over his body, she didn't care where. Sometimes yelling his little peewee was going to get it, and
slapping his penis.

The only time she didn't hit him when he cried was
one day when some people showed up and said they
were going to take him away from her. He'd cried pierc-
ingly, clinging to his mother's leg, not wanting to go.
His mother shrieked at the man and woman who'd come
to the house, asking how they could take away her baby,
stroking his hair as she said that.

The people—social workers, he now realized—left
that day, and in case they might every come back, his
mother packed up what little they owned and they
moved.

They lived with people she told him to call Aunt so-
and-so, or Uncle this or that. He accepted they were relatives until he got older and understood what being a
relative meant. When he'd start asking questions about
how they were related, his mother would tell him to shut
up.

He was eight the first time he saw his mother having

sex with one of his "uncles." It was the third or fourth
place they'd lived in two years. A small brick row house
that always smelled of deep frying fat.

He came home early from school because it was a half
day for teachers. Had quietly entered the house, always
careful not to disturb anyone, having been told by his
mother to be polite and courteous so he would blend in
with the family.

He heard the noise upstairs and thought his mother
was in another fight with someone, but, standing in the
hall, the door half opened, he saw his mother naked on
the bed. His "uncle" was on top of her with his shirt on,
his pants down around his ankles, moving viciously
while his mother grunted as though in pain.

He didn't understand what was happening, but knew
enough not to ask questions. The experience left him
even more empty and confused. He blamed his reaction
on his "uncle." Within days, those feelings turned to intense hatred.

In the first outburst of temper he'd ever known, as
though he'd gone mad, he went into his uncle's bedroom
one night and started tearing apart his clothes, ripping up
the thin paperback books and magazines with pictures of
naked women he found under his bed.

His uncle caught him, whipped him severely, would
have probably killed him had his mother not pulled him
away. The next day, they moved across the city to live
with other "relatives." His mother was not that angry
with him, which was surprising.

On the drive over, a new bond seemed to be established between them. She talked to him in a voice he'd
only heard her use with grown-ups, as though he was a
man now. "You know more than you look like you
know, don't you?" she asked him. He hadn't known
what she'd meant, but said, very proudly, "Yes."

His mother started to cry, saying how he'd done that for her, wasn't it wonderful how her little man had come to her rescue. He had no idea at the time his uncle had been forcing his mother to go to bed with him so they could keep living there; that he was a dirty vulgar man who used his mother in all sorts of "unnatural" positions. She'd put up with it only because they needed a place to stay, because what she was making as a dime store clerk couldn't pay any rent.

But after her "little man" came to her rescue, they had to leave, and she was glad for *him* to have made the decision for them.

After that, she had many more men, but was always careful to tell him it was all right. "Mommy likes this man," she'd say. "I really really like him. It's okay, you understand?" He'd say he did, but he didn't. Because all the men were just like his uncle to him. He hated them all. He did spiteful things, scratched the paint on their cars, spit at them, tore up the gifts they brought for his mother or the cheap toys meant for him.

As punishment, his mother whipped him hard; sometimes the men did, too. He took it, wouldn't fight back. He found that by counting the blows, like his mother reeling off his punishment years earlier, he could concentrate on the numbers and not the pain.

The only one he never did anything to—not at first— was Henry. He thought Henry was an ugly man. He could tell his mother didn't act right around him, like she was playacting. Henry treated his mother differently from other men. When Henry took his mother on a date, he was taken with them. Like a family, his mother said happily. And Henry never went upstairs with his mother, never made noise he'd hear through the walls.

Henry hadn't been coming around too long when he and his mother sat him down one day and said they were going to be married. That he could call Henry "Father," but only if he wanted to. He didn't want to, but since his mother encouraged him, he called jerk Henry "Father," which seemed to make them happy, like everything was going to be fine.

Father/Henry never paid much attention to him, which he didn't really care about. They lived in the nicest house he'd ever seen. He wore new clothes. Other kids stopped looking at him like he was a reject. He made a few friends, but knew all along—even when his mother assured they'd found a home now, that Henry was going to be a good father to him—it wouldn't last. Something would happen and they'd move again.

A year and a half later, his mother had a baby. He'd been frightened by the prospect of a brother or sister, but when Alice arrived, he fell in love with her. She was so tiny and fragile. She needed protection and he vowed *he* would be her protector. Henry certainly couldn't be. Henry was a skinny man who always had to get bigger men to help move things around the house.

He was only ten years old at the time, and kids in gym class talked about lifting weights to make themselves stronger. He saw middle school boys doing it, saw their arms getting big. He started lifting weights, determined to be strong enough to protect his baby sister.

Soon, he began to fantasize about Alice and him running away; he would take her someplace safe. He told her good-night stories about it, expanding the fantasy, talking about nice houses they'd live in, nicer even than Henry's. And how he would never let Henry and other men like him lay on top of her with their pants down and do violent things to her. He would protect her from men like that.

By the time Alice was a year old, he was more in love with her by the day. He no longer played with friends, but rushed home after school to be with Alice. He'd feed her, play with her, tell her stories. His mother was overjoyed. Henry, too, until the night Henry found him giving Alice a bath.

He'd helped bathe Alice before, but always when his mother was holding her because Alice was so small. That night, though, for the first time, his mother said it was okay for him to give Alice a bath on his own. He was overjoyed at the prospect, being finally given the one task he hadn't been able to do by himself. Now he was all Alice needed. He could do everything.

But when Henry saw him soaping Alice between her legs, wiping where his mother said was very important to keep clean, Henry grabbed his arm and roughly pulled him away. Demanded to know what he was doing to Alice.

"Giving her a bath," he explained obviously, but Henry screamed that's not what he was doing, he was doing dirty things to her. Henry's face turned beet red, and he slapped him on the arms and head, weak man's punches he barely felt, thinking at the time, "I'm stronger than you, Henry. I could kill you right now. Grab your throat and strangle you to death."

From that day on, although his mother tried to convince Henry otherwise, he wasn't allowed to be alone with Alice. He was devastated. A tension crept over the house. Henry was always watching him. He heard Henry and his mother arguing about him, Henry claiming he was molesting Alice.

The accusation made him crazy inside. To spell the anxiety, he lifted weights relentlessly, doing it until his arms trembled from strain and his heart beat rapidly against his chest. He muttered through deep breaths how he was going to kill Henry. Kill him and take Alice where she'd be safe.

His anger spilled over into school. He became uncontrollable. He got into fights with boys two and three years older and beat them mercilessly, knocking out teeth. He was suspended numerous times, eventually sent to a special education school.

At home, Henry yelled at him, but he could tell Henry was scared of him now. Henry had seen what he'd done to kids at school. Henry must have sensed he was next.

By the time he was seventeen, most of the past four years as a runaway, he'd been in juvenile court three times. The last time for a fight in which the nineteen-year-old he'd beaten had lost an eye. They were going to send him to a juvenile detention facility, or, as an alternative, he could join the armed forces.

He took the marines, but never made it through boot camp. Three weeks into basic training, he'd had five fights. Other recruits called him a psycho. He did the balance of basic training in the stockade, a total of a year there. And then they gave him a dishonorable discharge.

He was close to Florida at the time; it was April, so he hit Daytona Beach and hung out with the spring breakers. Eventually made his way down to Miami and hooked up with Jamaicans, intrigued by their music, culture, and ganja.

He'd never done drugs his entire life, but once they turned him onto them, he finally found what he had been missing. The calm the sinsemilla laid over him was wonderful.

His thinking became fuzzy, but that was okay, quite a relief after so many years of pain. He'd get stoned and dream about his sister, Alice. He was still determined to get her away from Henry. To take care of her himself.

In Florida, he did some robberies with the Jamaicans.

Two days after his eighteenth birthday, he got busted. His service record and juvenile offenses bought him a year in jail. More time to lift weights and also to learn.

Lots of guys in jail talked about how it was dumb to get caught, how they weren't going to get caught again once they got out, planning schemes to commit perfect crimes. He listened to them, thought how right they were, all along doped on ganja that was easier to get in jail than outside.

Two months after his release, he got picked up for committing a "perfect crime." Another robbery, this time with aggravated assault tacked on top. He got a ten-year sentence, did three and a half easy years; no one messed with him.

He wasn't the biggest guy in the block by a long shot, but he was the wildest. They called him Hurricane because that's what he looked like in a fight, fast and powerful. Very strong, quick hands. Once taking hold of a guy's throat and not letting go until the guards knocked him unconscious.

He hung with Jamaicans in prison. Found one of them very spiritual, a guy who taught him how to focus his energy. Who said he could really be something if he wanted, but he'd have to stop hanging with losers, would have to march out on his own. He learned how to meditate. How to control his anger, channel it.

The Jamaican also introduced him to belladonna, said it was the most beautiful experience in the world. He had some for him, a little dose he should save until he got out. Give it to a lady friend and watch her eyes while making love to her. See her respond like never before.

He didn't tell the Jamaican there weren't any lady friends in his life, and never had been. While sex had interested him for a long time, he'd suppressed those feelings from going beyond masturbation. Remembering how he'd seen his mother taken so violently as a child. How she hadn't wanted it done.

He tempered his desires with pornography, finding suggestive pictures to look at, making himself come while thinking about real women posed that way. Maybe a woman he could give some belladonna to, let her experience the drug's pleasure while he watched.

By the time his first parole hearing was scheduled, he seemed a much different person. The anger on the outside had turned inward where it was focused like the heart of a bomb, inert, waiting for a fuse.

The Review Board was impressed. They honestly believed he'd been rehabilitated when they cut him loose. They congratulated themselves on the fine innovative programs the corrections system had undertaken.

Out of jail his second trip, he decided it was time to go home for a while. He hadn't talked to his mother in eight years. Hadn't seen Alice, either. She would be fifteen, he thought, around that age, anyway.

His Jamaican friends had a connection for him back in Baltimore: a network set up in a tiny area becoming known as Little Kingston, where drug-running posses were making inroads.

He took the train into the city and walked to Henry's house. It looked different, much smaller than he'd remembered. He knocked on the door and Alice answered. Seeing her, all the love and emotion he'd suppressed over the years came flooding back. He hugged her and she screamed.

Immediately, he released her, watched in horror as she ran upstairs. He started after her. She didn't remember who he was. How could she not remember? All the stories, how she'd looked so happy when he'd told her how he was going to take her away from Henry.

Upstairs, Alice screaming, "Daddy! Daddy!"

Henry rushed out of the bedroom. Looking even more weak and pathetic than years ago. Fear struck his eyes, seeing who'd come into his house, who was back.

Henry told him his mother had died of leukemia two years ago. They'd tried to contact him.

He was surprised how unaffected he was by the news of his mother's death. Was nearly astounded to hear himself tell Henry his mother was a whore, that Henry had been lucky not to get syphilis from all the men his mother had fucked before him.

Henry began to tremble even before his hands were around his throat, choking the life out of him, leaving him to die as gurgling cries of spittle ran over his lips.

Alice witnessed her father's murder. She screamed horrendously and slapped wildly as he tried to hold her and said it was all right, that they were better off with Henry dead, that it was what they'd wanted for such a long time.

Alice remained hysterical until he forced belladonna down her throat. An uncontrolled dose. The Jamaican never told him how much to use.

Alice went into wild convulsions in his arms, but he believed her to be in ecstasy, as though having the intense pleasure of sex without the dirty contact. Her eyes opened widely, beautifully. And stayed that way once she was dead.

He felt a rush of excitement, an unthinkable arousal holding her dead body. He shook undressing her, continued to shiver carrying her lithe naked body to her bed. He propped her in a position like the women in the magazines he liked and masturbated looking at her. He had never known such intense pleasure.

The experience left him overly excited. Emotions changed through his body as though fired by electricity. He forced himself to focus. He had to get rid of the bodies, make sure the police never found them. They never did. They found the next bodies, though, but that didn't matter because they weren't going to find him.

Now, four years later, he prowled Baltimore streets, looking for a new body. Maybe someone not so young this time. Someone a little more experienced.

22.

Carla Griffin left The Patios At Knollwood shortly before nine P.M. She opened the iron gate and passed under the archway, holding the gate as it closed, easing it shut. Her back to the street, her mind was distracted by pleasures she was leaving behind.

Hours she spent with Mickey Blane passed so quickly. She wanted to be with him all the time, and felt miserable when she wasn't, depressed and anxious. It didn't always have to be making love to him, either. Seeing his face, smelling his cologne, talking on the phone, she settled for anything. Because that's all she could have, maybe forever, definitely while Mickey's father was still alive.

Carla glanced back at the front windows of the apartment she'd just left, knowing Mickey remained inside. She'd like a final glimpse of him, a quick wave. So intent on her desire, she didn't see the man coming up on her from behind.

Liz McKinley started shooting pictures of Carla the moment she exited Building A. Carla crossing the brick walk. Carla outside the gate, on the sidewalk.

Liz shooting all that until the man came up on Carla from behind. Grabbed her. That's when Liz threw down the camera and jumped out of the car.

The man had Carla by both shoulders, holding her steady. "Are you all right?"

Carla tested her ankle, having turned it sharply.

"I startled you. I'm sorry. But from behind you looked exactly like my fiancée." He was a tall man with a weak jawline. Wearing a long-sleeve Polo short, unusual for the summer. "She lives here. My fiancée," he clarified when Carla appeared puzzled.

"Oh, God." She exhaled deeply. "You did startle me." She touched the front of her T-shirt blouse. "My heart's beating like a bird."

"Is your foot okay?" he asked. His hands remained on her shoulders.

Carla put weight on her ankle, testing it. "Fine," she confirmed. "I just turned it a little."

"I really am sorry. But like I said, you looked just like Janice. Your hair especially." His grasp of her shoulders lingered unnecessarily.

Carla became uncomfortable.

He finally withdrew his hands. "You were leaving?"

"Yes. I'm parked just across the street."

"I'll walk you to your car. This isn't the greatest of neighborhoods for them to build these expensive apartments. Urban renewal." He rolled his eyes.

Carla knew this was one of the safest sections of town. She started toward the street, leery of him. "That's all right."

He touched her bare arm. His fingers were moist. "I really don't mind."

"I'm fine. Thanks." She ran between cars. Horns blaring as she hurried across the street.

Cut off from her, the man waited for a break in traffic.

Carla fumbled with her keys, unlocked the door and got in, relocking the door as the man jogged over.

He tried to appear casual. Smiling. He tapped on her

window. "I really am sorry," he called through the glass.
"Maybe we could have coffee some time."

Carla started the Honda. "I don't think so." She pulled
abruptly from the curb. Tires squealing.

Liz called, "Smile," to the guy with the beard who'd
followed Carla Griffin to her car. He was standing in the
spot vacated by the Honda as Liz cruised past and
snapped his picture.

"Hey, hey, what are you doing?" he shouted, running
toward her in khaki shorts and sockless loafers. He had
thin, hairless legs; a somewhat strange-looking forty-
year-old guy, probably a horny poetry professor who got
off reading suggestive prose to freshman girls.

Liz tossed the Canon onto the passenger seat and sped
away. "Creep."

He decided they weren't married. Not the way they
danced together. Not in this club. A grocery store converted to a nightclub. Lots of outdated neon glitz. A
black velour backdrop behind the DJ for God's sake.
Blue-collar partiers and loud music. Bass thumping like
a sonic boom, drowning out high notes—just give 'em
that rhythm, keep 'em moving.

He sat at the bar, drank straight scotch—paint-thinner
house brand. Watched the guy and girl dance, and
thought about the girl. The kinky outfit she had on. A
man's suit and tie, but no shirt. Wide lapels on the
jacket, and only one fastened button. Showing incredible
cleavage the striped tie couldn't begin to hide, not the
way she danced. Wild motions, tits and tie moving lust-
fully. She also had a panama hat, a slick look with her
long hair bouncing out beneath it.

Her guy loved her outfit, too, no doubt about it. A
weight-lifter jock, displaying his girlfriend. *Hey, look at*

this body she's got, not afraid for people to see her half naked, tits dancing out of that blazer. Letting people gaze at her knowing they wouldn't try taking her away from him, not a guy that big.

Which was okay with the man at the bar; all he liked to do was look. Although he liked looking at them stoned and dying better than dancing. He wondered if he could talk her into dancing for him before he fed her belladonna.

He hoped he wasn't going to have to hit her with the drug first. But some of them didn't cooperate. The ones who didn't go for him had to be forced. Just because he didn't appeal to them didn't diminish the fantasy. Once the fantasy started, you had to go with it. Denying fantasies was not good.

The ones he had to force were more trouble. You had to worry where you did it, how long you took. The best ones went to motels with him, even paid for the room. Almost all of the first women did, but he'd been more patient back then, spent time warming them up, telling them lies.

It was in Jamaica—during his four-year exile—that he'd begun to feel restless, bored by conversation. So he just started taking them. Tourist women he found walking the beach at night. Put them out quick, stripped them in the sand, loaded in the belladonna, and watched them die.

Kay, the one he'd done in the pron stall two days ago, had been one of the first "volunteers" in a while. She'd been drawn to him. Which was good. He wasn't so busy he couldn't spend a little time with them, just so it wasn't any place too public.

He wondered now how it was going to be with the one he was watching dance. Look at her, letting her he-man stick his hand inside her blazer, right on a tit. He had a feeling she'd be the bossy type. Even if she did feel like cheating on her stud, she'd have a lot of questions. And he didn't have time for that.

He was on a timetable. He couldn't stay in the city that much longer. Had to keep moving. But the hunger came in such intense periods. He could go months without—over a year at one point—but once he got started again, well, it was damned hard to stop.

He drank more scotch and felt the hint of a buzz, enjoying conversation with himself. Thinking how The Kroop would disapprove of this. The Kroop would want him figuring out how he was going to do the job: kill Greg Aronson.

Yeah, yeah, yeah, business, business. He'd hit Aronson soon enough. Had driven by the house once already. Saw the sign on the front driveway advertising what kind of alarm system they had, knew that would be a problem, but he'd get around it. He just didn't want to think about how he was going to kill Aronson right now.

He wanted to watch the girl dance. Feeling the heat of the club make him sweat. The leotard he wore under his clothes was itching a little, itching to make something happen.

He swirled melting ice against scotch and fantasized. Imagined the dancing girl completely naked, lying on her back. Those big tits, probably implants, would sit up on her chest at attention, wouldn't fall back against her rib cage like natural ones. She'd be firm. The paint brush would glide over her tits like glass, leave bright red trails of color. She'd start convulsing from the belladonna, jumping in ecstasy as the paint dried.

He'd feel the thrill watching her, maybe get off once, then do it again after she was dead, after he had a chance to pose her. A really, really hot pose. Something that would make even the cops turn on when they found her stone hard in death.

He finished his drink, paid for it, and walked outside. All very anonymous. Just in and out. A faceless guy no one would realize had been there.

But once out in the parking lot, walking toward the rented Dodge, he heard footsteps behind him.

"Hey!" A young woman's voice. Talking to him?

He turned and saw her smiling. "I was going to buy you a drink, but you got out of there in such a hurry." An attractive girl, late twenties. Thick chestnut hair she'd spent lots of time getting just right, flowing over the shoulders of a see-through purple blouse beneath which she wore dressy lingerie. A short white skirt. Long legs in high heels bringing her to within a few inches of his height. And best of all: great eyes, beautiful, big blue eyes.

He returned her smile. "I've had enough of bars for a while. I'm going to take a drive."

"Oh. Okay." She was disappointed.

Through his smile, he felt anger. Scratch the dancer now. Someone had noticed him. He couldn't risk being put in the same club as the dancer if the cops found out where she'd been the night she died.

The new girl suggested, "Can I go with you?" Coming on to him. "It is a nice night for a drive."

When he heard the front door open, Griffin folded shut the police file on Dunbar Waddy. He looked at the clock even though it would only be five minutes later than when he'd checked the last time, which had only been five minutes after the time before that. Ten twenty-five P.M. She'd been gone nearly five hours.

He waited in the big chair in Cassie's room, listened to Carla's footsteps cross the hardwood floor. She hesitated short of the door.

"It's okay," Griffin said, meaning he wasn't holding Cassie.

Carla moved half into the doorway, placed a hand against the frame, and leaned gracefully against it. Griffin wondering if she knew how beautiful she looked.

"You all right?" he asked.

She nodded, all signs of anxiety now erased. "Just tired."

"Did you eat?"

Another nod. "I'm going to call it a night, Jimmy. Sorry about earlier." She turned toward her bedroom.

How long, Grif? How long you gonna put up with it?

Tracy Deil already had a hotel room. In the Hilton, less than five miles from the dance club.

Tracy was a sales rep for a national swimwear company, a former model turned aspiring exec in town to drum up new accounts. Outgoing, aggressive, not at all afraid of meeting new people, especially not the man she'd seen in the club.

She'd thought him handsome enough, probably smart, maybe a little lonely or even shy the way he stayed to himself. Tracy thought he might have been married; he didn't seem interested in talking to any of the single women, hadn't even looked her way the whole time she'd been looking at him. But he didn't have a wedding band, not the crease of one recently pocketed. She'd decided to buy him a drink just as he'd paid for his and walked out.

He'd been worth following. So she'd gone outside to walk away from the smoke and noise of the bar. Why not? Tracy was prepared. She had condoms in her small leather clutch. Knew she looked good in her outfit.

She hadn't expected him to have that kind of car, though. She'd pegged him as a restored Camero driver, maybe a '65 Mustang, definitely a convertible. She said something about it, driving around the city, windows down, warm air spilling through the cockpit, checking out city lights. He said it was rented. Like her, he was in town on business, interviewing for jobs.

They talked about that for a while until he became sketchy about details of the kind of work he did. Tracy assumed he wasn't having much luck hunting for work, didn't want to talk about it. He became a little tense. She asked if he wanted to have another drink somewhere. He looked over at her, eye to eye, said he was really in the mood for something more intoxicating.

She thought he'd meant going to bed with her, but then he asked if she did drugs, had ever heard of belladonna. An incredible *gentle* rush, he pitched. Very sexy. Like being on the beach in the tropics. Breezy.

Now they were in her room and she was on it. An experience like nothing she'd ever had before. Better than marijuana or coke. On this stuff—she was going to have to remember the name—the room seemed so bright, as though the tiny table lamp was the sun, big and white, making her glow all over. Peaceful. Exotic.

She let him undress her. Everything came off so urgently. He barely touched her body although she wanted him to. Arousal was flowing between her legs.

Once she was naked, he spread her arms and legs, left her in that pose as he removed his clothes and lay on top of her. Not naked, though, wearing something. Like a big stocking. She felt his erection contained by it, pressing over her thighs.

"This is so good." She sighed.

He hummed appreciatively. "It gets better." He reached for the small satchel he'd carried to her room and got the paint.

23.

"Mickey's not in yet?" Griffin asked Lynn, one of eleven pool secretaries in the City Attorney's office.

"I haven't forgotten you, Jimmy." Lynn removed operator-style headphones and stretched, taking a break from the pleading she had up on the screen. "Soon as he comes in, I'll buzz you."

"I've been trying to call him since last night. He doesn't answer home, in his car. Now he's out on some 'emergency'?"

"I wonder what her name is, too." Lynn smirked. "You know, Jimmy, you could have that many girls if you were single. Could have almost that many being married."

"Shame, shame," Grif scolded. "From the lips of a newlywed."

Lynn breathed on her wedding band, buffed it against her blouse like a trophy. "I waited for you, Jimmy, but, no, you kept hanging around with that Carla woman."

Griffin liked Lynn, one of the only women he'd ever talked to about the problems he and Carla were having. Lynn, unlike his police friends, told him to hang in there. That anything worthwhile was worth waiting for. "Besides," she'd say, "if life was perfect, would either of us be working here?" Lynn shared Griffin's opinion of Richard Marish.

Griffin went back to his office, where he'd been for

two hours—since eight forty-five A.M. Waiting for
Blane. He was determined to take another crack at con-
vincing him the FBI should be called in. Griffin figured
if he could work Blane into agreeing with him, they
could double-barrel Marish. It had worked before, especially if they could make Marish think it was his
idea.

Griffin's phone buzzed, Lynn announcing over the intercom, "Rawley Jenkins?" Not recognizing the name.
"On four."

Griffin picked up. Heard lots of commotion in the
background. "Any luck—?"

"What the hell's going on, kid?" Jenkins demanded
angrily. "What the *hell's* going on? I got cops and homicide detectives and your buddy Mickey Blane down
here, all over my ass."

"What?"

"Talking about having found another body."

"I'll be right there."

"I hope they ain't chewed me up by the time you do."

"Goddamn," Griffin cursed. "Welcome to the circus."

A trio of TV mini-cam vans, representing each of the
city's network channels, were parked in the circular
main drive to Memorial Hospital, satellite dishes ready
to beam live reports if something got hot. Reporters
framed against the hospital backdrop read urgent scrib-
blings from their notepads.

A duo of city cops assigned to scene control pulled
back bright yellow sawhorses to allow Griffin into the driveway. Griffin nodded to them, fresh-faced kids probably
two months out of the academy. He didn't know either of
them.

Fran Zimnoch, a veteran TV reporter who made it her
business to know every ranking cop and prosecutor, cut

short taping her story's intro and waved her cameraman to where Griffin was getting out of the Taurus.

A print reporter saw Fran make the break and beat her to Griffin. He was a disheveled young guy who probably had to shave once a month. Asking Griffin if he had any comment. When Griffin replied, "About what?" the reporter didn't know how to follow up, not that sure what was going on himself.

"Jimmy, Fran Zimnoch." As though she had to introduce herself. She held out her free hand, microphone and notepad clutched in the other. "Give me a quick minute, okay, Jimmy." She turned a welcoming handshake into a reporter's martial arts move, steering Griffin to the side of marble entrance steps, screening him from other reporters. Knowing they'd get him in time, she just wanted him first. "What've you got, Jimmy? Is it Bright Eyes? Is Dunbar Waddy back?"

Griffin was cringing, but only on the inside. The smell in the air was distinct: shit hitting the fan. Another body, only this one wasn't covered up. The story was out now. "I'm just getting here, Fran." Griffin in control.

A warm day had her perfume kicked into overdrive. A heady scent to it, aggressive, like Fran herself. "I want to roll the tape, okay, Jimmy, even for a no comment."

"Fire away."

Fran spun her finger in a tight circle, signaling her cameraman to start shooting. She didn't bother fiddling with her hair or adjusting the collar of her blouse. Maybe she wasn't pretty enough to make national news—fuck them—she was after a story, not a beauty prize.

Looking into the camera. "I'm with Jimmy Griffin, chief investigator with the City Attorney's office." Turned to Griffin: "Four years ago, you were the homicide detective on the Dunbar Waddy case. The Bright Eyes serial killer who drugged women to death and left them naked in suggestive positions. Waddy was convicted, but was freed on appeal and never found. Today another woman has been murdered in a similar style. Jimmy, is this Bright Eyes again?" Dramatically. "Is the city's worst nightmare back?"

Griffin looked at her, very comfortable in front of a camera, a talent Richard Marish not only demanded, but had sent him to seminars to practice. He even had a little bit of a television voice, a touch lower than normal, distinct pronunciation, but not speaking too slowly as though stalling for a thought. "Fran, we're in the early stages. It's very dangerous to speculate, but whether it's Dunbar Waddy or another perpetrator, you can be assured our office is going to put a manpower blitz on it. Everyone remembers the tragedy of the last case. It's not going to be repeated. I give you my life on that." Griffin gestured toward the hospital. "I've got to get inside."

"Certainly."

Griffin walked behind Fran Zimnoch, controlled urgency in motion. He managed to avoid all other reporters except one: Liz McKinley.

She came in stride with Griffin up the marble steps. " 'I give you my life on it?' " she moaned. "What kind of crap is that?"

Griffin smirked. "An interview tutor called it suicidal overstatement. He had a lot of categories for bullshit, that's the only one I remember."

"Nice."

They were in the front hall, heading for Rawley Jenkins's office. Hospital routine was distracted by the buzz of rumor and celebrity. Staff members watched TV crews on the front steps and passed wild gossip. One overwrought nurse said she'd heard Bright Eyes was loose in the building.

"So much for my scoop," Liz said. She checked her watch: about an hour to deadline. Her laptop was in the car. She could put the final touches on the story she'd worked up on diskette and file it by modem in time, just tell layout to leave space for photos and film she'd FedEx later. "Any idea what this's about?" she asked Griffin.

"Nothing more than I told you on the phone." Griffin had called Liz from his car on the ride over—a deal was a deal.

"Cute. Our boy must have a real taste for it these days. How do you figure he went four years without?"

Maybe, Griffin thought, he was in a hospital recovering from bullet wounds.

Griffin entered Rawley Jenkins's outer office without knocking. A fierce argument was going on behind the inner-office door. None of three voices was Jenkins's. One belonged to Mickey Blane, demanding, "That's the way it is. Period."

"You're insane," an outraged voice countered. "We're going to sue your dick off."

A third voice tried to calm the second.

The inner door flew open. A uniform cop led the way out. He was followed by two suited men, corporate stiffs in gray suits, short haircuts, silk socks, and wing-tip shoes, one man very red in the face. Griffin immediately pegged them as hospital lawyers.

Rawley Jenkins towered close behind. Missing the jacket to his Montgomery Ward suit today. A certain oddity to his walk, instinctively ducking the doorway even though he cleared it by inches.

Another uniform cop had hold of Jenkins's arm.

Mickey Blane brought up the rear.

Christ, Griffin realized, they had Jenkins in handcuffs.

That's why his gait was strange—his arms weren't swinging. He raised chained wrists for Griffin to see.

Griffin sidestepped the lead cop to get at Blane. "What the hell's going on, Mickey? What the hell's—?"

"Get back to the office," Blane snapped, not looking at him. "You're off the case."

"What're you talking about?" The rolling blockade of bodies pushed him aside. "Mickey, what the hell are you doing?"

"Get back to the office," Blane yelled. "*Now!*"

The group proceeded into the main hall, attracting attention. Jenkins looked back at Griffin, didn't have to say a word. His expression spoke volumes: *That fucking Dickie Marish!*

Unlike Richard Marish, Mickey Blane wasn't always able to stare someone down while arguing with them, especially if they were a friend. "The PR people said to do it," Blane defended.

"It's crazy, Mickey," Griffin accused. "It's goddamned crazy."

"The decision's made."

"Thanks for the consultation."

"And what would that have accomplished, Grif, huh? Nothing. Just like this conversation. It's not the way you'd do it. Fine. We appreciate that." Making it sound like it was Blane and Marish against Griffin.

They were in Blane's Jaguar, parked outside Central District, Griffin having followed Blane's caravan there from Memorial Hospital. Rawley Jenkins was inside being processed and taken before a commissioner to set bail.

Blane's sports car idled smoothly, air conditioner shooting out cool air that failed to reduce the effect of hot sunshine streaming into Griffin's half of the car.

Blane's custom-tailored suit jacket hung behind his seat; his white shirtsleeves were rolled up. Blane wasn't wearing his gun again today.

"I know you don't like it," Blane conceded. "I'm sorry."

"No you're not. You're getting just like him. You never used to think like Marish. Not this much. It's like a disease."

Blane wouldn't look at him, staring instead over the long hood of the Jag.

"And now," Griffin added, incredulous, "you're letting Frank Wallace and homicide take over?"

"It's their case. It's a murder."

"And I'm out?" Griffin confirmed.

"You're out."

"That's great." Griffin leaned sideways against the door, glaring at Blane. "Just great. Gratitude still goes a long way in this city. About an inch past friendship."

"It's not personal."

"The hell it's not. You're yanking me off the case because you think it's going to look bad for the office. The same guy who missed Bright Eyes last time in charge again now. Only I didn't miss him, did I, Mickey? I blew him away! Because of what he did to Diana and Jeremy. I blew the fucker away! For you! At least, I thought I did. . . ."

"Don't you think I know that!" Losing control, Blane's voice cracked slightly. "Don't you think I know that *every* minute of *every* day of my life. That I *live* with what happened?"

"No, Mickey. I really don't." Griffin considered his friend, not yelling back, lowering his voice, realizing where they stood. "I think you're too caught up in your future. I think when you buried Diana and Jeremy, you erased them from your mind."

"You son of a bitch! Goddamn you to say that!"

"Tell me it's not true. Tell me within a month of your wife being dead you weren't fucking half the secretarial pool."

"Maybe that's how I tried to cope."

"Oh, yeah." Griffin laughed sourly. "You were a real martyr. If it moved, you wanted it."

Blane abruptly swung his left fist for Griffin's face, an awkward motion in the confines of the car. Griffin would have deflected Blane's hand even if his friend hadn't struck the rearview mirror. Blood broke through the skin on two of Blane's knuckles.

Griffin kicked open his door in anger. "you're a sorry sight."

"Go to hell."

Disgusted, Griffin walked away. He left the passenger door open, thinking, let the rich boy reach over and close it himself.

He went in the side entrance to Central District. In a few hours, he'd regret the argument. Blame it on Marish for corrupting his old friend. In the meantime, he needed to check on a new friend.

"I didn't tell 'em nothing, kid. Not a fucking thing." Before being placed in the holding cell where he was now, Rawley Jenkins's personal effects had been taken away—belt, tie, and shoelaces included.

The front of his pants drooped despite a sizable gut. Jenkins didn't care; his shirttail covered what his pants didn't. "Dickie Marish charging *me* with obstruction of justice. Ain't that a gem."

"I'll talk with your lawyers. I'll tell them you—"

"Forget those lawyers. Don't waste your time." Jenkins waved his hand as though moving stale air from his face. "Those suits don't know dick. Bunch of Ivy League make-believes. They look good sitting on the hospital board, but they're no good for this kind of thing. I still got some contacts in the system. Don't worry about me."

Griffin stood close to the bars of Jenkins's cage. Adjacent cells were separated by a concrete wall. A luxury Jenkins would lose when moved upstairs, the first of many transfers in a process referred to by defense lawyers as musical jail.

Perhaps the bureaucracy had unintentionally designed its pretrial detainee policy this way, but the net effect was lawyers usually couldn't find their clients for the first twenty-four hours after arrest, much less talk to them.

"Let me at least get you a bail bondsman," Griffin offered.

"Forget it. They got me on a hundred grand retainer."

"Jesus. Who set it?"

"Who wrote it down, or who ordered it? Come on, Jimmy, Dickie Marish's got this thing rigged from head to toe. Only he don't know a couple things."

"Like what?"

"Let's not talk about it here. I mean it's nice of you to come visit, I appreciate it. Hell, your old man got me shot, he never sent a get-well card." Jenkins reached through the bars, reassuringly grabbed Griffin's arm. "We'll get together tonight."

"Tonight?"

Jenkins clued Griffin with a quick wink. "I'll be out by then. I'll call, show you what I found last night."

When the phone rang, he knew who it was. The only person who knew he was here.

The Kroop, asking: "What are you waiting for?" Meaning why hadn't he done anything about Greg Aronson yet.

"This weekend," the man replied coolly. "I need a Saturday or Sunday to get in the house."

"Call me as soon as it's done. I'll have your package delivered. There's going to be a plane ticket in it as well. One way. Use it." The Kroop hung up, not sounding too appreciative, but ten grand was probably thanks enough.

24.

"Souvenir for the wife and kids." Lenny Shane, prurient photographers of the dead and maimed, handed Griffin a Polaroid of Tracy Deil's naked corpse. "Pretty sweet, huh. Look how this guy positions her, facedown, ass way up in the air, spread those legs. Too bad she was bye-byes." Lenny flicked his finger dead center in the print. "Although, me personally, I go to the trouble to paint a nice red design on the front of her, I think I'd leave her faceup . . . but that's me."

Griffin immediately saw the similarity between the dead woman and victims four years ago. She was posed just like Bright Eyes had done two of the others.

"Keep it," Lenny invited, wrongfully believing Griffin's interest in the photo went beyond the job at hand. "I got more." Lenny pulled a mini Tracy Deil portfolio from the pocket of his safari jacket, adroitly fanning snapshots like a card shark.

Lenny took Polaroids for his own amusement; "official" police photographs were done on the duo of Nikons strung around his neck. "You missed the real thing." Lenny tilted his head toward the king-size hotel bed; a bare mattress made pricy accommodations look cheap. "They just bagged her an hour ago. The tweezers boys were in here looking for fibers before they let us in. Big hubbub over this, Grif. You running the show?"

Griffin shook his head, concealing anger about being pulled off the case. "Frank Wallace."

"Oh, shit," Lenny moaned. "Fuck-up Frank. If he was half as good as he thought he'd still be terrible."

Griffin didn't comment. He was preoccupied with the thought that Dunbar Waddy really was back. The theory—the fear—seemed confirmed by what had happened in this room. The odd part was, Griffin couldn't picture it: Dunbar Waddy—the man he'd chased and shot, thought he'd killed four years ago—had been in this very room, less than twelve hours ago.

Maybe he didn't *want* to believe Waddy was back. Because that meant Griffin was responsible for this woman's death. Jane Doe, too. If he'd recaptured Waddy four years ago, brought him to trial for Blane's wife and son—or, hell, if he'd even succeeded at killing him— this woman would still be alive.

Lenny said, "You see Frank yet?"

Griffin blinked, put the photo in his suit pocket. "No."

"Yeah, well, he's down in the lobby. Setting up a portable command post. You know he loves to organize. Make little file folders for all his evidence, use cut out tabs for dividers in his case binder. Too bad he spends all that time playing with paper and never catches nobody." Lenny spit out a little piece of something he felt floating around in his mouth. "You know, I heard Marish got the mayor to open up the rainy day fund. They're actually going to pay overtime on this one. Wallace's got fifteen cops interviewing hotel guests. But, you know, they ain't gonna find nothing. The lab boys were looking frustrated. Place was wiped down, no prints. No sign of a struggle. No skin or blood under her fingernails. Nothing running out of her ass or pussy. No loose body hairs on her. This guy's very slick, Grif. But he made a big mistake comin' back after all this time. He ain't gonna slide out from under you twice."

"It's not my case, Lenny."

"Uh-huh." Lenny gave Griffin a knowing look and leaned close. "So what're you doin' here then? You got some friends gonna buy the place?"

"Just looking around." Griffin pointed to the bathroom; behind a closed door came the sound of pipes rattling. "I assume Johnny's in there?"

"Who else?" Lenny snapped a quick Polaroid of Griffin, handed him the undeveloped print as it fed from the camera. "One for the kids." Lenny assumed everyone had a houseful of children like he did.

Circles from the camera flash dancing in his vision, Griffin knocked on the bathroom door.

"Yello," Johnny Gibson replied cheerfully. "Gimme a sec." Tools scraped across the tile floor. Gibson cussed when he banged his head on something, said, "Okee-doke," when it was clear to open the door.

Griffin did so just enough to peer in.

Johnny Gibson, all five-five, 155 pounds, and sixty-three years of him, was contorted across the wet bathroom floor in a position only a three-year-old or plumber could manage. Wearing gray waterman's pants, worker's boots, and a gas station attendant's shirt, much of his "uniform" soaked with water.

The name the police department printed on Gibson's paycheck was actually George Gibson, but his having solved a murder case twenty years ago by dismantling a toilet and finding spent shell casings lodged amidst snarled hair in the drain trap had given him the nickname Johnny.

"Piss-poor job whoever installed this toilet," Johnny griped. "Piss poor. Fittings're all bent up. Big-ass kink in the drain from a glob of solder snot I don't know how it got in there. No pride in workmanship anymore, Jim. No pride."

The dismantled porcelain tank sat crookedly against the bathtub; beside that was Johnny's tool kit: a big Sears Craftsman box more fitting a construction worker than a forensics man.

Griffin squatted beside him. "You got anything?"

"Workin' on it." Johnny wore surgical gloves, had two fingers stuck down the drain. He turned to reach for his toolbox, but was a little short on arm span. "Wanna hand me a Ziploc outta there."

Griffin obliged. The top shelf of the Craftsman was neatly organized with tools and cellophane evidence bags with self-sealing tops. Griffin slapped a bag into Johnny's palm as though assisting surgery.

Fingers wedging deep into the drain, Johnny made a series of grunts, then pulled out a long, slippery glob of congealed hair. "Toilet fish, we call 'em. Make the Roto-Rooter men rich. Women," he said, carefully placing the dripping mass into a plastic evidence bag, "love cleaning their brush and dropping a big old tangle of hair into the toilet. *Scarumph!*" Johnny did his impression of flushing. "Down she goes till she hits the big turn and air bubble in the trap, sometimes gets hung up there until her husband comes along with a big dump to push its way through. 'Cept in this case, lady staying here had real long blond hair—she must've cleaned her brush, say . . ." perched on one elbow, Johnny considered his bagged catch, ". . . last night, maybe right after getting ready to go out on a date. 'Cause her brush was clean—I checked it. Look for your-self if you want. It's in a box in the tub."

Griffin was more interested in why Johnny found value in a seemingly worthless lump of hair.

"See, what happens is that after she gets that hair in

the toilet, someone else comes along and does their business, cleans up after themselves, flushes it down, figures that's that." Johnny fingered the wet hair, squashing it around in the sealed bag. "See those little bits of white papery stuff? That's shreds of toilet paper. See over here, this kind of pale gray ooze?"

"Yeah?"

"You and your wife ever fool around in the shower? Maybe in the bathtub, only you don't let yourself go inside her, you come out and shoot into the tub. Then go to clean the drain a little while later and there's this gluey stuff all over everything. That's what we got here. A semen sample."

"Johnny, you are beautiful."

"Yeah, my wife tells me that."

Liz McKinley asked the title lawyer in the city land records office how much it would cost to do the job in a hurry.

"How much of a hurry?"

"I need it last week."

"Three hundred?" he asked, feeling her out.

Liz made a face like who was he kidding, this guy wearing bad golf pants, hamburger juice on his striped polyester tie, and beer on his breath.

The lawyer countered his own offer, breaching a cardinal rule of negotiation. "*Two* hundred?"

"How long's it going to take?"

"Half an hour."

"Deal."

"Make the check out to Cash."

Liz was sure, she'd worked with Mister Cash before, also his partner, Pay To Any Holder.

To kill waiting time, Liz went to a bustling saloon on Water Street that had been around awhile. Dark booths and a brass railed bar. Liz sat at the bar in her leather skirt, where she got looks from young stockbrokers and bankers.

She'd dressed this way thinking it might be a look Griffin went for. Wondering how much it took to tempt him. Hard to tell. He seemed to be working his ass off, under lots of pressure, not sleeping with his wife from what she'd seen in his house.

Liz knew long hours and a lack of companionship took their toll. She blamed her wild streaks on working too much. Not that she got too absorbed in self-justification. Who did she have to answer to besides her paper? And they couldn't gripe.

Forty-five minutes ago she'd just sent in her story by modem, one helluva piece. Short of Liz Taylor deciding to have group sex with aliens, it would be the biggest headline of the summer—guaranteed. BRIGHT EYES IS BACK. You couldn't beat a good serial killer.

Plus, although she'd downplayed it with Griffin, the police file he'd given her was a real coup. It would reach Atlanta via FedEx by morning; there'd be plenty of time to strip it in with all layout being done by computer these days—mechanical cut and paste, no more X-Acto knives like when Liz started out.

And once the title abstractor finished with Liz's simple assignment, she was going to have something Griffin *didn't* know. Something that would make for one great trade. Liz telling herself that's why she was doing it—all business, get something to use for leverage—it wasn't just her dark curiosity raising its degenerate head. No, *that* would have made her bad.

"Lynn?"

The secretarial pool's newlywed turned toward Griffin's voice. He stood by his door. Having come back to the office with an attitude a few minutes ago, he now looked damned mad.

"Anybody been in my office?"

"I don't think so. No, wait a minute. Lorraine came around dropping off memos. She put one in there." Lorraine was Richard Marish's secretary. "Why?"

"The Waddy file's not on my desk. Where's Blane?"

"In conference with Marish. They're getting ready for Marish's press conference. It's pretty well fever pitch. They're not taking any calls," she said, seeing how Griffin was grinding his jaw. Calling after him, "Jimmy. *Jimmy*!" as he headed for the stairs that led to Marish's office.

The new girl next to Lynn asked what was going on. Lynn said, "A fight, I hope." She motioned for the other girl to keep quiet and follow her, giving Griffin a slight head start.

He went up the stairwell two steps at a time to Marish's floor, emerging into a quiet hallway with thick carpet that absorbed footsteps like a muffler.

Marish's reception area was vacant, the ever loyal and fastidious Lorraine not manning her post—what Marish sometimes referred to as the last line of defense; Lorraine the Hun there to repel attackers aiming for her beloved boss.

Griffin, in a vague display of etiquette, knocked on the door to Marish's inner lair before grabbing the knob. Locked. He knocked louder.

Lorraine opened the door just enough to lay one mean eye on him. Fifty-six years old, jet black hair raked severely off her forehead and sprayed with enough aerosol to put her personal hole in the O-zone.

"Find anything else in my office you liked, Lorraine?" Griffin pushed the door open despite Lorraine trying bravely to hold him back.

Marish and Blane were side by side behind Marish's desk, backlit by hazy white sunlight pushing through lowered shades. Marish in his customary jury-pleasing blue suit.

Marish's public relations team had been called in: three men and one woman, none older than thirty-six; sharp dressers engaged in spirited conversation until Griffin appeared. Now there was silence.

Griffin looked right at Marish. "I want my file."

"You're off the case," Marish snapped.

"I wasn't off it yesterday was I, Dick, when you told me to cover it up."

"Goddamn it, Jimmy," Blane swore. A pair of Band-Aids were clumsily taped across his knuckles.

One of the PR men, tall and serious looking, stood abruptly. He asked Lorraine to close the door, a much quieter order than his aggressive stance forecast.

Lorraine obliged.

"Can we discuss this with a little decorum?" the tall man suggested.

Griffin looked at Marish and Blane. Tried to keep the rage from his voice. "You can't take me off this case. You want Frank Wallace to run it, that's fine. Just don't goddamned shut me out."

"It's a problem of perception."

"Who are you?" Griffin barked at the PR man. "Some advertising whiz, thinks up jingles for diet drinks and used-car lots?"

Another PR man slapped his pencil against a legal pad with disgust.

"Grif, come on . . . ." Blane pleaded in his "old friend" voice, as though he hadn't tried to sucker punch Griffin a couple hours ago. "Let us get through this afternoon, okay? This's been very stressful on everyone. We've got a live press conference at six to get ready for."

"Give me the file and I'm gone."

Marish continued to glare at him, but said nothing, waiting to see how Blane would handle the confrontation. And Blane knew it. "You don't need the file. Why don't you go home and take it easy."

"I can catch this guy."

"Like last time," the third PR man mumbled sarcastically.

He'd no sooner said that than Griffin had him by the shoulders of his Savile Row suit. Dragged him out of his chair. Threw him hard enough against the wall to knock crooked a line of framed photos of Marish posed with city notables.

The pencil slapper hollered, "Jesus Christ!"

Blane came around the desk. "Goddamn it, Grif!"

Griffin pushed Blane aside and got in the face of his new enemy, a pissed-off midtwenties bodybuilder with a trendy haircut. The fit PR man sprang to his feet and glared at Griffin.

Griffin demanded, "Tell me about last time. Tell me how it *really* happened."

The pretty PR boy had put in some gym time rocking a heavy bag, but bags stood still. The punch he threw at Griffin had decent leverage, but no quickness.

Griffin sidestepped the blow. Grabbing his assailant's wrist, he jerked his arm forward and clipped him behind the ear with the butt of his hand.

The guy went sprawling across soft carpet. He tried to bounce to his feet again—show his buddies he hadn't been affected—but he wobbled on unsteady legs, inner ear spinning from the blow.

"Get out, Jimmy," Blane ordered. "Right now! Before it gets worse."

"I want the file."

Blane shook his head. "No way." Self-righteous with authority.

Next to Blane, Richard Marish seemed to be propping "his boy" up. He looked victorious.

Griffin stared at the two men, frustrated.

After a few moments of hard quiet—when it was clear the fight was over—the tall PR man, who remained calm throughout, said to Blane, "Tell him about the phones."

Blane exhaled determinedly. Put his hands on his hips. "Reporters are going to be calling you. Here and at home. Wanting to know about the case. Don't answer your phone. Or your door. They're going to try making you look bad."

Griffin shook his head. "What difference does it make? You've already done that for them." He turned and left the room.

Outside, Lynn and her friend were spying from the hall. Having gotten a glance inside, she told Griffin, "Damn, I heard somebody go down. I was hoping it'd been Marish."

Griffin took Lynn's elbow and led her toward the stairs. "I want you to run me a copy of the old City Attorney file on Dunbar Waddy. I got the police file the other night, but that was *my* old file. I need to see what was going on from this end, see what someone might have missed. You have any problem doing that?"

"None whatsoever."

Jack Karupka had a check on his desk for a quarter of a million dollars, made out to his client, a wealthy doctor who'd been conned on an investment deal. A legal limited-partnership swindle the doctor could have kept from getting screwed on if he'd let Karupka look over the papers *before* he'd signed and handed over his check. But doctors were notoriously cheap like that, not wanting to pay for advice, figuring since they *made* lots of money they'd be naturally shrewd investing it. Wrong.

Once The Kroop took his forty-percent fee, the doctor was going to be short about fifty grand, but he'd still be kissing The Kroop's ass for getting back anything for him. Once the limited partnership folded into Chapter Eleven, every document in perfect order, there was nothing the doctor could do to recover his money, legally. Which was why he'd called Karupka.

That had been two weeks ago.

Since then, Karupka had met once with the doctor, then saw the partnership's bankruptcy attorney, explaining he was getting into the case, discussing this over a very expensive lunch—Kroop's treat. No threats, no muscle, just The Kroop's reputation.

Within an hour of having paid for lunch, the partnership lawyer called his clients, advised them unless they came up with an offer for the doctor, they were likely to return home one night and find their house had burned down—a little mechanical failure in the basement. If they were lucky. If they were unlucky, the house might burn down with them in it. And no, it didn't matter that the partners only owned houses in Switzerland. Karupka had people who knew how to ski and yodel.

So now, after one hour's worth of work, Karupka had his client's money. He'd also made a tidy fee for himself. But he couldn't pause to enjoy success right now. Right now he had another problem, one that made the noon news and hourly bulletins since. A problem named Bright Eyes. An old client with whom he'd had a deal.

25.

Griffin tried phoning home for the entire hour it took Lynn to copy the City Attorney's four-year-old case file on Dunbar Waddy. The line was constantly busy. Terrific, reporters had probably been calling, so Carla had taken the phone off the hook.

Griffin scribbled a note and asked Lynn to fax it to Carla at home. His wife had a fax board installed in her computer that stayed on-line during working hours.

The note read: *Don't answer the phone. Sorry for the reporters. If you need me, to talk or to be there, call my pager and I'll be home fast. Otherwise, see you around 8:00. Love, Jimmy.*

Lynn, reading as Griffin wrote, said, "Pretty sweet. I'll make sure she gets it."

Griffin went out the back way, slipping past reporters setting up for Marish's press conference. The crime beat paparazzi sharpening their talons like falcons set for release after warm kill.

In warm shadows of the parking lot, Griffin saw the aged Ford LTD out of the corner of his eye. The once illustrious detective-issue four-door pulled out of a parking space and headed for him. A rumbling engine somehow held in place by a rusty frame and hopeless body.

Rawley Jenkins was behind the wheel, back in custody of his tie, shoelaces, and belt. Window down, he rolled up to Griffin, said, "Whaddayou been doing in there? I been out almost two hours."

Seeing the big man slightly improved Griffin's mood. As though Jenkins was an antidote to Richard Marish's poison. "You obviously didn't put up this heap as collateral."

"Don't insult my memories, kid. Besides, I'm out on recog."

"Pretty good trick."

"I told you, I still got some contacts." He pointed a meat-hook thumb toward the passenger door. "Get in. I got someone I want you to meet."

Rawley Jenkins drove like a cop, heavy on the gas, quick on the brake, working the pedals with two feet, not the high school driver's ed. right foot for gas *and* brake. The hell with that. Keep the left foot a quarter inch off the brake pedal, ready to burn those disk pads in a split second.

He knew side streets and cut-throughs, eliminating ten minutes off the trip across town. Avoiding traffic if not trash cans set out in the alleys, having knocked over at least five and given a couple others stiff spins like big bowling pins as he clipped them with a rusty bumper.

"I'm usually more law abiding," he assured Griffin, "but I want to make sure we finish with this guy in time to catch Dickie's press conference. I love a good comedy."

Griffin doubted he'd find humor—dark or otherwise—in anything else that happened today. Especially not since Jenkins was headed toward the part of town known as Little Kingston, where immigrating West Indians had been forced by police crackdowns, essentially cornering them as far as possible from highways "respectable" middle-class commuters traveled into the city.

There was no urban renewal here. Run-down flag-
stone and brick buildings, many painted in multiple
shades of bright turquoise and yellow like back home in
the Caribbean hillside.

Busted-out windows and doors. Aluminum-sided huts
set up in alleys. Bold, graphic flags—red, black, and
green—proudly displayed. The smell of jerk chicken,
curry, and cayenne on outdoor grills making the hot
early evening seem even more suffocating.

Jenkins announced, "Like being in the jungle, ain't
it?"

Rastifarians sporting long dreadlocks hung on street
corners making little effort to conceal spliffs of ganja.
Their women were hooted and whistled at, grabbed for,
wearing colorful hand-sewn dresses or short skirts with
halter or outdated stretch tube tops.

Reggae music—Bob Marley, Third World, Steel
Pulse, Black Uhuru—pulsed hypnotically from boom
boxes and through opened windows. Background
rhythms like a movie soundtrack that played twenty-four
hours a day.

A corner restaurant that had been an Irish bar back in
the fifties was now called Ocho's. A sun-faded poster of
Bob Marley was taped inside one greasy window.

There were no spaces at the curb; Jenkins didn't care.
He double parked, blocking a lane of traffic with the
LTD, telling Griffin, "They figure only a cop would park
like this. Keeps you from getting screwed with."

Jenkins popped open the glove compartment and
withdrew the snub-nose .357 Colt Python he'd had
strapped under his arm yesterday. He stuffed it in his suit
pocket. "Let's go, kid."

As Jenkins and Griffin emerged from the LTD, a trio
of Jamaicans dispersed from the corner. Jerkins warning
their backs, "Don't fuck with the car."

Jenkins pushed open Ocho's screen door with the arrogance of a gunslinger. Griffin was right beside him.

Inside, seven small tables were covered with stained paper cloths. A mismatched collection of wood chairs was only occupied by five patrons, all of whom stopped eating and made sure their hands were in plain sight.

Jenkins nodded to the clientele. "Thanks for your cooperation." He headed for the kitchen, a badly ventilated area that hadn't seen an honest health inspector in five years.

Grease filters dripped onto scalding hot cook surfaces, flash fires waiting to happen. A tired waitress sat on a stool pushed into a corner; the dark nipples of her pendulous breasts showed through a dirty white T-shirt.

On the stove, strips of marinated beef cooked alongside black beans and sizzled the potent aroma of cumin. A long-armed cook tended the well-seasoned pan. Sweat ran off his ebony face. He looked at Jenkins as though facing a prophecy. "Beer in deh coolah." He gestured toward an insulated Coleman packed with ice and bottled Heinekens.

Jenkins bent down and grabbed two bottles, uncapped them on an opener screwed into a butcher-block table. He gave Griffin one. "Like nothing else in the States. Unpasteurized. Smuggled in from Saint Croix."

The cook dumped the contents of his pan onto two plates, spooned on liberal portions of mango chutney, and pushed them toward the waitress. As though rising from the dead, she came off the stool and carried the food into the restaurant.

Jenkins watched her the whole time.

Griffin's father used to do that, too; denigrated blacks to no end, but still stared at black women with a raw kind of lust no Caucasian seemed capable of raising in him.

The cook crossed his arms. Not afraid, but uncomfortable. He wore a sleeveless shirt that exposed lean arms, one of which sported a crude prison tattoo on a sinewy bicep.

"Beyer, here," Jenkins said, gesturing to the cook with his beer, "learned to cook in City Jail. Was paroled out of there, but was right back at it, breaking and entering. *Gotta have those drugs.*" Jenkins's voice mocking the cook as though doing a bad Jolson.

Griffin didn't like how this—whatever it was—was going down. He said, "What's the point?" Wanting to get to it. There wasn't any sense ragging the guy.

Jenkins made another gesture toward Beyer, every action trying to put the cook down, making him seem worthless. "Beyer knew Dunbar Waddy, didn't you, Beyer?"

"I tole you dat, mon."

"Now tell him," Jenkins said firmly.

Beyer appeared resigned, a man without options. Without looking at either intruder, he said, "Knew Dunbah back five, six years. Hunt wit' 'im all deh time. Did some house together."

"Breaking and entering," Jenkins clarified.

Griffin knew the reference.

"Dunbah sometimes went on jobs wit' me was a little stoned. Seen? Not makin' good decisions. Sometimes we'd find a 'ouse looked like was empty, but turned out to 'ave people in it. I'd want to get away, not wantin' to deal wit' no people comin' on us wit' a gun. But Dunbah crazy fuckah sometimes. Want to mix it up wit' dem."

"Tell him about the one apartment."

Beyer didn't respond for a few seconds; delay his only means of defiance. "One night, Dunbah said he'd found us a good apartment. Not too far outta deh city. Close to deh interstate. We drove out dere, went in t'rough a glass door. Dunbah tell me to get deh stereo and computer out deh ot'er rooms, he gonna go into deh bedroom. I said, h'okay. Was puttin' away deh stuff when I 'ear dis noise from deh bedroom.

"I look in, see Dunbah got dis big-ass knife, 'olding it to dis lady's throat. Got her nightgown torn off, fuckin' her hard, while she cryin', whimperin' for 'im not to kill her."

"Tell him about after," Jenkins ordered.

After beat of hesitation, shorter this time, then: "Deh night we do dis, May fifteen, four years h'ago. I never forget deh date, mon. Seen? Because dat deh night one of deh women murdered deh prosecutor say Dunbah killed. One of deh Bright Eyes women. But dere's no way Dunbah could do dat woman, because we been out in deh county doin' dat woman's apartment. You check dat county case, you find it never been solved."

Jenkins said, "Tell him the other part."

Beyer looked at Griffin. "When Dunbah get caught rapin' dat other woman downtown—"

"Leslie Connors," Jenkins clarified, the third Bright Eyes victim, the thirty-five-year-old housewife.

Beyer nodded. "Dunbah get snagged for dat and de police talk about 'im killin' dese ot'er women, he call me from jail. He say I gotta testify for 'im. Say deh night one of deh women was murdered was when he in deh county wit' me."

"What'd you do?" Griffin asked.

Beyer wiped a greasy cloth over his perspiring face. "I'm not sure who to call, Dunbah didn't say, so I try deh City Attorney office. Say I got information about Dunbah, that he couldn't have killed one of those women, because he was wit' me doin' a house. But I tell dem I can't say just what house unless they gonna let me go on it. Seen, Dunbah said it was okay wit' him, for me to sell him to get free of it myself. 'Cause it was his alibi."

"I never heard about this before," Griffin said. "You sure you called the City Attorney's office?"

"Yeah, mon. Deh City Attorney. Deh tell me dey send somebody to see *me*. Which I say, I don't know, I want a lawyah, but deh say not to worry about it. Dey 'ave a man come to see me wit' a paper says I'm getting munity."

"Immunity," Jenkins corrected, acting superior.

"Seen. So dis mon come out. Look about like 'im." Beyer pointed at Jenkins. "Got no paper about the munity, but he gotta big-ass gun he puts in my mouth, say I ever mention anyt'ing 'bout havin' an alibi for Dunbah again, he gonna blow my head off."

Griffin reacted with a mix of surprise and doubt. "Someone from the City Attorney's office told you that?"

Beyer avoided Griffin's eyes. "Dat's right."

Griffin turned to Jenkins. "Nobody who looked like you worked for the City Attorney's office back then. Gerremo was the only investigator and he rarely left the office. None of the prosecutors were your size."

Beyer didn't care if "Griffin didn't believe him. 'I jus' tellin' you what 'oppened, mon. Dat's what he tell me to do." Referring to Jenkins.

"So for all this time you keep quiet because you're afraid of this guy who came to talk to you. This big guy who put a gun in your mouth and threatened to kill you, right? That's what you said?"

Beyer nodded. "Seen."

"And all of a sudden you're not afraid of him anymore?"

"Mon, four years h'ago, dat other mon threatened to kill me if I talked. So I don' talk."

"You're talking now," Griffin countered.

Beyer pointed at Jenkins. " 'Cause *he* threaten to kill me if I don't."

"You don't believe his story?" In the LTD, driving back across town, Jenkins leaned his sizable frame against the center armrest, doing damage to it with his elbow. "All coerced statements aren't lies. Besides, how would he know to tell me a story like that? All I asked was the last time he'd seen Dunbar Waddy."

"You happen to run a check on where *Beyer's* been the last four years?"

"You're thinking maybe he was in jail. That he and Dunbar could have been doing these women together. A pair of Bright Eyes. Maybe Waddy got busted on it and Bayer laid low. Maybe he got nabbed on something else and is in jail for four years. Gets out and starts doing more women." Jenkins glanced at Griffin. "That's what you're thinking, right? Sure you are. 'Cause I thought the same thing. Which's why I talked to Beyer's parole officer. Beyer's been out over two years and been clean." Jenkins smiled. "Next theory?"

26.

Liz McKinley attended Richard Marish's press conference courtesy of the thirteen-inch color TV in Carla Griffin's bedroom/office. Liz was beginning to like this city. So far, she'd been awakened by Griffin's call: another murder—fantastic, conveniently occurring in time for her to make her Friday noon deadline. She no longer had an exclusive story, but *what* she did have—namely the entire old police file—would pulverize everyone else.

At the hospital, she'd gotten an up-to-date look at Mickey Blane in the flesh. Having forgotten how hot he was. Though Liz would still take Griffin if given the choice.

Seeing Blane and Griffin go at it—Blane telling Griffin he was off the case—had been a bit surprising, but pressure did strange things to friendships. And Liz wasn't worried about losing her "in." No way would Griffin let the case go, she was sure of that.

After the hospital, Liz took her little sojourn to the City Land Records office, getting a list of all the owners in Building A at The Patios At Knollwood, where Carla Griffin had gone yesterday.

From Land Records, Liz went to Griffin's house, having arrived here just after three-thirty. The idea had been to somehow—she wasn't exactly sure how—run the names of those condo owners past Carla, see who made her eyes widen. Only Liz had found Carla walking out the door, suitcase in one hand, Cassie in the other.

Carla had been quite edgy and distraught, apologizing for not wanting to talk just now, but she had to go. Where, she wouldn't say, but Liz thought that was okay, she had a pretty good idea.

Carla had started up the stairs to take Cassie to Mrs. Pulaski—their baby-sitter—when Liz asked if she could use the bathroom. Carla said sure.

Liz used that opportunity to go into the back bathroom and check where Carla kept her diaphragm. Tah-dah—it was missing.

Liz flushed the toilet to keep up her act, came out of the bathroom as though having just washed her hands, only to find Carla had, in her apparent haste, forgotten about her.

Carla had locked the deadbolt from outside with her key, leaving Liz inside.

Liz waited a few minutes, figuring Carla would surely come back; when she didn't, Liz found herself in the highly lush position of having free rein of someone's house. It was playtime.

From the looks of him, Rawley Jenkins would be at home in a studio crash pad apartment, same sheets on the bed as last month, empty cardboard toilet paper rollers overflowing the trash can, an old TV dinner on a folding table in front of the sofa. But that wasn't Jenkins's lifestyle at all.

He lived in the restored carriage house of a city mansion. His doorway tucked back on a brick-paved side street, ornate streetlamps glowing like replicas of old London town. An iron gate enclosed a small entry patio that looked like a setting for afternoon tea with a small working fountain and antique ice-cream-parlor chairs set around a dainty table.

As the gate hinges squeaked, a fat cat jumped off an inside windowsill and was waiting for Jenkins to come in. The big gray fellow rubbing with obvious pleasure against Jenkins's shins.

Jenkins turned on the lights. An octagonal foyer led to stairs left, a hall to the kitchen straight ahead, and a living room to the right. Modern art on unframed canvases was displayed on every wall. The furnishings were tasteful, some antiques, some reproductions, bordering on expensive.

"Not my place," Jenkins said, sounding almost apologetic.

"You got the key," Griffin pointed out.

Jenkins scooped the cat in his own big paw and slung him over his shoulder. The feline was quickly at home in that position. Walking into the living room, Jenkins said, "After my wife died, I sold our place. Wasn't the same living there without her. I rented an apartment for a while, bought this fatso cat and another one that ran off. This here's Ollie. Stan went AWOL on us."

Jenkins plopped down on a white sofa littered with spots of gray cat hair. He gestured for Griffin to make himself at home. "It was kind of lonely, so I started looking into roommates. It's a good way to live for a guy my age. Ex-cop who can cook. I share this place with two girls right out of college. Kind of like the daughters I never had, although these two I don't have to feel guilty sneaking looks at when they run from the shower to the bedroom in a towel that can't quite cover all the good parts."

Using a remote control, Jenkins flipped on a color TV fitted snugly in an armoire. "I make them feel safe—like they've got a daddy they can run home to—and looking at them gives me something worth waking up for every day besides that shit job at the hospital. They're in Europe for a couple weeks."

"Nice arrangement," Griffin said, wondering what else Jenkins could do to surprise him. Odd how you formed a picture of someone you'd known for years, only to find you didn't really know them at all.

Jenkins kicked off his shoes, put his feet up on the couch. Ollie remained on his shoulder. Jenkins remoted on the TV and, mocking an announcer's voice, said, "Here he comes. Every con man's idol, Diii-ick Marish."

Marish's press conference was being carried live. On the screen, white lights of TV cameras cast unflattering shadows across Marish's face. He stood behind a podium on which was carved the symbol of his office, as though Marish was the damned President. His hair looked particularly shellacked in place, perhaps fearful a sudden gust of wind might whip through the City Attorney press room.

Mickey Blane was beside Marish, pride of the PR folks, looking like a *GQ* cover boy.

Griffin remarked, "Amazing how you suppress true feelings about someone who writes your paycheck."

"Shit, kid. We all gotta make a living. You're no different from anyone else. You think I like answering to that board of trustees in the hospital? Nobody there's done an honest day's work in his life."

Marish read a prepared statement. Detailing Tracy Deil's murder, how the modus operandi was similar to Bright Eyes's, although possibly the work of a copycat. Warning the city to be cautious, but not to panic. Assuring that incredible manpower was being detailed to the case. How *he* had persuaded the mayor to open up the Rainy Day Fund to cover police overtime.

Griffin said, "You know he's doing this live because

he thinks he gets burned letting them tape his press conferences. That they edit him to make him look bad, or bury the story completely. He goes on at six-oh-five, he's right there in prime news time. And watch, he'll take questions, but the people he points to are shills. Judy Kulligan and Maury Laza. They'll ask questions the PR people fed them earlier." Griffin became more disgusted the longer he watched. "The guy's shit."

Marish's posture behind the podium was like a swashbuckler getting ready for a sword duel, trying to convey a sense of power. "We are double-barreling this case from the get-go. Nothing will impede us. We have already charged Rawley Jenkins, security chief of Memorial Hospital, with obstruction of justice for his attempted cover-up of another murder that follows the Bright Eyes MO."

Jenkins stroked his cat, said, "Hey, I made the news. First time since I got shot. This time I'm gettin' screwed. What a scrapbook." Jenkins tried to smile; Griffin sensed him burning.

Marish finished his statement, which amounted to nothing more than an unpaid political announcement, then took questions.

"Kulligan or Laza?" Griffin asked Jenkins. "Who's your pick?"

"You call it."

"Kulligan," Griffin said. "She's a woman and Marish will think that looks better since this is a sexual serial killer."

Marish pointed front center. Judy Kulligan stood.

Jenkins said, "I owe yah a beer."

"Now watch Marish look concerned, very deep in thought, like he appreciates this is a woman's issue, violence against women, like he gives a good goddamn."

Kulligan asked a seemingly rough question—did Marish feel responsible for not being able to keep Dunbar Waddy imprisoned four years ago—but Marish's PR people had him loaded for a response.

Marish practically leapt over the podium, verbally attacking the judge who released Waddy on bail pending appeal last time, Marish outraged that a convicted killer had again been released into society by a liberal bench.

This was also Marish's opportunity to put his arm around Mickey Blane, recreating the pose of the old press conference; he recounted the savage killing of Blane's family with the same vigor today as four years ago.

Sober this time, Blane stood beside Marish looking dead into the camera, strong and poised, like facing personal history and beating it back.

"Good God," Griffin complained. "Turn it off."

Jenkins was about to do just that when Maury Laza shouted at Marish, "What about Jimmy Griffin? He was the detective in charge of the police department's investigation last time. Now he works for your office. What's his involvement in this case?"

Marish responded staunchly. "James Griffin was, effective five-fifteen this afternoon, placed on administrative leave pending an investigation to be conducted by a special prosecutor as to whether or not he aided and abetted Rawley Jenkins in the cover-up of an as yet unidentified victim and also . . ." Marish hesitated for dramatic effect, ". . . whether James Griffin was in any way responsible for a breach of duty in failing to follow up leads in the case four years ago that would have resulted in the capture of Dunbar Waddy."

A general uproar rose from the press corps. Marish waved off any more questions and left the podium, Mickey Blane just off his shoulder, pacing Marish stride for stride.

Griffin looked at Jenkins as though studying his face. Jenkins asked, "What?"

"Just checking for lipstick marks. I see you didn't get a kiss either."

"Kid, professional whores never kiss when they screw."

Liz McKinley spent an hour searching Carla Griffin's bedroom, looking for a diary, letters, pictures, anything juicy. There was nothing good, which Liz found suspicious, as though Carla had purposefully cleaned out all her memories.

Liz did get a close look at the lone framed photograph she'd seen yesterday. An old shot looking even more historic with its colors faded. A small handwritten date in the bottom right corner, fifteen years ago. A picture taken at the beach: Carla, Griffin, and Mickey Blane in swimsuits. They'd been eighteen at the time. Blane in the center of the trio, sporting a rich kid's smile, arms around his two friends.

It was while Liz studied the expressions in that photograph that an unrelated thought occurred to her. She should have realized sooner: the computer. Where better for Carla to conceal something? Amidst all those electronic pathways, locked doors of technological access barred by passwords and hidden files. A world where information that sometimes seemed lost was actually right there.

Liz turned on the computer. While it was booting, she saw a memo Carla had group faxed two hours ago, advising approximately a dozen law firms she was shutting down early for the weekend.

The computer came up, greeting Liz with a colorful menu, ready to guide her into an array of programs loaded on the hard drive.

Liz picked up the telephone and called Atlanta, charging the toll call to her paper.

On the third ring, a polite Southern accent answered.

"Mrs. Dunleavy. This is Liz McKinley from *America Exposed*. Is Todd there?"

After a few minutes of cordial chat, Mrs. Dunleavy said she'd get Todd.

Twenty seconds later, an extension was picked up. Todd, quite cheerful, greeting, "Hey," in an accent as sweet and charming as his mother's.

"Busy?" Liz asked.

"Wait a second." Todd covered the mouthpiece, shouted for his mother to hang up the extension. As soon as there was a click, Todd whispered eagerly, "We gonna talk dirty today?"

Liz getting sultry, half panting, "You know the day you turn eighteen, provided that makes you legal, I'm going to drive out to your house and do incredibly nasty things to you."

"Yeah, yeah, tell me." Todd urged, doing his dirty old man voice.

"Absolutely. In the meantime, I've got this little computer problem. I'm at someone else's machine. An IBM clone. I need to go through the hard disk—maybe some floppies—looking for names. Help me out."

"The machine got a modem?"

Liz peeked behind the computer case. Amidst a tangle of wires were two phone lines, one running in, one out. "Could be just a fax. No, wait a minute, I've got a menu option up on the screen for a comm program."

"Fire it up.

Liz hot-keyed a communications package to life, the screen flashing changes before opening a new menu. We're on line."

"Gimme the number, I'll try it out."

"The number . . . ?" It wasn't written on the computer anywhere. Liz checked Carla's work stationery. Two phone numbers were listed, one for voice, the other marked DATA/FAX. She related it to Todd, who then hand-held her through a few quick system tests and commands, verifying how Carla's machine was set up.

The process was a little awkward, like having sex for the first time, but Todd guided her through it. Then, when Carla's machine was ready to receive a call, Todd said, "Okay, here comes Harry," referring to himself by the pet name Liz gave him, an alias-tribute to notable porn star Harry Reams, Todd always bragging to Liz he was going to be more than she could handle when she finally decided to stop being chicken and went to bed with him.

Todd was a pretty aggressive, horny kid besides having won his age group in the County Science Fair every year since he was eight. He'd also been given a suspended sentence in juvenile court for hacking his way into the computer system of a major soda bottling plant, rerouting their delivery routes so it took them three weeks to get back to normal.

Liz covered that story for *America Exposed*, what had launched a continuing relationship with Todd.

Now, Todd tapped computer keys in Atlanta. A ring sounded inside Carla's computer, followed by a buzzing hum, a shrill beep, then Todd breathing deeply on the other end of the line. "Oh, I'm in you, baby. I'm in you!" That same message appearing simultaneously on the screen in front of Liz.

Liz speaking, and typing, "Do it, Harry, do me with that long pipe!"

Todd laughed. "Okay, lady, now quit playing. Get out of the way so a real man can do some work here. Gimme those names you want me to check out on this baby."

*   *   *

Trevor Bourbin met Griffin in an alley two blocks from the station, not having wanted to meet him at all. Bourbin pulled an unmarked car into the shadows and turned off his lights. He looked angry, having just been put on a double shift to work Bright Eyes.

By the time Griffin said hello, half a dozen squad cars had driven past the end of the alley, the police chief ordering lots of blue on the pavement for Bright Eyes to see.

"You knew the girl was dead, Jimmy Grif. You knew Jane Doe bought it and didn't tell me. Didn't tell me he'd gotten in the hospital and given her a dose. You fuckin' used me, man."

Griffin accepted Bourbin's right to be mad. "But if I'd told you, you'd be suspended along with me. It's lucky you didn't know." A sorry excuse and they both knew it.

"Fuck that, man. You tell me everything, let *me* make the decision. I told you not to leave me hangin' out."

"I didn't," Griffin insisted. "I hurt your feelings, I'm sorry, but now *I'm* hanging out." Griffin punched his own chest for emphasis. "Marish's serving up scapegoat for dinner and I'm it."

"So what'm I supposed to do?" Bourbin demanded, as though nothing should be expected of him, not from Griffin, anyway.

"I need you to help me out."

"The kind of help you need I can't give you."

"I can get this guy, but Marish's got me shut out."

"How'm I gonna help you when *I* don't know what's goin' on?"

"All you have to do is ask questions for me, that's all."

"Like what?"

"Like if the semen Johnny Gibson found in Tracy Deil's hotel matches Dunbar Waddy's blood type."

"You call 'em and ask yourself."

"I tried before I called you. All questions have to be cleared through Frank Wallace and he told me go fuck myself. That I'd screwed the case when it was mine, I wasn't getting the same chance now that it's his."

Inside the unmarked cruiser, Bourbin's face was nearly concealed by darkness. Only pale green diodes from his radio formed a hint of shadows across his wide nose. "That's all you need to know? Blood type on the semen?"

"And if it matches."

Bourbin hung a heavy hand over the steering wheel, looked straight ahead. "I don't fuckin' believe this . . . You got nerve. *Balls*." Bourbin shook his head, decided, "Okay, I'll check the lab."

"Thanks." Griffin backed away.

Bourbin gestured for him to stop. " 'Nother thing. FBI called today. Got me the name of the choreographer in Jamaica put on that dinner show. The fake human sacrifice where the hexagon gets painted on? I called the guy. He says it's not based on any religion or ritual. He just made it up, thought it looked sexy."

Todd Dunleavy was able to operate Carla Griffin's computer from his home in Georgia thanks to a program he'd written he called *Todd's Remote Control*. Once inside, he probed around with hacker and utility programs he'd also written.

Cross-checking the list of names Liz gave him, he came up with a couple matches, but almost every time it was a common name found in a WordPerfect text file, a pleading or memorandum of law Carla had prepared for work.

Liz suggested a batch of new words to try—words
Todd liked lots better. *Cock. Pussy. Vagina. Breasts.
Kiss. Tongue. Orgasm. Climax. Penis. Hard-on. Nipples.
Love. Infatuation. Obsession. Adultery.* Liz figuring if
Carla kept any type of diary or journal—and didn't all
depression patients do that, suck Prozac and write notes
of self-analysis—one of those sweet terms would likely
be in there.

It didn't take long at all before the computer started
flashing a boxed message on the screen: FOUND. FOUND.
FOUND. FOUND. Lots and lots of FOUNDS, miniature explo-
sions of them.

"My kind of lady," Todd said over the phone. "Maybe
you could bring her with you for my eighteenth birthday.
I'll give you both a ride."

Liz hit a veritable jackpot. Carla kept a diary and it
was on disk. All of it. Broken down into years, a separate
file for each, dating back to when she was a teenager.
Having transferred all her written ledgers into the computer; putting them under phony business-sounding file
names; changing file attributes to hide them from normal
menu screens; even going so far as to lock them from access with passwords in case someone got that far.

But Todd Dunleavy wasn't just someone. He got it all
for Liz, every last byte, transferred into readable files, no
passwords, even made a copy for himself. A little late-
night reading when the cable stations he pirated weren't
running soft porn.

Within half an hour Liz knew who Carla was sleeping
with, the number of the condo she used at The Patios At
Knollwood, and who owned it. One of the names she
knew, the other she didn't.

27.

Griffin was unsure what kind of mood he'd find Carla in. He prepared himself for the worst and tried to summon the energy to deal with it.

He could see from outside that the living room was dark. Carla was probably hiding in her office/bedroom, lights off so any reporters knocking on the door would assume no one was home. Not a bad idea.

Griffin expected at least one stubborn guy with a notepad and pencil waiting to ambush him, but he made the trip to the porch unscathed.

He unlocked the door and went in. The door to Cassie's room was open, but the night-light was off. Carla probably had Cassie with her, Griffin seeing a strip of light shining out beneath her bedroom door.

"Carla?" Wanting to hear her voice as a barometer of her mood before actually meeting eye to eye. It was always best to have some kind of hint so he'd know what "face" he should have on. "Carla?"

No answer. That wasn't good. The silent nights were the worst. Like torture, not knowing what she was thinking, only that it was bad and there wasn't anything he could do about it.

"Carla?" Starting down the hall, halfway to her door when he heard a trickle of water. A gentle splashing sound. Carla must be giving Cassie a bath. "Carla?" Going into her bedroom.

It was too quiet. No sounds from Cassie. The bathroom door was closed.

"Carla?" Griffin knocked.

The knob was unlocked. He turned it, looked in. "Carla?"

Liz McKinley said, "I am if you want me to be." She was reclined in a bathtub of warm water. Not having bothered to cover herself with so much as bubble bath.

Griffin stared in disbelief. "What the hell are you doing? Where's Carla?"

"You ask a lot of questions for a guy who hasn't slept with his wife very much for two years." Liz ran her hands through her hair, slicked it back.

"Get out of here."

"Why?"

"My wife comes home—"

"She's not coming home. Not tonight anyway. You didn't see her note?"

He hadn't.

"She left it on the dining-room table—had to leave for a few days, something like that." Liz was very nonchalant.

Griffin grabbed a towel and threw it at her.

Liz let it land in the water, picking it up only after it was soaking wet. "Nice." She plopped it soggily on the tile floor.

Griffin couldn't not look at her.

Liz said, "This is kind of my James Bond fantasy seduction scene. You know how James always used to come back to his suite on the Riviera or someplace like that and there'd be clothes strewn in a path to the bathroom, and there was this lovely named Miss Ample Buns or something like that waiting for him. Except you never saw anything good happen, which I figured meant maybe James was impotent. All those women and not a single orgasm. PG movies are so dull."

Griffin regained his composure. Almost like talking a jumper off a roof ledge, said, "Liz, this can't happen."

"Sure it can . . . if you want it to." Liz stood boldly. "Do you want to?"

Water dripped off her body, raining into the tub. Just when he'd thought he was over the shock of seeing her naked, this move hit him with a few extra amps of surprise. As though the tub had been a sort of transparent clothing. Now there was nothing to hide.

Liz grabbed the remaining towel off the rack and tossed it to him. "Dry me off, okay?"

Griffin started to hand back the towel.

"Trust me, you got nothing to lose."

Griffin felt the closeness of her body.

Liz put her hands behind her back, a relaxed pose, one shoulder slightly lower than the other, hip cocked. Her nipples were soft until Griffin touched them with the towel.

Liz clutched his forearm, felt the strength of him through the fabric of his shirt.

His eyes offered a thousand reasons why not, all moral, all valid. He released the towel and left the room.

Liz sighed. "Damn it."

Liz stayed, but just for dinner. They had Chinese food delivered to the apartment and ate from cardboard containers. It was awkward for a little while, but, for the most part, they acted as though the "bathtub" never happened. Perhaps it had been a simultaneous dream.

Only for a brief instance did they even refer to it. Liz asking, "If you weren't married . . . ?"

And Griffin replying, "In a second."

*   *   *

He had enjoyed himself last night. Tracy—or Ella as
he was calling her—had a wonderful reaction to belladonna. In the car, when he'd fed her a capsule, she'd
sucked it off his fingers with exotic interest, looking forward to the wonderful buzz he claimed it would give her.
A mild sensuous ride.

Her pupils had opened magically; she'd been very
aroused. Had wanted to make it with him in the car,
going so far as to reach for his zipper while he was driving.

But he'd said he had a thing about being in public,
that he was really rather shy, that's why he hadn't come
over to her in the bar—a lie she'd bought. Could they go
to her place?

Sure.

In her hotel room, she'd been ready to get right into
bed. He'd slowed her down. Said he didn't like to rush
it. That he wanted to watch her for a while, treasure her,
make *her* feel good first.

She'd said he was like no other man she'd ever been
with, usually it was slam, bam, out the door. And there
had been quite a few men she'd met traveling, although
she assured him she was cautious—only safe sex.

He'd guaranteed her he was very safe himself.

When he'd offered her more belladonna, she'd said
sure, if he did some with her. He palmed a capsule, pretended to swallow it. So she downed a second, much
more potent hit.

She'd been dancing out of her clothes for him when
the convulsions grabbed her. Stripped to black lace
panties, she struggled to stay on her feet.

It had been like watching her wrestle with a barbaric
ghost. One that eventually got the better of her, dropped

her to the carpet, made her shiver until her lungs stopped working and she suffocated.

Left with wide-open eyes, body supple in death, waiting for him to paint on the hexagon like he'd seen in that show in Jamaica—quite an erotic experience having watched a mock death play.

The paint dried to a tacky finish on her flesh by the time he was ready to position her on the bed. Her muscles had begun to stiffen slightly, but he was still able to force her into a provocative angle. Raising her ass, spreading her legs.

Standing at the foot of the bed, he'd felt the power surge through his hard-on as he took it into his hand, stroked himself until tremors of ecstasy shuddered through him.

Finished with her, he'd gone into the bathroom, cleaned his hand with toilet paper, flushed his fluid down the john, then went about wiping down the entire hotel room, having been very careful as to what he'd touched.

Now, he was tempted to kill another one even though the hunger really wasn't there. Just to show the cops they couldn't catch him. Fortunately, he recognized that sort of thinking was dangerous. He had a job to do for The Kroop and that should come first.

Still, he'd been getting itchy sitting in the motel room, waiting, passing time. Which was why he was out on the street tonight, back in the city.

Heartbeat picking up a few kicks when the Dynasty was side by side with a police car at a light. Thinking, *I'm here, you asshole. Right here, jerk-off. The guy you're looking for. Who you're never gonna catch.*

28.

Sara Krenshaw thought her assets were pale ivory skin, fake British accent, and the way her breasts looked in low-cut blouses boosted by an underwire bra. She wasn't crazy about her legs—which she considered a little heavy—or her stomach—which she felt was on the pudgy side.

So even on a hot night like tonight, she wore long leather pants to conceal her legs. Cruising the street with her silky blouse unbuttoned, showing skin and the lace edges of her bra.

Sara worked alone, no pimp, and had been whoring for seven years off and on, dating back to when she was a runaway at fourteen.

She wasn't really in the mood to hit the bricks tonight, but a job was, after all, a job. And she thought she was good enough at hers. She had an eye for details. Like how the guy in the four-door sedan had cruised by four times now, trying to look disinterested, but failing. Maybe he was a little shy. Felt uncomfortable picking up a girl in public.

It was just after ten, but already there were lots of people on The Block, a once-famed strip of neon and glitz; bawdy entertainment being slowly legislated out of existence, another fatality to changing times when even sex wasn't as innocent as it used to be.

Temptation lingered on every corner via audio, video,

or in person. Take your pick and pleasure. No one was deterred by the number of police cars out tonight.

Sara *had* heard something about a murder earlier, but not the details, figuring it was just another killing in a city averaging at least one shooting death per day.

When the guy in the sedan came by a fifth time, Sara turned the corner. She proceeded along a less traveled side street, slightly exaggerating her walk to entice him.

Headlights flashed across a vacant building beside her as the sedan made the same turn. He pulled alongside the curb, window down. Called out to her.

Sara—congratulating herself that she *did* know how to get the business—walked over to the man. Said, " 'Lo, love," in her fake accent, bending at the waist so he could look down her shirt at the creamy curves of her breasts.

Liz was still at Griffin's—just talking—when the eleven o'clock news came on.

Griffin had brought Cassie down from Mrs. Pulaski's and settled her into her crib. She slept quietly, but her mere presence in the adjacent room, her door partially opened, diffused the potential for seduction.

Griffin didn't want Liz to leave. He liked the way she made him feel, even though he couldn't bring himself to allow anything to happen between them.

If Carla walked in, he wasn't sure what he'd say. Figured he should lie, tell her Liz was working on a story. But then he realized that wasn't a lie, was it? So how come the truth seemed so incriminating? That he *was* attracted to Liz.

Just before the late news was about to show an edited version of Richard Marish's press conference, Griffin's phone rang. He looked at Liz, both of them thinking it might be Carla.

It wasn't.

"Jimmy Grif. Get yo ass to Center and Light. Word is we got another Bright Eyes. But don't say you heard it from me." Trevor Bourbin broke the connection before Griffin could thank him.

Outside the vacant building, a perimeter had been established to hold back gawkers and the press corps. Minicam units spilled bright light that illuminated half the block.

Inside, portable police floods washed over a rickety stairwell that only reached the second floor, the rest of it having fallen down sometime before the place had been condemned.

Plaster walls were chipped and full of holes revealing asbestos insulation. Crusty layers of lead paint peeled away from the ceiling. Rats had enjoyed free run of the place for years, dropping pellets of excrement that in part accounted for the ripe smell.

The homicide people who knew Griffin wasn't supposed to be there didn't stop him. Nor did Frank Wallace. Seeing the purpose in Griffin's demeanor, Frank wasn't quite so aggressive in person as on the phone.

Griffin and Liz were upstairs where the body had been found. The room now sealed off while the tweezers and microscope boys did their work.

The hallway was busy with activity, so many people they tripped over one another. Further complicating logistics was Frank Wallace's "ever-necessary" command post, consisting of a folding table, chairs, police radio, three cellular phones, portable fax machine, and boxes ready to accept inventoried evidence. For some unknown reason, probably something Frank had seen in a movie, there was also a huge city map taped to the dilapidated wall behind him.

"Frank," a bleary-eyed Lenny Shane whispered to Griffin, "is trying a new set of color codes for his case binder this time. Least that's what I hear." Lenny winked. He was waiting for the lab boys to finish, twin Nikons roped around his neck.

"We got ID," a plainclothes detective reported to Frank Wallace. "Sara Krenshaw. 9953 Cathedral Place. She's got a rap sheet. Prostitute."

Frank scribbled notes.

A sergeant in uniform told Frank he was assembling witnesses downstairs. Five at last count.

"Witnesses?" Griffin asked Lenny.

"Uh-huh. Supposedly went down like this: prostitute goes over to a john's car, they talk a little while, she gets in up front with him. She gets into a struggle with him *and* another guy who's in the backseat. The two guys haul her out of the car, one's got a rope around her neck. They bring her up here, rape her, beat her to death."

"That's not Bright Eyes."

"I know that. You know that. Everybody fuckin' knows that but Frank, which ain't gonna stop him from announcing this to the media in about an hour."

"How can he even consider it?"

"Come 'ere." Lenny waggled his finger, directing Griffin to the doorway so he could look inside at the body.

Liz was right behind him, gasped, "Oh, God," when she saw: Sara Krenshaw stripped naked, hanging from exposed rafters by a thick cord looped around her neck. A bloody baseball bat was on the floor beside puddles of semen that dripped from her vagina. There was also a can of spray paint on the floor, what her killers had used to paint a symbol across her naked body. Wide uneven lines of red that dripped skinny entrails along her stomach and thighs.

Lenny commented, "Nasty pricks did her couldn't even count. That's an *oct*agon they put on her, not a hexagon. Doncha hate copycats can't get the details right."

As much as Griffin never showed visible signs of emotion from the aftermath of brutal crime, this scene had unsettling effects. Witnessing a crime—although admittedly less than being a victim to it—made the entire judicial process seem inadequate. There could be no mitigating factors. No defense short of *not* having committed the act was even worthy of consideration. If you did it, you should pay. But it never happened like that.

Liz's reaction to the senselessness of murder was different. Having long abandoned hope for society, she viewed tragedy as a confirmation of her lifestyle. That the world was a terribly wicked place and being able to find an enjoyable niche in it for yourself was immeasurably valuable. Have fun while you could, because the next maniac's knife might get you.

Back home, Carla's white Prelude wasn't parked on the street; there were plenty of empty spots. She really wasn't coming home tonight.

Griffin asked Liz if she wanted to come in.

"I better not."

Griffin nodded, no sense letting a loose late-night decision ruin a tract record of fidelity. He walked Liz to her car. "I'll see you tomorrow."

She kissed him briefly on the lips and withdrew. "Don't feel guilty about it. Okay?"

He waited until she drove away before going inside.

Mrs. Pulaski was asleep on the sofa, mouth agape, snoring quietly. Wearing the same housecoat Griffin had seen her in a hundred times, yet it still looked brand new, perfectly clean; perhaps she bought them by the gross.

"Adda." He gently touched her shoulder.

She abruptly cut off a snore and opened her eyes in surprise, disoriented before remembering where she was. "Lordie. That fast I was dreaming." Her accent still held traces of her native Yugoslavia fifty years after being smuggled across the border.

"Thanks for coming down. It *was* an emergency."

With so much of her weight around her hips and stomach, Adda Pulaski had little leverage to sit up. She grabbed hold of the sofa back and pulled with a strong arm while giving a slight kick with her opposite leg. "Not your wife?" she asked, upright. "This emergency?"

"No. A murder across town."

"The madman I saw on the news?"

"No. Different."

"Mmmp." Mrs. Pulaski grunted. She tilted her head down and remained quiet for what seemed like a long time. Griffin thought maybe she'd fallen back asleep. When she looked up, the way pale light touched the creases and shadows of her face made her expression seem especially rich; soft furrows reflecting a sense more of experience than age. "Has your wife left you?"

Griffin was surprised by the question. While he had only known Mrs. Pulaski for two years, and only closely since the final weeks of Carla's pregnancy, he couldn't remember her ever asking a personal question. Thinking her either unobservant or disinterested in her neighbors' lives.

Adda said, "When she left today, she had a suitcase. And there was a note on your dining-room table. I saw it when I went to look in on Cassie."

"She just went away for the weekend. The man—the killer who was on the news tonight—is very upsetting for us. He killed our best friend's wife and child four years ago. You didn't know her then. My wife was a different person before that happened. It's been hard on her."

Adda nodded, looking at Griffin. "Hard on you, too." She stood and aimed herself for the door. Needing a few steps to get the direction right, her posture on the sofa having tightened an arthritic hip.

"Adda?"

She looked back.

"The woman who was with me tonight . . . She's helping me investigate the case. She's a reporter—"

"I didn't see any woman," Adda Pulaski said. With that, she smiled.

The underground parking lot at Liz McKinley's hotel was full. The attendant apologizing, "Convention in for the weekend. There's a public lot across the street if you want." He handed her a plastic chit. "There's a big pay board on one side. You can't miss it. Put this in the slot for your parking space. That way you don't have to pay."

Liz looked over her shoulder at the lot half a block away. She could only see the front portion of it; the rest was blocked by construction barricades set up around a building being rehabbed. "Little dark over there, isn't it?" Liz was not pleased.

"It's fine, don't worry."

Liz ungratefully grabbed the parking chit from his hand, figuring paying for this was the least the hotel could do. But why should this city be any different from the rest? Throw up a lot of buildings, then worry about roads and parking later—much, much later, like never.

She backed out of the entrance to the underground garage and onto the street. Waited for a few cars to pass, then cut over three lanes and went down the crossing street to the public lot.

A police car drove by, making Liz feel secure for

about three seconds, but then the cop turned left at the intersection and was out of sight.

Liz bumped the Thunderbird up a concrete apron onto the macadam surface. The parking spaces were extremely narrow and the only open spots up front were for subcompacts.

Liz proceeded slowly toward the rear of the lot. Medium-rise brick buildings, one of which appeared abandoned, created walls along two sides of the square area; the third edge was bordered by the construction job. Of five pole lamps, two were burned out.

Liz telling herself, Great, this is the kind of place people get beat up and the cops shake their heads, wonder how someone could have been so stupid as to be there in the first place.

She found a spot between a ten-year-old Cadillac and a nondescript four-door sedan. Got out of the car wishing she hadn't worn the not-so-demure outfit meant to entice Griffin. Wishing he was here with her.

Liz started toward the pay board, metal box attached by serious bolts to a concrete pillar. A faceplate divided the board into numbered sections, one for each parking spot. Liz plunked in the chit she'd been given, turned around, and screamed when the man came up behind her.

29.

Griffin called Liz's hotel room just after nine-thirty Saturday morning. When she didn't answer, he left a message with the hotel operator.

The paper had been printed too early to include Sara Krenshaw's murder and the local TV stations weren't about to interrupt cartoons to give details of a grisly killing, so Griffin listened to AM news radio to see if Frank Wallace had actually declared her a Bright Eyes's victim.

Waiting for the top of the hour, when they ran local stories, Griffin drank regular coffee—not French Roast—and ate plain toast with jelly—no croissants from Sutton Place. When that was finished, he made scrambled eggs. Had just finished them when the Sara Krenshaw story came on.

She got top billing, a graphic description of her killing, followed by edited portions of an interview with Frank Wallace. Frank saying he could neither confirm nor deny this as another Bright Eyes's killing, but his tone made it clear he thought it was. The story cut back to the newscaster, who reported that neither City Attorney Richard Marish nor Assistant CA Mickey Blane was available for comment. Griffin figuring they were huddled with the PR people, plotting strategy as to how to best "sell" this most recent development.

Griffin switched off the radio, went into the living

room, and picked up the old CA file on Dunbar Waddy. In weight alone, it was at least three times bigger than the police department file. Stuffed with preliminary motions, case research, witness interviews, correspondence, and trial entries.

The trick, as always, was to avoid becoming bogged down by the volume of pages. If he began to sense he was staring at a new page—not absorbing it—he'd know it was time to take a break, get up, move around the house, play with Cassie a little while, then go back to it fresh. A method Griffin had used successfully for the year of law school he'd squeezed in between personal disasters.

The first inch of pages contained copies of the police department file he'd already reviewed. He checked to make sure nothing was different or out of place, then moved into the CA case notes.

They proved little more than worthless memos from Investigator Gerremo. All based on his version of conducting witness interviews, which was to make phone calls from an air-conditioned office, never putting more than four thousand business miles a year on his office-issued car.

There was no mention in the file of the Jamaican cook Jenkins had found, Beyer, providing Dunbar Waddy with an alibi. Griffin still wasn't sure what to make of Beyer's story; it was so bizarre it begged to be believed, but Griffin couldn't accept it without some collaboration.

Pretrial motions in the file appeared routine, most having been prepared by an assistant for signature by Blane. What caught Griffin's eye was the *State's Automatic Discovery and Request for Discovery.* A boilerplate form, but there were two versions in the file. The earlier-dated version had been stamped with the word DRAFT across the first page, although it clearly wasn't a draft version; it was on CA stationery, paper with a red double stripe running along the left-inch margin of the page, the official moniker CITY ATTORNEY'S OFFICE, embossed in the lower left corner.

There was only one meaningful change between the draft and final version; all the other changes were no more than cosmetic.

STATE	* IN THE
vs.	* CIRCUIT COURT
DUNBAR WADDY	*
Defendant	* Case # CR-19587-18
* * *	* * *

STATE'S AUTOMATIC DISCOVERY AND REQUEST FOR DISCOVERY

NOW COMES, Michael K. Blane, Assistant City Attorney, and in compliance with Rule 4-263(a) of the Rules of Court Procedure, says as follows:

1. The State is not in possession of any relevant material or information regarding whether the State used a search and seizure, wiretap, or eavesdrop in gathering evidence in this case.

2. The Defendant made an oral statement, to wit:

(a) When asked: "What were you doing to that woman?" Answered: "I didn't rape the bitch. She uhh never said for me not to do anything to her. I didn't kill her, neither. She was uhh there on the floor, not wearing any clothes. Just laying there when I walked in. She was moving. Her eyes was open. She saw me come up to her. I said, 'I got something I think you want,' and asked if she wanted to see it. She nodded, so I uhh opened my pants and showed it to her and she looked like she wanted it, so I gave it to her."

(b) When asked: "How did the duct tape get put over her mouth?" Answered: "I don't know."

(c) When asked: "What were you doing in the apartment in the first place?" Answered: "I want a lawyer."

Interrogation ended at that point.

3. The Defendant did not make a written statement or confession.

4. The Defendant has not, at this time, been identified by a pretrial identification procedure.

~~5. Information known to the State at this time which tends to negate the guilt of the Defendant as to the offenses charged herein or which tends to reduce his punishment therefore is attached hereto as Exhibit "A."~~

5. The State is not, at this time, in possession of any information that tends to negate the guilt of the Defendant as to the offenses charged herein or that tends to reduce his punishment therefore.

It was the altered paragraph five that concerned Griffin. He could see how running off standard forms, many of which were the same in case after case, Blane's assistant could have included the wrong fifth paragraph. Except for the fact that an exhibit was referred to. That wasn't part of the boilerplate. Someone had to have typed in the line about there being an Exhibit A, as though looking right at it while processing the pleading.

Griffin checked all through the file. No Exhibit A.

He went to the work-log page, where a record was made of which CD employee did what on the file.

Jamie Brooks had prepared both versions of the discovery motion. Griffin remembered her as a young, efficient assistant prosecutor. Fresh out of law school. Very aggressive. Highly recruited by law firms, but had opted for lesser pay in order to get more court experience.

She'd left the CA's office shortly after the Bright Eyes case. Rumor had been she'd gotten into an argument with Blane; that she wouldn't sleep with him during those wild drunken months Blane went on the prowl after losing Diana.

Griffin couldn't remember where Jamie Brooks had gone to work after the CA's office. He hadn't had contact with her since.

He checked the metro phone book. No listing.

In Carla's office, he pulled the Maryland Bar Association Lawyer Directory off the shelf. The green pages listed every attorney licensed to practice in the state. Griffin hoped Jamie Brooks hadn't gotten married, or had at least kept her last name.

There she was, BROOKS, JAMIE S. An address and phone number in Carroll County, little more than an hour west of the city, near where Griffin used to go hiking. Being Saturday, Griffin called Jamie Brooks's home number long distance. When he got an answering machine, he tried her office.

A woman answered on the second ring. Small law office, working on a Saturday; he should have guessed.

"Brooks and McAlister."

"Jamie Brooks?" Griffin thought he recognized her voice.

"Speaking."

"This is Jimmy Griffin from the CA's office downtown. How've you been?"

Silence at the other end of the line.

"Jamie?"

Not responding at first, but, finally, "Yes?"

"If this is a bad time, I'm sorry. But I was going through an old case file and had a question about—"

"Exhibit A."

Griffin was stunned. "Yeah . . . that's right. Exhibit A."

And Jamie said, "Not over the phone."

Griffin had come back into the apartment for Cassie when the phone rang. Sweating from the heat, he answered with an impatient, "Hello." Thinking it might be Carla, ready to make *her* feel guilty for a change; because Mrs. Pulaski was out, he was going to have to take Cassie out to Carroll County with him. Already having set up her car seat in his Taurus.

"Sounds like you're having my kind of day." It was Liz.

"You just caught me going out the door." He told her about Jamie Brooks.

"Pick me up at my hotel?"

"Ten minutes?"

"Good. I'll tell you all about Ralph Young."

"Who?"

"A guy I slugged in the parking lot last night."

Greg and Michelle Aronson lived in separate bedrooms in a big stone rancher on Seminary Avenue, twenty minutes north of the city line. A prestigious neighborhood sought so religiously by upwardly mobile professionals that real estate values continued to climb even through slow market periods.

It was a scenic locale among winding lanes shaded by graceful maple and oak trees. Jaguars, Mercedes, and BMWs parked like trophies along brick driveways and inside garages left open this summer Saturday.

Homeowners toured green lawns on expensive riding mowers, which had become status symbols of their own.

Greg Aronson, however, was not one of those men who cut his own lawn. He was out back in his Ralph Lauren shirt and LLB shorts, arguing with a supervisor from the pool service company about having to pay for a replacement pump valve when he'd just had a new valve installed last fall.

The pool man trying patiently to explain how this was a different valve, but Aronson didn't want to hear anything about that; to Greg, a valve was a valve, not knowing a damned thing about the mechanics of a swimming pool, only that it was costing him too much to swim in his.

Like most arguments with rich people, this one went around in circles. Aronson acting as if he told the pool man about replacing a valve last fall for the fifteenth time, it would suddenly make the situation different from the first fourteen times he'd said it.

Meanwhile, Michelle Aronson was locked in her bedroom, trying to concentrate on a pile of magazines and ignore as best she could that she was still shaking.

Last night, around three in the morning, Greg had come into her bedroom, thrown the covers off her, pulled up her nightgown, told her to shut up, and raped her. When she'd struggled—which sometimes made him stop in the past—he'd hit her in the stomach with his fist, knocked the wind out of her, then stuck himself inside her while she was still gasping for breath.

When she'd said she was suffocating, he grunted, "I don't care if you do," and came inside her.

Now, the magazine shook so violently in her grasp, Michelle laid the heavy issue open across her pillow to hold it still. Her bedroom still smelled of his sex. She wanted to wash the sheets, but that would mean leaving the room.

If she could kill Greg herself, she would. She didn't want to have to depend on someone else to help her, having always been independent until she'd married Greg. Slowly, steadily, he'd taken all that away, made it so there wasn't anything she couldn't do without his okay.

Michelle not having any idea the answer to her prayers was less than two hundred yards away, jogging along the sidewalk in a one-piece nylon suit more typically used by bicyclists than runners.

30

Griffin drove the Taurus twenty miles over the fifth-five limit, figuring he'd have to slow down once he hit the country line and his badge would lose its influence. He had his course charted via map: I–95 to the Baltimore Beltway to I–70, then north on Route 32 to Carroll County's county seat, Westminster. Where Brooks and McAlister had their offices.

Cassie was secured in a car seat in back, gumming on a plastic rattle.

Liz sat beside Griffin, having said, "Oh . . ." seeing Cassie was along for the trip. Liz thought Cassie was a cute baby, but the idea of putting up with screaming for a couple hours wasn't something she looked forward to. So far, though, so good. Cassie was quiet.

Griffin filled in Liz on last night's copycat murder, then asked, "So what's this about a guy in the parking lot?" Griffin asked Liz.

"Last night, I get back to the hotel and the underground lot's full. So this dweeb sends me to some hell-hole across the street. It's dark and isolated, like there's a big sign: muggers welcome. I get out of my car and this schmuck sneaks up behind me. Trying to be cute. Like he was going to scare me, then make a pass. The creep. He'd probably been sitting in his car waiting for some woman to terrorize."

"And you hit him," Griffin confirmed.

"He deserved it. I turn around and there he is looking goofy, reaching out like he's going to touch me, what am I supposed to do? Be another scream no one reports to the police? Unh-unh. I nailed him."

"You're tough."

"Hey, make fun if you want." She was clearly miffed.

Griffin liked conversations with Liz. Lively. "You hit him hard?"

"Busted his nose."

"No kidding?"

"Yeah, it's over here like this now." Liz put her forefinger to the tip of her nose and pressed it to the side. "He yooks yike dis," she described, using a nasal tone for effect. "The police took my statement this morning. That's where I was when you called. You know a cop named Underwood?"

"No."

"Anyway, he thought it was pretty funny. He said they weren't pressing charges, but had to make a report because the guy's talking about suing me." She shook her head, frowning. "I should sue him."

Once the city's silhouette of concrete and steel vanished behind them, the interstate wound luxuriously through suburban neighborhoods. Meadows and farms sprawled across a rolling landscape.

Griffin pointed out animals to Cassie and made the obligatory corresponding sounds. Liz wasn't into it, but went along, prompted by Griffin, thankful to stop playing substitute mommy once Cassie dozed off.

Westminster, the county seat, was like a setting from a Christmas garden. White wood-sided houses with gable roofs. Church steeples rising above dark green trees that framed hilly streets.

The eastern edge of Main Street had gone slightly

"tourist" with antique shops, restaurants overpriced by local standards, and bed and breakfast inns; all designed to lure city-weary couples for a peaceful day in the country.

An overall sense of calm, quiet, and slow. Older couples window shopping. Young parents holding their children's hands while crossing the street. Hanging baskets of begonias and fuchsia on nearly every porch front.

"Cute place," Liz said, ". . . for about two hours."

At least twenty policemen Griffin had known on the force had escaped the city for places like this, wanting to raise a family where there weren't so many temptations or crazies. John Blum having told Griffin, "One night, just one night I want to *not* hear a siren or glass breaking." A few, the restless ones like Liz, went stir crazy and returned to the city, but most stayed and wondered why they hadn't gotten out sooner.

Griffin thought about it sometimes himself, but having been born and raised, lived his entire life downtown, it didn't seem like a real possibility. As though he'd be moving to a foreign country.

Former Assistant CA Jamie Brooks's office was easy to find. A converted town house with a front bow window overlooking Main Street. Sided in wood freshly painted shell white. A hand-painted sign, BROOKS AND MCALISTER, ATTORNEYS & COUNSELORS AT LAW, hung from the arm of a Williamsburg light pole. Beneath the sign was a brilliant pink hydrangea.

Griffin parked in the shade of a mature dogwood tree. He asked Liz if she'd mind waiting in the car with Cassie, unsure if what Jamie Brooks had to tell him might be inhibited by the presence of someone she didn't know.

Liz said, "Oh, sure, no trouble at all," dreading every minute she was going to be left alone with a baby.

It was ten degrees cooler than in the city. Less humid. A touch of crispness in the air coming off the mountains.

A worn stone walkway bordered by a carpet of blue rug junipers led to an oak entrance door. It was unlocked, so Griffin walked in.

The decor spoke subtly of small-town money and influence. A cathedral ceiling opened to a loft on the second floor, where Brooks and McAlister maintained their law library.

Jamie Brooks stood at the loft's oak railing, obviously not having planned to see clients today dressed in a tennis shirt, shorts, and running shoes.

"Looks like you're doing okay," Griffin commented about her digs. His voice echoed quietly off a high ceiling that gave the impression of standing in a much larger space.

"Not bad for two women running shop in what *was* pretty much an all-male community until we got here." Jamie's tone was a mix of pride and defiance.

Griffin was impressed. "Good for you," he said sincerely.

Jamie pointed out stairs to Griffin's right. Told him to come up and was there to shake his hand at the landing. She had the firm grip of an athlete, Griffin recalling she'd gone to college on a tennis scholarship.

She still looked as young as when working for Marish and Blane as an assistant CA, but was much more sure in the way she moved. Griffin deciding it came from Jamie having found a comfortable station in life.

"I heard the news last night. About Bright Eyes." Jamie stood beside a long wooden bookcase filled with *Atlantic Reporter* volumes. "I was wondering if anyone would call me about the old case. Didn't figure Frank Wallace would. Didn't figure you would either, seeing as

Marish made the public announcement you were suspended. Or is that just a ruse?"

"I haven't been back to the office to find out, but I think it's for real."

"Should I ask why?"

Griffin shrugged it off. "Mickey and Marish want a little distance between themselves and the cop who let Bright Eyes get away."

"Marish and Blane." Jamie shook her head. "Quite a team. *Quite* a team."

"Marish, mostly."

"Blane's the same way. Power hungry. Self-obsessed, but aren't all lawyers?" Jamie didn't mind castigating her own profession. She walked toward her private office between aisles of books. Griffin following as she said, "Well then, once and former infamous Detective Griffin, tell me what I'm about to do isn't going to get me disbarred."

"I don't know what you're going to do."

At the far end of the small library was a suite of two near identical offices. Both had windows looking into the library on one wall and over a quaint back street at the other. The textured wallpaper featured a relaxing free-form pattern. The desks were cherry. And, at least in Jamie's office, there was a wall safe.

"Actually," she said, spinning the combination, "this is somewhat of a relief. I always had the feeling someone was going to track this down someday. I guess I'm only good at keeping *other people's* secrets."

She opened the safe and reached inside, withdrew a thin sealed envelope on the face of which was hand printed, IN THE EVENT OF MY DEATH, PLEASE FORWARD UN-OPENED TO JAMES GRIFFIN, LAST KNOWN TO ME AS A HOMICIDE DETECTIVE, CITY POLICE, AS OF MY LAST DAY IN THE

EMPLOY OF THE CITY ATTORNEY'S OFFICE. The postmark
on the envelope was four years old.

Jamie said, "I mailed it to myself so the postmark
would prove the date. Sorry about the in-the-event-of-
my-death stuff. I was younger, a little more vulnerable to
my imagination at the time." She handed the envelope to
Griffin.

"What is it?"

"Exhibit A."

Greg Aronson was still arguing with the pool service
supervisor, the debate growing more heated, when the
man in the long-sleeve jogging suit broke course with
the sidewalk. The jogger diverted between the long
picket fence that ran the entire length of the Aronson's
acre and a half and the tall line of leyland cypress that
secluded their house from neighbors' views.

The man knew he was taking a chance. Someone
could see him, but that would be okay, just so they didn't
notice him. It was a risk he had to take. He wasn't a
B&E man, history had proven that; he'd experienced
enough trouble with places not fitted with security sys-
tems to know not to mess with one that was. And this
house did have an alarm.

What he needed to do was get inside the alarm's
perimeter *before* the system was activated for the night.
Once he was in, he could hide until it was time.

He darted into the garage.

Greg Aronson was just on the other side of a hedge
wall, bitching something awful about valves.

The man had to work swiftly now.

Driving through the area on a scouting run, finding
the Aronsons' garage doors opened, he'd noticed a set
of interior stairs leading up to a storage area built into

tall roof eaves of the attic. He was assuming there'd be someplace to hide up there. If not . . . it could get dicey.

He ascended the stairs quickly, accessing the attic. The floor spanned the entire ceiling of the two-car garage. A few pieces of furniture protected by white sheets were the only items stored beneath the high-pitched roof. There was enough headroom to stand once he was six feet from the back wall. Unfortunately, it was insufferably hot. He hadn't properly considered the temperature. Sweat began pouring off his face.

There was no possibility of remaining up here for very long.

He was going to have to get inside the house itself.

"You thought someone might kill you?" Griffin now held the sealed envelope produced by Jamie Brooks. "Bright Eyes?"

"No." She chose not to answer more specifically, gesturing to the envelope. "Go ahead. Open it."

Griffin tore the seal and pulled out two sheets of paper inside. It was the original page one of the *State's Automatic Discovery and Request for Discovery*. Paragraph five, referring to Exhibit A, remained intact.

"That was my copy," Jamie explained. "I kept duplicates of most of my work. Some of the attorneys would make a slew of hand corrections, then decide they liked my version better, only they'd written over so much of it it was easier to go back to an original."

Griffin turned to the second page. Exhibit A.

"Fingerprints," he said. It was a page removed from a crime scene report. Prints of two fingers from the first knuckle to pad. The images of arches, loops, and whorls centered in the middle of a page marked at the top:

LATENT LIFT CARD

Lift No. 1   Evidence No. 3
CCN No. 7865442
Case description: Suspected homicide.
Victim: **LESLIE CONNORS**.
Location where latent was found: On victim.
Description of item that latent was found on:
"Sticky" side of duct tape secured over victim's mouth.

Jamie said, "Connors was the third Bright Eyes victim. The housewife the police caught Dunbar Waddy raping."

Griffin nodded.

"Apparently, when Bright Eyes put the tape over her mouth he didn't wear gloves. Just like the FBI said. He touched them with his hands knowing he was going to wipe everything down afterward and his fingerprints would be erased. Only with Leslie Connors, he had to do something he hadn't needed to do with the others. She must have been making too much noise so he put tape over her mouth. When he did it, he didn't have on gloves, and ended up holding the edge of the tape. Like this."

Jamie picked up a piece of paper and made as though about to place it over Griffin's face. Her index and middle fingers touched what would have been the adhesive side had it been tape. "His bare fingers leave a print on the part of the tape that goes over Leslie Connors's open mouth. By not removing the tape when he wiped the rest of the scene down, his fingerprints stayed for the lab boys when they pulled it off."

"I never saw this."

"I know you didn't."

Griffin was confident he knew the answer to his next

question before asking it. "They're not Dunbar Waddy's prints, are they?"

Jamie Brooks shook her head no. "When Blane saw the lab report, he went nuts. I'd already prepared the Discovery Motion to include the fingerprint report. He said redo it. He said there was no way Waddy's lawyer was getting that information. When I balked, he said it wasn't relevant."

"Not relevant? Fingerprints that don't belong to the defendant aren't relevant?"

Jamie held up her hand. "I know. *Believe me*, I know. But you remember the pressure we were under to make the case. And once Waddy had been caught, Marish and the police chief held a joint news conference. They said they *had* the guy. It was a damned celebration. They couldn't go back on that."

"Why didn't you tell me this?"

"Are you kidding? I didn't work for you. You were a cop, an outsider. I worked for Marish and Blane. And it was made very clear the information wasn't supposed to leave the office. In fact, Mickey said if I told anyone it would be the last thing I did. Which got me a little scared. That's why I wrote that blurb on the envelope. In retrospect, I think he meant he'd blackball me in the legal community. That it would be the last thing I did *as a lawyer*."

Griffin couldn't believe it. "Christ. They knew we had the wrong guy."

"Not the way Mickey saw it. He said Waddy's erection being inside Leslie Connors made a stronger case than some other guy's fingerprints on the inside of a piece of tape."

"Did anyone ever check out whose fingerprints they were?"

"Not as far as I know. Maybe if there had been more

killings. If the case hadn't ended the way it did . . ."
Jamie shrugged.

"But now there have been more killings. Mickey
never suggested I check this out."

"Maybe he doesn't want to admit concealing the fingerprints four years ago."

"Unless. . ." Griffin had a terrible thought. What had
Marish said at the news conference about a special prosecutor being appointed? Investigating whether Griffin
had interfered with solving the case four years ago.
"Christ. Maybe they're going to blame me. Say *I* never
told *them* about these prints."

31.

Griffin returned to the car to find Liz in the backseat, nobly attempting to quiet Cassie's crying. Liz definitely out of her element.

"I think maybe she's wet?" Liz said, pure guess, not knowing a damned thing about babies except they tended to be loud.

Griffin said, "You drive. I'll do this."

"Gladly."

Griffin settled into the backseat and undertook diaper duty as routinely as waiting all day in court to offer a minute's testimony. He quickly stuffed the wet diaper into a twist-tie trash sack he kept in an old gym bag turned baby carryall. The new diaper went on with experienced fingers.

"Pretty smooth, Griffin," Liz complimented. "Who'd have thought." She adjusted the seat, started the engine. "So what'd the lawyer have to say? Judging from the look on your face, I take it's bad."

"It might be."

"So where're we going?"

"Back to the city," Griffin said angrily. "To find Mickey Blane."

Unlike Griffin, Rawley Jenkins's involvement with the Jane Doe cover-up hadn't cost him his job, temporar-

ily or otherwise. In fact, the board of trustees was likely
to give him a raise.

In his hospital office now, Jenkins considered the fax
Griffin had transmitted to him from Carroll County: a
fingerprint report that had *not* been in the police department file on Dunbar Waddy. Griffin having asked Jenkins to get one of his old cronies in the department to
check it out on the sly.

When Griffin first met Mickey Blane, freshman year
of high school, his father told him, "Jim-boy, don't ever
depend on a kid like that. Kid's got money, *family's* got
money, he don't need nobody else. Soon as you serve his
purpose, you're gonna be a ghost to him. He'll barely remember you were ever his friend, that's how fast he'll
write you off. Rich folks're like that. It might seem like
an even deal most times, give and take, but you watch,
scales're always tilted in their direction, like house odds
at a casino. They hit you for half a point advantage on
every roll, over time you dig one helluva hole."

Saying that, Charlie Griffin had been drunk, as usual.
Besides which he had a real jealous paranoia about people with money. Given that, and his general surly nature—a man who, when drinking, hated everything and
everybody, including his own family—Griffin had dis-
missed the remark. Or tried to.

Over the years, however, echoes of his father's warning clung like the worn-out skin of a snake. Because
while Griffin did consider Blane his closest friend, there
was no denying Mickey was extremely self-centered—
like Jamie Brooks said. Blane's career, attaining status,
took priority. What other people thought about him was
extremely important, because Blane loved being envied.
He wanted to be a man every other man wanted to be,
and every woman wanted to go to bed with.

But concealing evidence in a criminal trial went far beyond conceit. That Blane had willfully undertaken a wrongful prosecution was unthinkable. Griffin hoped that's not what had happened, that there was another explanation; either way, he was going to find out.

Confront Blane face-to-face. If only he could find him . . .

Griffin was back in the city now. Late afternoon. He hustled down the block to where Liz and Cassie waited in the Taurus, parked in a yellow zone. Cassie was irritable from the heat and being restrained so long in a car seat. Liz wasn't looking too happy about the way her day had gone, either—playing chauffeur/baby-sitter.

Griffin shook his head. "He's not in the office." They'd already been past Blane's condo. "Maybe the athletic club." Griffin got in back with Cassie and tried to soothe her. Simultaneously directing Liz on the best route to the club.

Liz wondered if she should keep her mouth shut. Maybe it wasn't her place to say. After all, she'd just been nosing around—for her own perverse enjoyment.

Ultimately, Liz just ended up saying, "I think I know where Blane is."

In the backseat, Cassie cradled in his arms, Griffin looked for Liz's eyes in the rearview mirror. His expression asked how in the hell she'd know something like that.

Liz kept her eyes on the road. Griffin never verbalized the question, but Liz felt his stare prompting her for an answer. When they were a block away from The Patios At Knollwood, Liz, pretending to be defensive, said, "I don't just sit around hotel rooms waiting for you to call, you know. I'm an investigative reporter. I look into things."

Griffin maintained his silence.

Proceeding slowly along the block, Liz began to think maybe this wasn't a good idea. She considered turning around, saying she was wrong, that she *didn't* know where Mickey Blane was. How could *she* possibly know where *Griffin's* best friend was.

But then Griffin sat forward, said, "That's his Jaguar."

And parked two cars in front of that was Carla's white Honda.

Liz watched Griffin in the rearview mirror. He blinked twice to break what had been a brief stare. His entire body grew rigid. His breathing quickened and became audible.

Liz was honest enough to know most people derived some pleasure—admittedly or not—from other people's pain. To a large degree, that's what the newspaper she worked for was all about. Voyeuristic sadism. But this was different. She felt bad for Griffin.

She turned toward him. There was a new question in his eyes: how did she know? There was also a glimmer of hope, as though seeking some unincriminating answer as to why his wife and best friend were together.

When Liz said, "I'm sorry," that shred of faith was extinguished like a candle's flame pressed out between two fingers.

Silently, Griffin resecured Cassie in the car seat.

The baby screamed, wanting to be held.

Griffin said, "Where are they?"

Liz said, "Two-D." Knowledge gleaned from having hacked into Carla's computer diary-on-disk. When Griffin opened the rear door, Liz reached back and grasped his forearm. His muscles felt violent, coiled to strike. "Leave your gun?" she asked. "I don't want to think I'm getting someone killed."

"It's all right," he replied, but clearly it wasn't. He

kept the .45 holstered inside his blazer and started across the street.

Afterward. it seemed like a blur.

Although he'd been there, Griffin felt emotionally detached, as though having watched a silent dream. Moving, but not consciously directing his actions. Speaking, but not thinking the words.

He'd gone inside the building. The uniformed concierge tried to stop Griffin's advance toward the stairs. Griffin wasn't sure how the man ended up on the floor, but there he'd been, looking afraid until Griffin flashed his CA badge.

Going up the steps, his heart pounded so loudly it was all he'd heard.

On the second floor, the evenly lit hallway seemed to throb as his pulse thrust pressure against his eyes.

He'd never felt so disoriented in his life—what he later guessed was shock. Never. Not when his father had gone raging drunk in the street. Not seeing how Blane's Diana and Jeremy had been slaughtered. Not chasing Dunbar Waddy and killing him. Not in any aspect of police work no matter how threatening.

Knocking on the door to 2-D, he'd stood to the side so if anyone looked out they wouldn't see him through the peephole.

He had to knock a second time.

The knob turned. The door opened a crack.

Mickey Blane peered outside with the chain still latched.

The door burst open—Griffin assumed because he'd hit it with his shoulder, maybe kicked it, he couldn't honestly say. Only someone else was on the floor again. Blane this time, wearing silk pajama bottoms, no top, blood oozing through his nose, mouth, and a gash in his forehead; the edge of the door had smashed against him.

Blane's eyes showed terror and dread, his worst fear realized. Not that he'd cheated on his friend, but that he'd been caught.

Carla, alerted by the noise, came running down the hall from the bedroom. She wore a long white night-gown unbuttoned between her breasts, a purchase from the Victoria's Secret catalog she'd shown to Griffin, but had never worn for him.

Carla clutched the front of the nightgown over her breasts. Her mouth moved, but there didn't seem to be any sound coming out, at least nothing Griffin heard over the boom of his heart.

Carla backed away as he came toward her. One hand against her breasts, the other in front of her face as though to ward him off. So maybe he'd *looked* like he was going to kill her.

Griffin caught her outside the bedroom where she'd slept last night with Blane. Grabbed her wrist when he was attacked from behind.

Blane threw his arms around Griffin's throat and tried to pull him back. Griffin shrugged free of the hold. Pivoting quickly, he punched Blane's bare stomach and felt the air go out of him. Blane crumpled painfully to the floor, dripping blood onto plush carpet.

The hint of a scream slid over the deafening drum beat of Griffin's heart.

Carla slapped Griffin with both hands, arms flailing wildly like twin windmills.

Griffin backed against the wall. And let Carla hit him. Her fingernails scratched his face.

When Griffin next experienced daylight, it burned the cuts on his face, mixing sweat with blood and tears.

Somehow Liz had gotten him out of the apartment. Had him run with her back to the car. Made him slouch down as she peeled away from the curb.

Police sirens screamed past them. Someone in the apartment had heard the fight, the screams, and called the cops.

Cassie howled in the backseat.

Liz said it was all right, everything was okay.

Griffin knew that was a lie.

32.

Michelle Aronson didn't leave her bedroom on Saturday until two-thirty. That was when Greg went out. He didn't say where he was going. Michelle heard the Mercedes start up. Greg peeled wheels out of the driveway like a teenager. Greg always acting that way when he was mad—this time with the pool people. He was very pissy when he didn't get his way.

With Greg gone, Michelle fixed a peanut butter sandwich and sat outside until it got too hot. She would have liked to take a swim, but Greg told her two days ago not to use the pool until the "goddamned motherfucking pump" was fixed. Why a broken pump meant she couldn't use the pool, she didn't know, but you didn't ask Greg questions. He barked answers and quick explanations and if you didn't understand it right off, tough shit, you were a dumb bimbo and didn't deserve to know.

Michelle watched TV on the screened patio for a while. She liked baseball, but hadn't been to a game since marrying Greg, who despised the sport. Today, the Orioles were playing New York, losing.

Michelle had been a baseball fan since high school, when a kid she knew back then got drafted out of the twelfth grade. A great player who always had the misfortune of ending up on teams with second basemen having incredible years, first Ryne Sandberg with the Cubs,

then Juan Samuel in LA. Sometimes, maddening and un-
fair as it was, you needed plain old luck.

Michelle was thinking about luck, how she wished
hers would improve, when she went inside the kitchen
and heard something in the ceiling. It was a different
noise from the house-settling creaks that used to scare
her as a kid home alone. Much different. Someone was
up in the attic, walking around.

The house already looked different to him. It felt different. Griffin realized that, mentally, he was already
moving out. This was no longer where he lived, but
where he had once lived. When he was married to Carla,
when Cassie was a baby.

Thinking as though trying to project himself years
into the future and look back on what was his life now.
Trying to fast forward through the pain he knew was
going to come when the shock wore off.

Over and over, he replayed seeing Carla and Mickey
together. A luxury apartment. Mickey shirtless, hair tou-
sled. Carla still in her nightgown late in the afternoon,
like they'd been in bed together all day.

Each time he remembered more details, as though
wrestling off layers of a protective cocoon. Sounds he
didn't think he'd heard were suddenly audible to his
memory. Carla gasping, "Oh, my God," realizing Griffin
was there. Carla shrieking, "You killed him, my God,
you killed him," seeing Blane bleeding on the floor.
Carla telling Griffin to get out, sounding angry. *She* was
mad at *him*. Backing down the hall, Carla yelling, "How
could you do this? *How could you do this?*" Lashing out
verbally, then physically, slapping and scratching for his
face.

God, he ached all over. Pain that twisted and knotted
his entire body from the inside out.

Griffin was uncertain how long he'd been home—in what *used* to be his wife's office, what *used* to be his wife's bed. It was dark out now. Amber globes in what *used* to be Carla's garden cast warm yellow light through panes of the French doors.

Lying there, his instinct was to move out right now. It wouldn't take long except with Cassie. There would be a lot to move for her. And Griffin *was* taking her with him. He wouldn't fight Carla about anything else, but he'd fight for Cassie.

Liz appeared in the doorway, commenting, "So you are alive. Good. I was getting worried."

When she turned on the light, Griffin squinted.

"You look like hell." Liz approached with a washbowl and hand towel. She laid him back on a fresh pillow; the one he'd been resting on was streaked with dried blood. "You got some nasty scrapes."

It burned when she patted the cool cloth to his wounds, but that was a mild sensation compared to what he'd suffered already.

"Cassie okay?" he asked.

Liz nodded.

"Good." Griffin sat up, took the cloth from her, and went into the bathroom. He was used to taking care of himself. He felt awkward being waited on, always had.

The mirror confirmed Liz's opinion. He had some major scratches across his temple and cheeks. Down the side of his neck, an oozing scab crossed his jugular.

As he pushed the wet cloth over his face, weaker stresses reopened and seeped threads of blood. He rinsed out the washcloth and kept it with him, figured to dab where he was still bleeding until it stopped again.

He asked Liz how she'd found out.

Liz sat on the bed, hands braced against the mattress. "I followed her."

"Why?"

"I have a habit of being a snoop. I just wondered what your wife was like. So I followed her."

"Something made you suspicious."

"No." Liz lied. "I was bored, nothing was happening with Bright Eyes, so I followed her. To pass the time."

Griffin pressed the cloth to his throat and looked at it, considering a decreasing smear of blood. "How many times did you see her with him?" His voice was vacant, suppressing emotion.

"Once."

"Before yesterday?"

"Yes."

"Is that why you—?"

"Tried to seduce you? No. I did that because I wanted to. Hell, I'd've done it four years ago if I could've. Hope to do it again once this stops messing you up."

Griffin shook his head without any particular purpose, a vague gesture accompanied by a false smile and quiet grunt. He leaned an arm against the door frame. "I never followed her. Days she disappeared, having little fits, I just let her go. Never pressed her. Figured it was all up here." He tapped his forehead. "Not between her legs." The anger came quickly.

Without further warning, he roughly knocked a glass vase off the shelf above what *had* been Carla's desk. It hit the floor in one piece, spilling a puddle of water and a bouquet of cut lavender.

Griffin stared at the flowers, picked up the vase by its base, and smashed it into the computer screen. Tiny shards of glass erupted from the screen; the vase broke into bigger pieces.

Just as quickly, he became calm. As though analyzing what he had just done. Slowly, he crossed the room to Carla's dresser, looked at the old picture of him with

Carla and Blane, not overlooking Blane was posed between them even then.

Griffin smashed the frame against the wall. Removed the black-and-white print behind shattered glass and ripped it twice.

Liz asked, "You think that's enough?"

Griffin stared at the floor, the tattered photograph. "Yeah," he said defiantly. "That's enough."

Liz was glad Griffin hadn't asked too many questions about Carla and Blane. Because Liz had a lot of answers—more than she would have been comfortable reporting.

Carla Griffin's diary had been explicit.

Carla lost her virginity to Mickey Blane in high school. Having snuck out of her house late one Saturday night. Blane, eighteen, driving his father's Cadillac, picked her up, and took Carla to his parents' place. His mom and dad were out of town for the weekend.

It was warm and they went skinny-dipping. The pool lights were on and Carla could see Blane had an erection for her that never faded. A sight that fascinated and scared her, especially when he rubbed against her, said he wanted to make love to her, wanted to be her "first."

There had always been a special bond between Carla and Blane, one they were careful to hide from Griffin. Blane saying it was because he didn't want to hurt Griffin's feelings, knowing how much Griffin liked Carla; but Carla noted suspicions that Blane wanted their relationship kept secret so he could be one up on Griffin.

Regardless of motive, their sexual relationship became their private alliance.

It started that night in Blane's parents' bedroom. A luxurious place for Carla to, as Blane put it, "lose it." A huge bed, expensive linens, signs of money all around; everything Carla's family never had and never would.

Carla fell deeply in love with Blane that night and had never stopped loving him. But it always stayed a secret. Not even when Carla suspected Blane was playing her along as a convenient screw, that he didn't love her. She never directly confronted him with that issue.

The closest she ever came was when Blane was in college. Carla took the bus to Princeton to see him, slept with him in the frat house. She asked if he thought they might get married one day. Blane said not while his father was alive.

Blane's father didn't like him associating with Carla and Griffin, kids from the "bad side"—meaning, poor side—of town. Blane's father wanted his son socializing with people who could help him get ahead in life. Sons of captains of industry, that old thing.

When Blane began dating Diana, a relationship that had his father's blessing, Carla was hurt. Blane always had other girls, but none seriously. For the first time, a chasm developed between Carla and Blane; it deepened when Blane and Diana were engaged, worsened still when they were married.

Shortly thereafter, Carla married Griffin. A man she told herself she could "learn to love."

Reading that passage of the diary, Liz figured Carla never made it to class. She never was able to feel for Griffin what Blane raised in her. A fact Carla realized herself, only *after* she and Griffin were married. Because she couldn't stay away from Blane.

Carla and Blane began to see each other again after they were married. Blane told her it was fate, they were always going to end up together.

Blane began talking about divorcing Diana once his

father died, that Carla would leave Griffin and they would finally be married.

Liz wondered why Carla hadn't seen that as a fuck-me lie, the crap women—and men—fell for when they so desperately wanted to believe the person they loved so much loved them back.

The night Blane's Diana and Jeremy were murdered by Dunbar Waddy, Blane hadn't been home. He'd been in a hotel room with Carla.

Racked by guilt—the thought that had Blane been home he could have saved his wife and son—Carla and Blane didn't see each other after that. How could they ever be together again?

Six months later, that changed. Blane called, said he missed her. And "fate" drew them back together again.

They grew more serious. Blane told Carla he was going to tell his father about her, that maybe he wouldn't object now that Carla had established herself as a successful paralegal.

More lies, Liz thought, but Blane was running out of options. Sooner or later, even the most naive lover has enough and calls it quits. Still, Blane was able to string out that line about going to his father for almost a year.

By that time, Carla was talking about leaving Griffin whether Blane would marry her or not. She didn't love him and couldn't keep up the lie any longer. Carla had even set a date to leave when she became pregnant.

Liz figured Blane must have been ecstatic hearing the news. Carla's pregnancy bought him more time.

"More time," Liz had commented reading that part of Carla's diary, "to keep using her."

What Liz hoped now, for Griffin's sake, was that he never found out about the rest of it. Some things—especially in matters of personal trust—you were better off never knowing.

Sitting with him in the living room, ten o'clock Saturday night, they shared delivered-in Szechuan beef and sesame noodles. Griffin ate, but didn't say much. Liz ran a hand through his hair and onto the back of his neck. She kissed his cheek, whispered, "You're gonna be fine."

At that moment, Rawley Jenkins happened to step onto the porch outside. Seeing Liz's kiss, his expression asked what the hell was going on.

Liz let him in. Jenkins eyed her suspiciously. Tossed an envelope to Griffin. Said, "I got the boy belongs to your fingerprints."

33.

Greg Aronson banged on the locked bedroom door, yelled, "Have you got the goddamned windows open in there!"

"No." Michelle kept her response short to conceal the quiver in her voice. At an hour she was usually dressed for bed—something bland that might turn Greg off if he broke in to rape her—she wore jeans, a long sleeve T-shirt, and tennis shoes. Not daring to move beyond arm's reach of the phone.

"You sure?" Greg demanded impatiently.

Normally, she'd consider—although wouldn't speak—a sarcastic answer, *Am I sure the windows are closed? You moron, there's two windows. How can I not be sure?* Tonight, she was too afraid, so she merely said, "I'm sure."

"Well, I'm trying to turn on the goddamned alarm and it won't ready. A window's open or something, goddamn it." Frustrated, Greg banged the door again with his fist and started back down the hall.

The home's intricate alarm system was configured so that before it could be activated, all windows and doors had to be closed, all motion and heat detectors free from positive readings. So Greg was going to have to find what the problem was: what was open, hot, or moving.

Michelle thinking, he'd find it all right. Find whoever

had been up in the attic. Someone who knew The Kroop. Someone who'd come to kill Greg.

She tried to keep calm, make everything seem routine—just like The Kroop instructed. She couldn't run out of the house; that would be suspicious. She had to hang in there . . . and in a few hours it might all be over.

"Christ, kid," Jenkins mumbled, "I'm damned sorry. And with Blane for chrissakes. That little shit." Jenkins sat on the striped love seat by the window, his size turning it into a comfortable chair for one. His suit was rumpled from being crushed by his body throughout the heat of the day and now into the night. "Maybe you want to forget this whole thing now. I don't blame you. It's no skin off me."

Griffin felt drained. Only through "trained" instinct—plow ahead, get the job done, don't quit—did he manage to reach for the fingerprint analysis Jenkins had run for him. Jenkins obviously having called in more than one favor to get such quick results from an FBI computer scan. The turnover time was usually days, not hours.

"Do we know him?" Griffin asked, opening the envelope, wondering how many more buried surprises the day had in store.

"Not me. But he's local. Got a record. Name's Stephen H. Deke. Goes by Stevie."

Griffin didn't recognize him.

Liz, cautiously, reached into her big shoulder bag and turned on the miniature recorder. "Deke as in geek?" she asked, wanting to get confirmation on tape. "D-E-E-K?"

"No." Jenkins spelled it correctly for her. His feelings toward Liz having apparently warmed since their first meeting in his office. He no longer considered her with snarling venom, though his eyes did spend undue time on the shape her breasts put to a thin summer blouse.

"FBI record's in there, too," Jenkins said. "Deke had a few beefs down in Florida some years back. Been clean for almost six years save one little scrape up here. An assault case that got nol-prossed about five months before the first Bright Eyes."

Griffin read Deke's physical description. White male in his late twenties—the FBI psychological profile had nailed that four years ago, estimating Bright Eyes would be white male, midtwenties, the correct age at the time.

Jenkins said, "Guess who got Deke the nol-pros?"

Griffin looked up. "Blane?"

Jenkins shook his head. "Jack Karupka."

Griffin's surprise showed through his weariness. "How'd this guy end up with an expensive suit like The Kroop?"

Before Jenkins could answer, Liz said, "I know that name," offering her statement with some hesitation not because of knowing *who* Karupka was—which she didn't—but because of *what* she knew Karupka was: namely, the owner of the apartment in which Mickey Blane and Carla Griffin had been having their affair.

When she told Griffin that, he went back to the bedroom, emerged moments later fully dressed, Liz able to detect from the bulge inside his blazer the .45 was holstered in place.

"Jimmy?" Liz followed him to the front door. "Jimmy?"

Griffin ignored her.

Liz looked to Jenkins for help.

The big man didn't get up. "Hey, kid, come on, don't do something stupid. What're you gonna do?"

Liz had Griffin's arm. Not enough strength, but enough presence for him to pause.

"I'll be back in an hour."

*   *   *

Greg Aronson was so agitated his face felt hot. Goddamned alarm system, goddamned pool valve, goddamned *house*. Nothing worked right. All this expensive
shit and not one good goddamned piece of it could run
an appreciable length of time without requiring some
redneck, uneducated repairman to come around and hose
Greg with a huge bill for fixing something that never
should have broken in the first place. *Goddamn it!*

He'd been all through the house, checked every window and door. All closed. So he comes back to the alarm
control panel in the foyer and the READY light still isn't
on. So what could it be? How come the goddamned
thing wasn't working right? And damned if he was
going to get out the manual and read it. Screw that. He'd
paid four grand to have this system installed, he
shouldn't have to read a goddamned encyclopedia to
make it run. Four fucking grand, it should work goddamn it. Just work.

He started toward the basement steps, about to check
the cellar again when the READY light came on. What
the hell? Well, there, anyway, it was okay. Probably the
damned humidity causing the problem. Greg started to
punch in the activation code when the READY light
went back off.

"Shit." He bet it was Michelle, goddamned Michelle
opening and closing a window in the guest room just to
screw with him. *The bitch!* He'd fix her. Pay a little visit
in the middle of the night. Work her over. Stick it to her
while she begged him to stop, knowing all along she
liked it. Hell, loved it. He knew she was having orgasms
even when she was fighting him. She couldn't fool him.
Thought she could, but no way. Bitch. Why the hell he'd
married her, he could never understand. He must've
been blind. All the shit she gave him now.

Greg was so angry he didn't hear the basement door opening behind him.

He froze seeing him there. Scared.

"What do you want?" Mickey Blane tried to be brave. His voice sounded strange projected through a bandaged and broken nose.

Drops of dried blood stained the front of Blane's button-down shirt. His lips were swollen from being hit by the door Griffin kicked open hours ago. A tooth knocked loose but not out had been secured in place, but throbbed like hell with the novocaine wearing off.

Blane had spent the last five hours in his private physician's and dentist's offices, having enough pull— and money—to interrupt their respective Saturdays.

Now, he walks in the door, figuring to collapse into bed after a nightmarish day. Only Griffin was waiting for him.

"What do you want?" Blane asked it louder this time, but no less fearful.

In Blane's living room, Griffin sat in a leather chair by a brass standing lamp. The light was switched on low. He'd used a key to get in—an arrangement friends often made with one another, leaving duplicate keys so someone could take care of their place while they were away.

Griffin wanted to ask how long it had been going on, Blane sleeping with his wife. Didn't they think he'd ever find out? Or didn't they care?

"What do you want?" Blane shouted. He was trembling. Maybe he'd wondered what it would be like if Griffin ever *did* find out about his affair with Carla. Maybe he'd thought he could talk his way out of it. Blane was used to talking his way out of everything. That was his job. He was good at it. Too good, maybe, because it left him falsely secure that talk could settle everything.

"Sit down, Mickey," Griffin finally said. His quiet tone was shadowed with outrage.

Blane hesitated. Would he be better off trying to out-run Griffin to the front door? Get out? Call for help?

"Sit down!"

"All right." Blane held both hands in front of him as though to deflect Griffin's anger. He sat awkwardly, un-sure what posture to assume. Reflex told him to lean back, casually cross his legs, that I'm-in-charge effect, but he couldn't pull it off. He tried putting his elbows on the armrest; that didn't work, either. He was too fidgety. Ended up tilted forward, forearms across his knees. His jaw ached; talking made it worse. "Christ, Grif, what do you want? To hear me say I'm sorry? That it won't hap-pen again? You call it. I fucked up. I've got no ex-cuse . . ."

Griffin allowed Blane to ramble, knowing damned well there wasn't a sincere feeling in it; Blane was merely trying to find magic words to take the evil out of Griffin's eyes.

". . . It just happened, for chrissakes. We've known each other for so long. You get lost in emotions. Things happen. It's one of—"

"Stephen H. Deke."

"What?" Blane blinked, as though moving his eyes would improve his hearing.

"Stevie Deke."

Blane appeared to go pale.

Griffin said, "You should be afraid, pal. I killed the last man who murdered people *I* loved. Although I won-der if you loved Diana and Jeremy as much as I did. And I don't mean loving them the way you love Carla, be-cause I didn't love your wife with my dick."

"Christ, come on." Blane began to panic; the situation was getting worse, not better.

"Were you screwing around on Diana?"

"Jesus Christ, why bring—?"

"Answer the fucking question!" Griffin demanded. "Were you screwing around on your wife?"

"Yes," Blane blurted out. "You knew it. Don't act surprised."

Griffin shook his head. "Unh-unh. You never told me. But maybe that's because I would've asked who it was with and you wouldn't have wanted to tell me it was Carla."

Blane pressed his hands to his face.

"It was, wasn't it, you fuck! You were screwing my wife when Diana was still alive. Weren't you? *Weren't you!*"

"Yes, all right! Yes." Blane's hands came away from his face so abruptly, his head appeared to explode from his grasp.

"Goddamn you!" Griffin slammed his fists against the leather chair and stood.

Blane jumped up, thinking Griffin was coming for him.

"Sit down!"

Blane did as he was told, close to sobbing, muttering, "Oh, Jesus, Grif, Jesus. What do you want?"

Griffin stared him down.

Blane appeared to wilt. Being in a room decorated as a trophy to his wealth offered little relief. All the plush furnishings, expensive objets d'art, limited edition oceanographic prints in handmade oak frames. Some arguably priceless items suddenly made valueless against the prospect of losing his life. Which from the way Blane looked, seemed to be foremost on his mind.

Griffin stood in the middle of the room, his silhou-

ette outlined in pale, hazy light from the brass lamp behind him. His shadow prevented direct light from striking Blane. "How long have you been in The Kroop's
pocket?"

Blane gripped the arm rails of his chair.

"You pinned the Bright Eyes case on a guy you knew
didn't do it. You suppressed Stevie Deke's fingerprints
and intimidated an alibi witness so Waddy's lawyer
wouldn't have any defense to raise. You did all this so a
guy The Kroop represented a few months earlier could
walk away from it."

"That's bullshit," Blane replied, trying to spit back-
bone into his denial, but coming up empty.

Griffin's jaw tightened. "You never wore your gun,
Mickey. The day I told you Bright Eyes might be back—
the man who supposedly killed your wife and son, a man
who, it might figure, would be after you—and you never
put on your gun. You were never scared. Not about that.
Because the man who really killed Diana and Jeremy
was dead and you knew it. Not Bright Eyes. But Dunbar
Waddy. I killed him. It was the man *you* let get away
who came back. The real Bright Eyes. That's what you
were scared about—about being found out."

Blane stared into his lap and shuddered violently, as
though demons inside him had grabbed hold of his soul
and were shredding it apart.

"How much did The Kroop pay you, Mickey? What'd
you get paid to prosecute the wrong man?"

Blane screamed, "Jesus, Grif. It cost me my wife and
son! Wasn't that enough? Wasn't losing them enough!"
His cries became uncontrollable. Blane balled himself
up in the chair, arms wrapped around his legs, thighs
drawn into his chest. "Christ, Grif, please . . . *Please!*"

"I'm taking you down, Mickey. I'm taking you down
hard."

*   *   *

Michelle Aronson heard them running down the hall toward her bedroom. Greg crying her name, sounding like a child. "Help! Michelle. Help!"

A loud rumble of bodies hit the floor. Hard wrestling noises as arms and legs banged the walls. Glass broke: a picture falling off the wall or a vase knocked off Greg's grandmother's antique sideboard.

Michelle covered her ears as though not hearing would help, her mind racing, *My God, it's happening, it's happening*. Unable to comprehend it was real.

On the other side of her locked door, Greg made sounds she'd never heard from him before: a harsh hissing, then a whimper. Like a helpless animal brutalized by a savage hunter.

The confrontation didn't last ninety seconds, and then it was done. There was only one man breathing in the hall now. A deep, satisfied sound.

Michelle became dizzied, gasped repeatedly, "My God, my God, what have I done, what have I done?" Yet while experiencing terror, she was also fascinated. That something like this could actually happen. *Had* happened. She had seen a man about having her husband killed, and now he was dead. Greg was dead.

Michelle eased quietly to the door, fingers cold from fear. She grasped the doorknob, turned it with one hand while holding in the lock button with the other to smother the sound it would make being released. She slowly edged the door open and peeked cautiously into the hall.

34.

Stevie Deke had pretended Greg Aronson was his stepfather. That fantasy had whirled maliciously into his
mind while waiting—hiding—all day in the house.

Having found his way from the garage storage attic
into the main attic, treading his way through roof trusses,
sniffing dust from pink insulation, finding his way into
the master bedroom closet via a set of pull-down stairs.
From there going to the unfinished basement, sitting in a
storage closet, his back against the cool concrete wall,
waiting, thinking, dreaming about the first man he'd
killed. Henry, his stepfather.

How he'd put his hands around Henry's throat and
choked the life out of him. Hearing air press from his
nose as though squeezing helium out of a tiny hole in a
balloon. Watching Henry's face seem to swell. Eyes roll
back on their way to a lifeless stare. Not belladonna
eyes, but satisfying all the same. A good way to kill *a
man*.

Now, hefting Aronson's corpse over his shoulder,
Stevie Deke carried him into the master bedroom.
Dropped him like a sack on the bed.

On the dresser, he saw a photograph of Aronson's
wife. Very attractive.

Hearing her move around the house earlier, he'd con-
jured up an image for her role in his fantasy. Thinking

about her as an older version of his half-sister, Alice—the first woman he'd ever seen with bright eyes.

He was disappointed to see from the photograph that Aronson's wife didn't look more like Alice, but he was so deep into it that just calling her by that name would give him pleasure.

Now, with Aronson dead, he removed his gloves, put them in the belt pouch, and went to the room at the end of the hall. He tried the knob. When it didn't turn, he called her name—her new name—"Alice," softly, reassuringly, the same tone he used when promising his half-sister he was going to take her away from "all this."

He told Michelle—Alice—it was okay to open the door. She was going to *have to* open the door.

Michelle whispered faintly, "Please go away."

He understood she was afraid. He assured her he was here to save her.

"Oh, God, please," she begged, "please just leave. Please."

He didn't want to have to break down the door, but when he heard her trying to inch open the window and sneak out on him, he had no choice.

When he burst into the room, her back was to him. Michelle was afraid to see his face, imagining it would be horrible. She had the window raised a few inches, now threw it up the rest of the way. Fumbled with the screen, unable to slide it free of its channel.

Before she could scream, he caught her throat in the powerful bend of his arm and pulled her back. Her cries choked off, he slammed shut the window with his free hand.

Michelle became so panic-stricken she couldn't move. Her eyes pressed shut; her hands clutched the arm

locked around her throat. It was far worse than Greg.
This man was so strong. She began to hyperventilate.

He kept calling her a name she didn't recognize.
Alice. Putting her down roughly on the bed. Lying beside her. Telling her it was all right. She should relax.

"I'm here to save you from this, Alice. It's okay now."

Michelle feared this was not someone The Kroop had
sent to kill Greg, but a madman. She tried to scream but
his hand dug into her throat. She became light-headed.

When she finally opened her eyes and saw him, she
was even more afraid. A sick hunger danced across his
pupils.

"Please," she gasped, forcing the final ounce of air
from her lungs. "Please . . ."

He released her throat. She rolled over and gagged
into the bedspread. Vertigo clearing slightly from her
mind when he grabbed a fistful of her long, dark hair
and jerked her head back. Michelle opened her mouth to
scream, but before the cry came out, a plastic dispenser
was down her throat, scratching her palate, shooting
warm, sour liquid she couldn't help swallowing.

Some of it went into her lungs and made her cough,
but before long, tension was sapped from her body, replaced by a dreamy warmth. When he turned her faceup
and pushed the medicine dropper between her lips once
again, squirted in another loaded rush of belladonna,
Michelle swallowed it willingly.

He said, "It's going to be fine now, Alice. Just fine."

He looked beautiful to her now. An erotic face. His
fingers much more gentle now as he undressed her. His
skin appeared dark blue; then Michelle realized it was an
athletic or dancing suit of some kind. Skintight all over.
Especially between his legs, where the fabric's force
trapped his hard-on.

"It's me, Stevie," he told her, pulling off her pants. He

grasped the waistband of her panties and rolled them down smooth, long legs. "I've come back to save you, Alice. To take you away from all this."

Michelle felt wonderful all over. Every place he touched her seemed to turn her on. As though her clitoris had dispatched feelers from her vagina to the rest of her body and his fingers knew the path.

Her throat felt a smooth wet pressure. She quivered as the slippery line moved along the side of her breast, stopped momentarily, then continued down her side to her waist.

He drew the paint brush over her hip bone, stopping just above the edge of her pubic bush, tracing the red line parallel to the upper crest of her vagina, lingering there, then moving to the right side of her body, finishing the hexagon he'd begun at her throat.

She was beautiful. Maybe more so than Alice. Positioned on her back, her breasts laid heavily against her rib cage, causing two legs of the pentagon to curve around their shape. Her nipples tightened like sugar cubes. Her waist was so slender. Legs long and lean. But best of all were the irises of her eyes. Wide open, glossy, seldom blinking. Sparkling blue like the Caribbean Sea he'd swum in every day while exiled by The Kroop to the islands. Her pupils were expansive black dots. The most arousing sight he could possibly imagine. Thrilling him with fantasies of servility. A body for his taking. To do with whatever he wanted. No restrictions. No expectations. No demands. Only to please himself.

His mouth became dry as his craving increased. His cock, hard against the tension of the bodysuit, throbbed mercilessly, an ever-present reminder of arousal.

She was lapsing into unconsciousness by the time the hexagon was complete. He was free now.

He carefully put away the jar of paint and the brush, zipping them inside the waist pouch along with the unused belladonna.

He positioned her on the bed, stretching each arm toward the headboard posts. Turned her face to the side so that she was looking away from him. Bent her knees so the soles of her feet touched together, creating a stress along her inner thighs.

He stood at the foot of the bed and shed his bodysuit from his shoulders to below his hips. Reveling in how his cock seemed to jump free from its entrapment, no longer contained by elastic, but jutting straight out for Alice.

Taking a breath, he wrapped his hand around his shaft and moved it back and forth, slowly at first, then more quickly, reaching a rapid pace that swelled pressure from his testicles through his shaft, warming his hard member until semen spasmed from his glans and made a sticky puddle in his palm.

Once he'd come, he inhaled a series of deep breaths to steady a slight twinge of energy still quaking through him. And then set about his task of cleaning up, wiping down wherever his ungloved fingers may have touched.

Jimmy Griffin tried to believe he was finished with his wife. It was over. Period. Except for the divorce, the unavoidable fight for Cassie, he'd have nothing else to do with her.

So why then, on his way home from Mickey Blane's condo, was he driving by The Patios At Knollwood, circling the block looking for Carla's Honda? Feeling relief when he didn't find it. Thinking for a moment maybe she'd be home waiting for him. To apologize. Tell him how much she loved him. How Blane had seduced her and her depression had caused her to reach out and try anything to feel better.

But when he returned home, her car wasn't there.

Griffin was tired walking up the front porch steps. Running on too much adrenaline left him sapped. He felt like he was climbing a sheer rock face in the state park, not stepping up six-inch risers.

Liz opened the door, worried.

Griffin tried to remember the last time Carla had waited up for him. It had been years.

Liz asked if he was all right.

Rawley Jenkins wondered that, too, drinking bottled beer from a six-pack he'd gone out for while Griffin was at Blane's.

"The Kroop paid him off," Griffin said. "Blane prosecuted Dunbar Waddy even though he knew he wasn't Bright Eyes."

"Jesus." Liz sighed.

Jenkins didn't seem too surprised. Then again, not much caught his blind side. "So whaddayou gonna do about it, kid?"

"Find Stevie Deke." Griffin placed a heavy hand on the mantel as though holding himself up. "And stick him in Mickey Blane's corrupt face."

Jenkins sipped beer from a long-necked bottle, effortlessly emptying half its contents. He smacked his lips, said, "Okay."

Griffin, forcing logic through tired synapses, said, "In the morning, I'll call a friend at SSA, see if she'll run Deke's name, find out if he's been working. I'll check his past record, look for acquaintances, old addresses, family. Start hitting the streets. Maybe check Customs and Immigration if he's gone in or out of the country recently. He had to be somewhere the last four years. A guy who has this much fun killing people can't have stayed quiet that long . . ." Griffin tried to consider other possibilities, but his mind was going numb, recycling tiresomely through the same thoughts.

Liz hooked her arm inside his. "Come on. Let's put you to bed."

Jenkins said, "I'll see myself out." He set his third empty on the floor. Slipped two fingers through the cardboard handle of his six-pack and carried its remains toward the door. "See you in the morning, kid."

"Your father called while you were out." In bed, Liz lay cozily against Griffin from behind, their bodies fitting together like two spoons. "I told him you were out. That I was the baby-sitter. I don't know if he believed me or not. He sounded worried. He'd read about Bright Eyes in the paper."

Griffin was so tired, but he couldn't seem to fall asleep. His mind wouldn't get out of gear. "What'd you tell him?"

"That you were going to nail the bastard."

The Kroop was facedown on the massage table in the athletic wing of his penthouse office. Rows of recessed ceiling lights were dimmed so his view of the city skyline dominated not only on the east window wall, but three mirrored walls as well.

Connie, Karupka's chef/companion, pressed her thumbs deeply between The Kroop's shoulder blades, working out tension that had crept into his muscles.

Connie reached for the phone when it rang. The front of her robe fell open, her breasts coming exposed for The Kroop to see from different angles depending on which mirrored wall he chose.

Without speaking to the caller, Connie handed Karupka the receiver and went back to her massage.

On the other end of the line, a familiar voice said, short and sweet, "Griffin knows."

Mickey Blane briefly considered suicide, but the moment passed. A spoiled brat's instinct.

His world was coming apart. All because of his best friend. Because Griffin didn't understand how it worked. You couldn't talk to him about it. Blane had tried over the years, plenty times. Especially since bringing Grif into the CA's office, giving him a cozy investigator's job.

Hell, Griffin didn't understand the job was like early retirement. Gravy. Blane having rewarded Griffin for that night on the Marrow Street Bridge. Christ, killing a man for him.

Blane owed Griffin for that. Which was why he'd set him up in the investigator's job. Having to talk Marish into it. A position where Griffin could sit back in an office, make phone calls, flirt with the secretaries, screw half of them if he wanted, and never have to go out on the street again. Like Gerremo. Just hang out, get a paycheck, do something that looked like work, fake it.

But not Grif, hell no. Griffin had to be out there running the streets, getting involved in cases, actually investigating. Which was okay, Grif wanted it that way, why not? But of all people to be involved on that rare occasion when a deal with Jack Karupka went south.

Blane would never be able to explain Karupka to Griffin. How taking money or favors from The Kroop wasn't a bribe, it was life. Because if you didn't take the money, you were out. Hell, everyone who mattered took money from The Kroop. Marish. Everyone! It was never direct, always through contributions to a reelection committee, or buying hundreds of tickets to $50-a-plate fund-raisers under various aliases to get around campaign contribution regs.

You took money from Karupka because it was good business. Jack made deals, but they were fair. He never looked to get anything where he wasn't giving equal value in return.

Like Stevie Deke. Okay, Deke was a murderer, a little sick. He had this thing for busting women out on drugs. Maybe Jack made a mistake ever using Deke, but everybody made mistakes. No sense getting burned just because of one error.

So four years ago, Jack had come to Blane with a proposal. It was the day after Dunbar Waddy had been caught; Blane and Marish having already announced they had Bright Eyes. Jack, very somber, said he had bad news. Waddy wasn't Bright Eyes. Jack's client, Stevie Deke, that's who they wanted. But Jack couldn't let them have Deke.

Stevie Deke had done jobs for Jack before—muscle work. Not only did Deke know too much about Jack's operation; he was one of Jack's boys. Part of Kroop's Troops. A guy who'd risked his freedom and life for Jack on jobs before. Jack felt obliged to protect Deke just like he dried out the East bloc boys who turned alcoholic on him.

You had to admire Jack for that. Admire him, too, for ratting out his own client to Blane. Jack could have sent Deke into hiding and left the CA's office with an unsolved case. A real black eye. Because they'd have soon found out Waddy was the wrong guy.

Those damned fingerprints on the inside of the duct tape. Deke's fingerprints. Left when he'd taped the third victim's mouth, needing to keep her quiet while he went out for more belladonna, a heavier hit because it looked like the usual fatal dose wasn't going to do her.

Only Dunbar Waddy, wandering around the building, probably looking for something to steal, came across this stoned naked woman and decided to rape her. The woman died anyway—it just took a little longer for the drugs to take effect—and the cops caught Waddy with his dick hip-deep inside the woman.

Christ. When Jack had told him that, Blane became sick to his stomach. But Jack had a deal that would wash them all clean.

Jack told Blane to cover up any evidence that hurt the CA's case and go ahead and prosecute Waddy—a guy with priors who deserved to burn if not for this case then for others. Offer Waddy a plea he'd be stupid to turn down. In return, Jack would get Deke out of the country and promise Deke wouldn't come back, end of story.

Blane had hoped Jack could find a way to make Waddy and Deke disappear. Have them both killed. But that couldn't happen. Jack wouldn't do it. The only way Jack would ever take out one of his "troops" was if they screwed him. That was the only reason people he used would understand. A guy reneges on a promise, a deal, you could whack him. Just because it wasn't convenient? No way.

To sweeten the pot, Jack had thrown in ten grand apiece for Blane and Marish. The deal was done.

It had been easy to prosecute Waddy, an inarticulate Jamaican with a propensity to violence. It would have worked, too, only when the judge balked at deportation come sentencing, Waddy's people raised money for an appeal.

Worse yet, Waddy's new lawyer was a lot sharper than the PD, who Karupka had paid to "go through the motions" and plea out Waddy; the new lawyer was finding holes in the State's case big enough to drive a car through. She raised allegations of ineffective counsel on a posttrial motion, made reference to Waddy passing a lie detector test that he wasn't Bright Eyes, and a judge ends up deciding the unthinkable and lets Waddy out on bail pending appeal.

All of which was about to create one hell of a mess for the CA's office when Waddy, out of jail, gets frazzled on crack cocaine and goes looking to damage the system that had set him up. The first symbols of his injustice he'd found were Diana and Jeremy Blane. And he massacred them.

Blane had never considered his wife, Diana, any great loss; she'd caught him cheating and had threatened to leave half a dozen times. Besides which, Blane was tired of her; she no longer excited him sexually. It was Jeremy, the product of his flesh, for whom Blane wept. But Jeremy's death had *not* been The Kroop's fault. And since Griffin had killed Waddy, it was over.

Except, now somehow, some way, Stevie Deke—the real Bright Eyes—had returned.

Karupka knew it was a problem. As soon as Karupka found out Deke was back in town—the day after Jane Doe turned up in the porn stall—he'd called Blane and apologized for breaking his end of the deal.

Jack promised Deke would be taken care of—and soon. Jack asked Blane to keep the cops off Deke so he could handle it himself. Blane said that was fine. He'd already told Griffin to keep the case quiet even before he'd known about The Kroop's involvement.

Which Karupka said was why Blane was going to be Richard Marish's successor one day. Because he thought the right way. Blane was going far. With a guy like Karupka behind him, how could he miss?

As it turned out, however, Jack hadn't been able to settle things with Deke soon enough. Griffin had found out. Even after being thrown off the case—Blane doing that to protect Griffin—Grif had kept going. And now he knew. He knew too much.

35.

Michelle Aronson was rushed to the emergency room at 4:35 A.M. Breathing and pulse erratic. Pupils enormously dilated. The red hexagon painted on her naked body alerting the staff to Bright Eyes's use of belladonna.

A maintenance dose of Haldol was administered. She was placed on a respirator and heart monitor and moved to a private, guarded room. Two police officers were placed on her door.

Frank Wallace, the city homicide detective in charge of the Bright Eyes case, was awakened at home to be advised there had been another attack.

Jimmy Griffin also got a phone call. Rawley Jenkins at 6:30 A.M., telling him to turn on the TV.

Griffin was awake already, feeding Cassie bottled formula, feeling slightly less groggy than last night, but not by much. He hadn't been able to sleep. Felt disoriented in his own house. The scratches Carla had skinned across his face and neck burned his conscious more than his body.

In his boxer shorts, Griffin carried Cassie to the living room and switched on the TV. Saw a live report: Frank Wallace about to hold an at-the-scene press conference, having set up another of his trademark "command posts" in front of a big stone rancher. Griffin knew immediately from the homestead's size it wasn't inside city lines.

In the background, a helicopter was first heard, then

seen, prowling the pink dawn sky, looking for Bright Eyes.

Frank Wallace scowled at the loud chop of the helicopter's rotors as though it was an impolite interruption. When the noise receded, Frank made his announcement. Reporting another Bright Eyes attack. A husband *and* wife this time. The husband apparently strangled by the killer's bare hands. The wife surviving so far; her condition cited as "guarded."

"We're dealing with a very sick, very deranged, abnormal, psychotic killer." Frank Wallace squinted because he thought it made him look tough while spewing adjectives. "He is powerful, extremely dangerous, extremely ruthless. Launching this surprise, terroristlike attack on a suburban couple. People in the vicinity should remain indoors, make certain all windows and doors are locked, and report any suspicious activity immediately."

Watching TV, Griffin had the phone lodged between his shoulder and ear. Cassie was cradled in his left arm, losing interest in the bottle.

Jenkins said, "Whaddayou think, kid? Should we report some suspicious activity?"

"Yeah, call the TV stations. Tell them two former cops are about to track down a guy Mickey Blane and Dickie Marish don't want found."

Jenkins arrived at Griffin's house within twenty minutes. Still wearing last night's clothes, breath smelling of beer. He and Griffin started working the phones.

Determining that Stephen H. Deke held a valid Maryland driver's license. The past four years indicated no violations, while years prior thereto were logged with numerous offenses, a few having transferred by reciprocity with Florida.

Deke's address was listed as Suite 205, Monroe

Street. A location that turned out to be a Pak-N-Mail outlet. Suite 205 was no more than one of fifty twenty-four-hour-access post office boxes in the store's foyer.

There weren't any vehicles in the state registered in Deke's name. Yet he was getting around somehow. Killers didn't take cabs. The locations were too widespread for him to walk. He was careful otherwise, he'd know stealing a car would be dangerous. Which meant he'd either bought a car under an alias, or rented or borrowed one. Buying under a false name was an unnecessary risk. All signs to date were that he operated on his own, which ruled out borrowing a friend's car. He'd rent a car, probably pay cash.

Griffin was calling rental agencies by the time Jenkins returned from scouting Deke's address. It was difficult finding someone in authority early Sunday morning, but even if Griffin was left talking to a $6.50-an-hour desk agent, he worked on getting them to reveal renter information with appeals to humanity and—when that didn't work—threats and coercion.

It was a frustrating, time-consuming process. There were almost forty car rental companies in the phone book—from the big national franchises to lowly four-and five-car mom-and-pop shops. And that didn't include auto dealers who rented out "loaner" cars when the floor-plan guy wasn't watching.

Places that didn't answer the phone or wouldn't volunteer information got personal visits from Jenkins and became quick to cooperate once he showed up looking mean and impatient, flashing a retired police department badge no one had the nerve to question. Jenkins called in every half hour complaining it was too damned hot to not have any luck.

Griffin was down to a final ten phone numbers when the front door opened.

Griffin hadn't seen them come onto the porch. The uniformed policeman entered first. He wasn't big, but very serious.

Carla stood just behind the cop's shoulder. She looked nervous, but defiant. Her short hair was freshly washed. Wearing business attire, she appeared efficient and—ironically—credible.

The cop offered Griffin a folded sheet of paper for his inspection.

Griffin set down the phone and stood.

"Sir, this is a Protective Order requiring you to leave these premises pending a formal hearing on charges that you are a threat to the safety and well-being of your wife and child."

Griffin snatched the court order and read it. It was dated and signed by a judge today—Sunday morning. "This is bullshit."

"Sir, you're going to have to—"

Griffin pointed accusingly at Carla. "How much did Mickey have to pay to get this, huh?"

"Sir." The policeman placed himself deliberately between Griffin and Carla.

Carla didn't say anything. Her arms were crossed. Tense as Griffin yelled at her:

"Did you also tell the judge how you and Mickey have been fucking each other for years behind my back?" To the cop: "Did she tell *you* that? How she's been fucking a guy I thought was my best friend?"

"Sir!" The cop came closer, offering final warning.

Liz emerged from Cassie's room and closed the door. "What's going on? You're disturbing the baby." She stopped, seeing Carla.

Carla shot a glance toward Griffin, who instinctively looked away, then came back to meet her eyes. Carla didn't appear shocked. The tension in her shoulders

eased, erasing the hard lines of muscles jutting determinedly along her neck.

Griffin thought, she thinks I'm screwing Liz. Swell.

The cop, interpreting the moment of quiet as indication
of settlement, stopped short of taking hold of Griffin. He
lowered his voice. "Sir," still being formal, "provided the
child is given to me, you can have some time to remove
your belongings."

Griffin held firm eye contact with Carla. He shook his
head. "There's nothing here I want. But I'm going to
fight you for Cassie."

Carla closed her eyes. "You can't win."

"Don't bet on it."

Regaining consciousness, Michelle Aronson was
vaguely aware of whiteness. For a moment, she thought
she was dead. Fear's cool chill came over her. The sound
of her own quick pulse increased from a whisper to
pounding in her ears. She heard voices, sensed activity.
Becoming light-headed without realizing she'd sat up
too quickly. Firm hands clasped her shoulders and urged
her to lie back.

"Hospital," she heard herself think out loud. "I'm in a
hospital."

A woman's voice—a foreign accent—told her that was
right. She *was* in the hospital. She was going to be okay.

Over the next hour, tended by doctors and nurses,
Michelle gradually regained her senses, notwithstanding
slight lingering effects of the belladonna.

Two police detectives were allowed in the room, both
men wearing suits and ties. Looking grave and concerned. Told by one of the doctors that if he felt his patient was too weakened to continue, he was going to stop
the questioning.

The first detective rested his hand on the bed rails.

"Mrs. Aronson, my name is Frank Wallace. I'm a detective. Are you feeling well enough to answer a few questions?"

Michelle panicked. Greg was dead. That's what they were going to tell her. They were going to find out that she had hired The Kroop to have him killed.

"Mrs. Aronson, did you see the man who did this to you?"

Did this to *me*? She thought.

"Can you hear me, Mrs. Aronson? Did you understand the question?"

The nurse with the foreign accent, a Pakistani, took Michelle's hand and stroked it. "Of course she understand you. You have to give her time to think. Her mind is jumbled from the drugs."

Michelle had a vague recollection of the man coming into her bedroom, grabbing her, squirting something in her mouth. Was that the drug the nurse was talking about? Or something they'd given her in the hospital?

Slowly, Frank Wallace repeated, "Did you see the man—?"

Her words constricted by a dry throat, Michelle said, "I want to see my husband. Can you let my husband in?"

Frank Wallace glanced at his fellow detective, the county homicide man assigned to Greg Aronson's murder.

Michelle raised her voice, showing tension. "Where's my husband?"

The doctor interceded, told the policeman that was all for now. As Michelle cried for her husband, the Pakistani nurse tightly held her hand. Soothed, "Later, dear. Later."

Michelle knew he was dead. Was excited, disoriented, and scared by the idea. But it had been done and, even through a residual haze of belladonna, she saw from the policemen's eyes they didn't suspect her. The Kroop had engineered a perfect crime. Greg was dead. And she was free.

                             *   *   *

Griffin had a new scene to replay in his mind today. Carla and the cop coming into the house. He thought about everything he *should* have said to her. That if he had the chance to do it again, he'd call her a whore. He'd wanted to at the time, but couldn't. God, she'd hurt him so badly.

He thought about it following Liz to her hotel, going up to her room, reestablishing contact with Rawley Jenkins. He tried to concentrate on the remaining car rental companies he called. But he couldn't stop thinking about his confrontation with Carla, over and over and over.

Telling Carla he'd fight her for Cassie. Carla, so damned smug and aloof, telling him he couldn't win. No doubt Mickey Blane could fix any court proceeding just like he'd found some judge to sign an ex parte order on a Sunday morning.

You can't win. You can't win.

Griffin kept hearing that over and over. And when he finally realized what she meant by it, he rushed into the bathroom and vomited violently into the toilet. He couldn't win a custody battle over Cassie. Couldn't win because Cassie wasn't his child. She was Blane's.

That afternoon, holding Griffin as he sobbed in her arms, Liz McKinley did something she hadn't done in years. She cried.

When the phone rang, she didn't want to answer it. Maybe she shouldn't have. Maybe it would have ended differently if she hadn't. But she *did* answer the phone. She did hear Rawley Jenkins, barely in control of his hunger on the other end of the line, say, "Tell the kid I got him. I know where Stevie Deke is. And *he's ours*."

36.

Rawley Jenkins's Ford LTD rumbled westward along the main highway out of the city.

Across the county line, at the first in a series of hills, dark thunderheads rolled in over the hazy summer horizon, turning a bleached white sky black-gray.

Griffin sat silently in the passenger seat. Dark rings under bloodshot eyes. The .45 Combat Commander holstered inside his blazer seemed to weigh a ton. On his way to meet Bright Eyes after so many years and even more lies.

"Kid, you haven't been drinking, have you?"

Griffin shook his head no.

" 'Cause the last time I had a Griffin backing me up, I got my ass shot off. I don't want history repeating itself."

"You want me to go in first, I'll go." Griffin spoke emotionlessly. His pulse was calm and steady.

Jenkins shook his head; he liked his plan better. "If Stevie Deke followed Waddy's trail he might've gotten a look at you. Me he doesn't know. Besides, I'm too old and worn out to be a cop, right? He won't suspect me." Jenkins looked at Griffin, watching him a good five seconds. There was little traffic to be concerned with. "Just be there covering my ass."

"Don't worry about it."

"And don't do anything stupid."

"Don't worry—"

"About it. Yeah, yeah, so you said." Jenkins watched the road.

Stone hills rose steeply on each side of the dual-lane highway. Thousands of acres of woods and parkland beyond. A forest of green seeming to change colors as storm clouds seeped across the sky like blood rushing through a wound.

Jenkins said, "We're just going in, getting Deke, turning him over the FBI. You tell them your story, right? All about Blane and Marish and Jack Karupka. No heroics. Nothing crazy."

Griffin nodded.

Jenkins mumbled, "*I* must be fuckin' crazy." He turned on the headlights as darkness came early.

Thunder rumbled in the distance.

Stevie Deke stood at the motel room window. Watching the approaching storm. Appreciating its violence.

Killing Greg Aronson had been unexpectedly rewarding. Making it a fantasy re-creation of murdering his stepfather. Pretending Aronson's wife was Alice: his stepsister—the first woman he'd killed, the one who'd started it all.

He'd always thought it appropriate Alice's name had begun with *A*, like the alphabet.

When he'd decided to kill more women, he'd wanted to do it alphabetically. Find a nice girl whose name began with *B* to do the second. But that was too restrictive; it inhibited his imagination.

He'd ended up taking the women who aroused him. Seduced or forced them. Filled them with belladonna. Watched them die. Watched their eyes brighten. Afterward, he gave them names to fit the alphabet sequence.

Occasionally he wondered what he'd do after he killed

Zelda. Maybe a double alphabet. Annie Ann. Amy Ann. Something like that. Whatever, he imagined it would take some time. Years. The sprees were enjoyable.

Now it was time to hide for a while. They'd never be able to catch him that way. A serial killer who worked in streaks. It probably hadn't been done before. The appetite was thought too difficult to suppress. But not for him. He was disciplined.

He'd take The Kroop's money for the Aronson hit, take the plane ticket—hopefully back to the islands— and enjoy another period of exile.

In the meantime, the girl sitting impatiently on the bed, no clothes on, legs crossed, one leg rocking over the other, chewing her gum, playing with hair so overpermed and dyed it looked like corn tassels, said, "This it? You just wanna look at me?" Not caring if that's all he wanted for a hundred bucks. Easy money. Hell, some guys, they call an escort service, pay a hundred, they wanted the world, and to go around and around and around.

And, at the moment, Deke wasn't even looking at her, which was of some concern. Him at the window.

She said, "You gotta friend coming, it's gonna cost more."

Jenkins did a drive-by past the entrance to the road-side motel. Few cars were parked inside the horseshoe complex. Sundays were slow for adulterers.

"Dodge Dynasty," Jenkins said. "You see it?"

"Near the back corner, right-hand side."

"That's our boy. Looks like he's home." At the first cut-through, Jenkins swung the LTD into a U-turn and headed back eastward. Getting a second look at the motel layout over the concrete half-wall separating the highway. "Room's got no back doors, only a rear window, right?"

"Looks it."

"Another window in front beside the door."

Griffin nodded.

"No other way in or out." A half mile past the motel, Jenkins did another U-turn and headed back.

Loose stones crunched under the LTD's tires as he wheeled slowly into the motel lot. His headlights cast a bright swatch over the small office and its drive-up check-in window. Jenkins looked straight ahead, not wanting the lady seated inside there to see him.

Fifty yards beyond the entrance, he backed into one of many empty parking spaces. Five doors from Deke's room, he turned off the engine and lights.

Behind the motel was densely wooded parkland. Trees blew against initial gusts of wind. The sky turning more black than gray.

Jenkins said, "Gonna rain like hell."

Griffin peered over his shoulder at Deke's room. A yellowed window shade was drawn. A light on inside. Griffin slid his .45 from its shoulder holster.

Jenkins took a breath. "Been a while since I did this. Hope my heart doesn't blow."

"Let me do it."

"Nah, kid, I'm joking with you. Gotta keep loose." Jenkins did a double tap on the steering wheel with his palms, expending a little anxiety. "You got me covered, right?"

"I'm there."

"Good. Fuck. Me, too."

When Jenkins opened the driver's door, Griffin switched off the car's interior light without taking his eye from Deke's room. He opened his own door an inch and kept it wedged there with his knee in case he had to get out in a hurry.

Jenkins opened the trunk. Took out a small paisley

suitcase. He smiled at Griffin, showing the frilly design. "Was my wife's."

"All right, all right!" the escort girl said, "I'm hurryin'."

This guy was a strange one. First he wanted her naked, now he wanted her dressed. The whole while he's looking out the window. She was hopping into her heels when he had her stand beside him.

Holding open the dirty curtain no more than an inch, he pointed to the parking lot: an old man carrying a fancy little suitcase, walking toward another room. Deke saying, "See the car he got out of?"

"Yeah. Broken-down old heap?"

"Looks like someone else is in there, doesn't it?"

"I don't know. Maybe, I guess. It's getting dark. I'm scared of storms."

"Walk over there and see who's in that car."

"Is that your friend?"

Deke said, "No," thinking, if someone's in that car, they sure as hell aren't any friend. And feeling angry about it. Having figured there was an outside chance something bad might go down today, and damned glad he'd set up this little contingency. Some people just weren't trustworthy.

"What do I say to him?" the girl asked. "If there is someone in the car?"

He had a hard grip on her arm, taking out his anger on her. "Just say you thought he was someone else, and come right back here. Right back."

"Okay, okay . . ."

Jenkins walked casually toward Deke's room. Trying to look like a traveling salesman, or whoever else might check into these fleabags. Staying close to the walls so Deke wouldn't be able to see him if he looked out.

One door from Deke's room, Jenkins glanced back at Griffin.

Griffin tried to wave Jenkins off.

A door to another room opened to Jenkins's blindside. A young woman coming out. Frizzy blond hair, orange stretch top squeezing small breasts. White cowgirl skirt slung provocatively across her hips, ripped into a daring mini.

Jenkins missed Griffin's signal. His back was to the girl; he didn't see her. He moved in front of Stevie Deke's door.

The girl was coming toward Griffin in the car. Right for him.

Griffin got out, held the gun inside his blazer.

Jenkins heard the car door, then saw the girl, flinched with surprise. Wondered what the hell was up.

Stevie Deke thought, son of a bitch. Not only was someone else in the car, but the guy was standing there now, obviously concealing a piece inside his blazer. Son of a bitch. Son of a bitch! Rage spun Deke's head even as he took those deep breaths the old Rastafarian coached as a cool-down method. Maybe it was a coincidence. Maybe— No, fuck, this was no coincidence. That fucking, fucking Jack Karupka!

The blonde kept coming directly toward Griffin, smiling as though she was supposed to know him.

Jenkins stood by the door to the room rented in Deke's name, watching, frozen. A look of, *Where'd she come from?* stitched in his expression.

Heavy drops of rain began to splatter randomly on hot asphalt.

The girl stopped suddenly, smile fading, as though

suddenly realizing something. Uttering words lost to the wind.

Griffin asking, "What?"

She called over the approach of the storm. "You're not who I thought—sorry." She turned and ran back to her room, squealing from the rain that fell suddenly heavy from a cracked open sky.

Griffin sensed Jenkins's relief. Jenkins waiting until the girl was back inside, then doing the damnedest thing: he opened the door to Stevie Deke's room and walked in. *Walked in.*

What the hell?

The blonde, back inside now, asked, "Do what?" asking her customer to repeat what he'd just said.

"Get over on the bed and make a lot of noise. Like you're having sex—getting laid and loving it." Telling her this without looking at her, still peering out the curtain.

"Just make noise?"

"Yeah," he whispered harshly. "Right now. Start it up. Go!"

"Do I take my clothes off?"

"Doesn't matter."

He was an odd one, but, sure, she could make noise. A little, "Ohhh, ahhh . . ." Looking at him. ". . . like that?"

He gestured an urgent motion with his hand, whispered, "Louder."

"Ohhhhh! Ahhhhh! Do it! Do it to me!" Shrugging as she made these noises . . . if this was what he wanted.

The rain increased, coming down in hard, deafening sheets.

Griffin started quickly along the walkway, slide-stepping the final few feet before the door to the room

Jenkins went in. Griffin's back to the wall. Kicking open the door, dropping in low, gun leveled across the small room.

Rawley Jenkins sitting on the bed, aiming a gun fitted with a silencer toward the door, lowering it when he saw Griffin. Jenkins with a phone in his other hand, telling Griffin, "Shut the door, kid."

Stevie Deke was pissed big-time. He was trying to push back the rage, but it was overflowing, like a pot of boiling water threatening to lift off its lid. These guys had come out to get him. That goddamned Karupka.

Time Stevie taught a lesson. Don't fuck with Stevie.

Talking into the phone, Rawley Jenkins said, "Jack, yeah, it's me. We got a problem. Deke ain't here."

Griffin stared at Jenkins.

"I can sit and wait all you want, Jack, you know me, all I got's time. But I don't know I want to hang around here longer than I have to. Some cops get smart and somehow find out Deke's here, I don't want to be loungin' around when they show."

Griffin said, "What the hell's—?"

Jenkins cut him off, pressing the mouthpiece to the phone against his jowly throat, making a cutting motion with his hand that held his weapon.

A clap of thunder rumbled the walls. Rain pounded the roof.

In the adjoining room, the girl with blond hair was making wild noises.

Jenkins listened into the phone, responded, "Okay," nodding, "okay, Jack. Okay." Getting instructions. Setting down the phone.

"What the hell's going on, Rawley?"

Minor problem. It'll work out."

"Work out! You're talking to Jack—Karupka?"

"Deke did a little work for Jack, but he's gotten a little out of control."

"And that's why you're here? For Karupka?"

"Uh-huh."

Griffin was stunned, becoming angry. "And why am I here?"

"Well, hope was, we'd make you a hero. I come out here, supposedly to give Deke a payoff for a job he did, only Deke doesn't get his cash and plane ticket, he gets a couple bullets. I shoot Deke, you take the credit for bagging Bright Eyes."

"Goddamn, Rawley, you've been in this all along! You son of a bitch. So that's why you covered up Jane Doe. Not for the hospital, for Jack Karupka."

"No, no. I had no idea what was involved at the beginning. I didn't remember any of that belladonna shit. Hell, that'd been four years ago. What I did at first was strictly for the hospital."

"So when did it *stop* being for the hospital and start being for The Kroop?"

"Last night." When Griffin glared at him, Jenkins said, "It's the truth. If it'd been earlier, would I have told you about that alibi witness your buddy Blane scared off the Waddy case? No way in hell. Jack called me last night. He knew Deke was a problem and had to do something about him. When he found out I was involved in this thing, he called off some other talent he'd been planning to use and got me."

Rain continued to punish the roof. On the other side of the wall, the blonde wailed how her customer was loving her like she'd never been done before.

"How'd The Kroop find out you were in this?"

"Your buddy Blane called *him* last night. Right after

you left his place, is my guess. But don't go getting yourself upset. It's better this way, trust me."

"I did until two minutes ago."

"Come on, kid, don't be that way. Relax. Everybody's gonna make out."

"Goddamn, Rawley. Goddamn." Griffin stalked the motel room. No way this could go down like this. Jenkins "hitting" Deke. No way.

Griffin looked over the room, a satchel bag on the ratty dresser near the bathroom, syringes and vials. Belladonna. They should have a warrant to be here. They had to get out, get a warrant, get Deke busted. Do it right this time. But damn it, they were so far "off the book" how were they ever going to make this case legit? Not chance Deke strolling on a procedural flaw. And Karupka. Damn! Griffin turning to Jenkins, "How the fuck did you ever get involved with The Kroop?"

"Don't make that sound like such a bad thing. I'll tell you, kid, after I got shot, that deal your father fucked up on covering—"

Griffin snapped, "Leave my father out of it."

Jenkins shrugged. "Sure. Okay. Sorry."

Next door, the girl screamed loudly she was about to come.

Jenkins said, "After I got shot, laid up in the hospital, no doubt gonna have permanent disability, I started getting lots of shit from the police department insurance carrier about a settlement. They offer me a lousy ten grand for a bum back that's gonna keep me out of work. Ten lousy grand. The insurance guy, he tells me he's sympathetic, he'd like to offer more, only his supervisors, 'they' won't let him. You ever notice how when someone wants to blame something on someone else, he always says 'they'? Throw it off on some faceless people, like it's a machine making these decisions, not a person. A 'they' you can't deal with. That's the beautiful thing about Jack Karupka. Jack knows who 'they' is. I went to him with my disability case, he settled it in thirty days. Got me twenty-five grand a year, adjusted for inflation, for the rest of my life. *Rest of my fucking life.*"

The blonde was getting into making noises. She pulled her top over her head, was shaking out her hair, moving around on the bed, when she screamed. Really screamed.

Her customer had a gun. A nasty-looking weapon. Aimed not at her, but the wall between them and the room next door.

Stevie Deke had never killed anyone with a gun before. Too impersonal. Not enough hands-on death for his tastes. And, goddamn it, it pissed him off to have to do it this way, but Jack Karupka, these guys in his room next door, they needed to get the message.

Deke had himself a little Uzi action about to happen here. A nice piece bought off a Jamaican gangsta' in Miami a few years back. He'd only ever fired it once, to make sure it worked. Kept it oiled and nearby. Loaded. Never, ever carried it on a "night on the town," just kept it where he slept to ward off surprises. In all his worst dreams, never expected to use it.

But here he was, finger on the trigger, the damned blonde turning into a screaming meemie. Hanging out in a room next to his regular room because he had some weird feeling The Kroop might try something fiendish like this. He'd seen a little conniving in The Kroop's eyes, figuring, at the time, that was just how lawyers looked. But, just in case, he'd hired the girl to be around with the thought of getting her to pick up the money from The Kroop's delivery boy, although he could tell from casing these two guys they hadn't come here to pay him.

So, goddamn it, he was going to need more than ten grand now. He was going to invoke the unwritten "penalty provision" in his deal with The Kroop. Triple his price. But first, these two guys. Send them back to The Kroop as a bloody message.

"So now you do these little jobs for The Kroop in return." Griffin didn't approve of the arrangement.

"Come on, kid. Christ, don't talk like a fucking angel. What's ever fair? Huh? In the court system? With lawyers? You gotta be kidding. Don't be like that."

Gun blasts sounded. Holes started leaping through the wall. Rapid-fire. A wild, fast line of eruptions. Bullets screaming into the room.

Jenkins lurching forward as a shot entered him from behind and went straight through him. Looking stunned as he fell to the floor.

More rounds blasting into the room, ripping a spray pattern that moved toward the front door.

Instinct having put Griffin on the floor upon the first blast. Crawling toward the foot of the bed, putting the mattress and box spring between him and the shooter. Someone in the next room set on auto fire. Eating them up.

Then, a brief pause. Reloading? No. A shadow flash outside the window. Movement toward their door. Kicking it open. A figure spinning into view—white guy, five-ten, pale T-shirt, jeans—weapon at waist height, looking to finish them off.

Griffin's .45 taking the first shots, two loud blasts that had Stevie Deke spinning back out of the doorway. Not hit, but retreating. Griffin firing a shot through the front wall. Scrambling to his feet as Deke spun back low into the doorway. Finger down on the trigger. Sprays of red light flashing as bullets laced over Griffin's head.

Deke running now. Griffin up and out the door after him. Visibility gone to shit in blinding rain.

Deke turned the corner beyond the last room; Griffin went wide at the same spot, using a parked car for cover in case Deke was there to ambush him.

Only Deke was flying now, sprinting down the side of the building, headed into the state park. Endless acres of forest.

Griffin chasing. Combat Commander in his grip. Splashing through puddles in thick grass. Adrenaline shooting through him. Flashbacks to another chase, another storm. Dunbar Waddy through downtown streets. Griffin the assassin then like Rawley Jenkins had been dispatched now.

Deke ran hard and fast across a short grassy clearing in back of the motel, cutting into the tree line before Griffin could get off a shot.

Griffin sprinting into the same clearing when a flurry of auto fire flashed out of the woods. Strange sounds around him as though the bullets actually were slicing big raindrops in half, looking to do the same to him when he dove facedown to the ground, sliding forward on wet grass, .45 lifted in front of him, pulling off two shots toward the direction of Deke's fire.

Griffin stayed pinned low in the grass for a few beats even when Deke stopped shooting, not knowing if Deke was hit, running, or concealed in the woods waiting for him to stand into a larger target. Griffin rolling onto his side, rising to a crouch. Not drawing fire, so he moved forward.

Running straight ahead now, ears pinched back for the sounds of gunfire, hoping like hell the next blast of orange firelight didn't explode in front of his face.

Griffin hurdled a briar patch at the end of the woods, but didn't quite clear it all. His back leg caught in stiff sticker branches, mean boys that ripped his pants and dug hard thorns into his flesh. He tore himself loose, feeling skin slashed by sharp prickers.

Thrashing through low branches, big leaves dripping water, Griffin penetrated the outer ring of the woods.

Trees created a leaky canopy against the rain. But where sheets of the storm slashed into the forest, mossy beds of clay and shale were slick underfoot. The woodland floor was uneven, difficult to cross quickly. So damned hard to see through darkness and rain.

But Bright Eyes was so close. After all these years. So many deaths. Griffin plowed ahead. Dove behind a big oak tree when the Uzi opened fire again. Less than a hundred yards ahead of him. Eleven o'clock. But not firing in his direction. Deke seeing ghosts in the woods?

The tree root had caught Deke's foot and turned his ankle, sent him tumbling forward, finger snapping off three bursts of the automatic before he loosened his grip on the trigger. Cussing loudly as he hit the ground. Needing to find a spot where he could lie and wait for the guy chasing him. Having missed his chance at the edge of the woods, looking to riddle the guy up with bullets, but his aim had been unsteady after running. Breathing so damned hard. Couldn't hold that weapon really still.

Deke trying to attain that calm edge, but the adrenals were pumping wild stress signals through his body. Something about that guy shooting at him. Having actually felt like he'd seen the guy's eyes. Just a split second. Looking at him while bullets flew. Something evil there. Not beautiful bright eyes like dying girls on belladonna, but devil eyes. Sinister.

Now in the goddamned woods where it was dark and

claustrophobic feeling. All the fucking trees like walls. Branches grabbing at him. Tree roots tripping him.

Deke breathing desperately through his open mouth as he thrashed forward. Rain falling through the trees and into his eyes and mouth. Seeing a brighter area of light down the incline to his left. Struggling toward that.

The trio of misfired shots were Griffin's compass, pointing him toward Stevie Deke. Back on target.

Pellets of rain dripped off his forehead in front of his eyes. Griffin moved stealthfully through the woods, ducking branches, avoiding swirls of sticker-laden vines that curled around the forest floor.

Deke's light-colored T-shirt waved like a flag through the trees. Griffin closing in on Deke, but angling a path parallel to him, tightening the distance from the side.

Deke trying to run but getting caught in dead ends. Paths snarled with vines like barbed wire, fallen trees. Deke turning abruptly in place, leveling the Uzi over the woods behind him, worried about Griffin, and Griffin taking cover, Deke not seeing him. But Deke had to feel him closing in. Less than fifty yards now. Slow, steady progress, Griffin constricting the distance between them, feeling a strange taste in his mouth along with the urge to spit. His glands producing saliva.

Deke moving toward brighter sky that glowed through the trees like a humid haze. Deke thinking that was the best route of escape. Not hearing the rushing water that lay ahead for the downpour of the storm, sounds Griffin knew from hiking Maryland woodlands.

Deke sprinted the final hundred yards of thinning forest, running toward the open expanse he'd sensed through the goddamned trees. Reaching the edge of the woods and stopping dead. He was on the edge of a steep rocky embankment, thirty feet up from a quick-moving river. A wide waterway.

"Deke!"

Someone calling his name. Deke squinting into the rain, looking down the tree line. Seeing no one.

"Deke! Drop the gun, Deke! Now!"

The voice echoed through the shallow valley that carried the river. Not sounding that close.

"Drop the gun!"

And then Deke heard the train.

Griffin shouted Deke's name a second time. Then a third.

Deke heard the train and started running.

Griffin fired the .45.

Deke panicked. The guy was shooting at him and Deke didn't know from where. Couldn't see him. Just heard the gun.

Deke hyperventilated scrambling along the edge of the forest, not wanting to be back in there, but those trees could stop bullets from hitting him. Three shots. Damned close. Snapping branches.

Deke running toward the train he heard, feeling its heavy presence make the ground tremble. Not knowing the area that well, but figuring if there was a train coming, maybe there was also . . .

. . . a bridge. Railroad bridge. Two hundred yards of iron crossing the river. And Deke was trying to get there, just far enough ahead of Griffin to use the bending hillside for cover.

Griffin couldn't get a line of sight for another shot. No sooner glimpsing Deke than losing him again, and no way to close his lead on this terrain. Fighting the edge of the incline for enough clear and level ground to set his feet, stepping in soggy imprints left by Deke moments earlier.

Deke was going to reach the bridge. Nothing Griffin could do to stop him. Another bridge. Another storm.

The hillside rolled into a wide swale that slid down to the tracks, Deke getting there, going down the incline on his butt, bouncing over rocks and scraping muddy ground. Sludge getting all over the Uzi, slopping into its barrel.

Deke didn't want to cross the bridge, but looking the other way down the tracks, he saw the train's white headlight through streaking rain. Five hundred yards away. Rumbling closer. Fast. The tracks on a narrow, steep pass cut through the hill. Not much room on either side. No way *around* the train.

Deke turned back and saw his pursuer round the bending hillside. He shook mud off the Uzi and fired.

Griffin went down in a hail of bullets. Chunks of tree bark flying around him. Leaves pulverized. Griffin maintaining hold on the .45 with one hand, grabbing a sapling at the forest's edge with another, using that young tree to keep from sliding over the incline, pulling himself behind cover as Deke emptied the Uzi and went running for the bridge—to cross over the river—only the bridge was narrow. No room for a train and a person to share.

The train might catch Deke before he reached the other side of the wide river. But might wasn't a good enough chance.

Griffin took the slope toward the tracks at haphazard speed, tumbling the final ten feet, intense pain snapping through his shoulder where he hit the tracks. Looking down the line and seeing the train coming at him. Horn blaring.

Griffin to his feet, struggling for balance, catching himself on a rail of the bridge. Running after Deke. The train so damned close.

Griffin shouting, "Deke! Deke!"

Bright Eyes halfway across the bridge, looking back, his depth perception making him think the train was right on top of Griffin, about to plow him under. Deke now realizing the bridge was too narrow, too long. Couldn't sidestep the train, couldn't outrun it.

He was going to hurdle the railing. Deke was going to dive into the river.

Deke hooking one leg over the edge, looking down, swinging the other leg over.

Griffin stopping, feet spread, two-handing the gun, military style. Train bearing down on him. Griffin firing the .45 from sixty yards as Deke went over the edge. Griffin watching him tumble toward the river. Falling as though he'd been shot. But through the rain, Griffin hadn't seen blood. Couldn't tell if he'd hit Deke, and if so, where. Was it a fatal shot?

The train blared. Griffin could have hung on to the side of the bridge, suspended himself until the train passed. But he really had no choice. Not this time.

He abandoned his gun and went into the river after Deke.

Feet first, hands cupped hard between his legs like sailors were trained to fall if they went over the side of a ship. Body slicing into cool, rushing water, hitting bottom fast, knees and ankles taking what stress the water didn't break.

No sooner above the surface than the river was carrying him on powerful current. Griffin using his arms and legs as steering rudders.

Fighting to keep his head above water. Already fifty yards from the bridge. The train howling behind him, sending vibrations down steel bridge supports that echoed through the river.

Griffin looking for Deke, spitting water that churned with silt and mud. Seeing an arm flailing. Just one arm, so he figured Deke had been hit by the .45. Deke spiraling in the river like an airplane with one wing.

Griffin letting the water sweep him faster, not fighting its pull, catching a surge.

Deke looked to be drowning. Coughing desperately. One arm splashing. Legs not in sight. Hit more than once by the .45 it seemed. Maybe dying.

Griffin swam forward, slicing through rougher water, grunting when his foot banged underwater rock.

Deke having no idea Griffin was behind him, not until Griffin grabbed his shirt and strong-armed him into a fierce squeeze.

Griffin feeling pure rage as the water took control, churning, pulling them under. Griffin feeling Deke's throat in the bend of his arm. Griffin tightening his hold. Deke gurgling for breath. Four years of anxiety. Torment. Corruption. His life torn apart from the inside out. His wife. His best friend. Cassie.

Griffin believed he might be dying. Drowning. That the water was taking him under. And if that was the destiny awaiting him today, Stevie Deke was going with him.

He clutched his arm unmercifully against Deke's throat, believed he felt the madman's windpipe crushing seconds before everything went black.

37.

Griffin regained consciousness in what felt like a hollow, pounding tube, as though an explosion had gone off inside his head and the aftershocks were still reverberating.

He smelled the antiseptic and knew: hospital. It hurt when he opened his eyes. Not a lot of light, but what there was carved into his pupils like daggers headed for his brain. His jaw ached. So did his shoulder. His ankle was stiff and swollen with a nasty sprain. Griffin taking inventory of himself. Assuming from the lack of med-tech goodies hooked to him, short of something feeding the vein in his left arm, he mustn't be too bad off.

Hearing a scuttling of feet, someone—woman's voice (nurse?)—reporting, "He's awake." Not sounding all that urgent, which he took as another good sign.

The strange taste in his mouth matched the smell in his nostrils. Earthy. The river. He remembered the river now. What had happened to him? Had Deke overpowered him?

A voice said, "Lucky you didn't drown."

Griffin squinted at the doctor standing over him, taking his blood pressure.

"You're okay. You've got a couple stitches in your head, a butterfly or two in your leg. Bruises, contusions, a severely sprained ankle, but no bone breaks. You'll live."

The doc trying to be lighthearted, Griffin responding, "Don't bet on it."

His caustic remark was immediately greeted by a celebrating, "What're you talking about, 'don't bet on it?' You're a hero, Grif. A goddamned hero!" Mickey Blane coming into Griffin's private room. Blane had makeup on his face to try covering cuts and bruises from the edge of that door. Show business. "How yah doing, buddy. Hell of a job out there. Fantastic!" Leaning over Griffin, whispering, "Don't say a word to anyone until we talk, okay? We can make this work. Everyone comes out smelling like a rose. Okay?"

Some guys had a lot of nerve. Griffin said, "Hey, Mickey?"

"Yeah, pal?"

"I didn't get hit that hard on the head. . . . You're going down. You *and* Marish *and* Karupka. Down and out."

Five hours later, around midnight, Griffin pulled the IV out of his arm and left the hospital. Liz pirated him past nurses' watchful eyes and into her rental car. Clutching him like she'd never hugged anyone in her life. Surprising the hell out of herself, how strongly she felt for him.

In the car, about to be embarrassed if she started to actually cry, she said, "Where to?"

Griffin said, "Wherever you can write."

"Laptop's in my hotel room."

"Let's do it."

The PR people, so well dressed and paid, tried to throw Richard Marish and Mickey Blane life preservers, but a nasty negative tide pulled them too far from reach too fast.

The initial story had been magnificent, and, Mickey Blane was right, it could have worked. Marish announcing their "ploy" had been a stunning success. That by decoying James Griffin as a suspended investigator, Bright Eyes had let his guard down and Griffin had snared him. An amazing shoot-out in a county motel. A chase through the state park, down to the railroad bridge, Griffin bravely diving into the flowing river after Bright Eyes, catching him in the open water. Bright Eyes drowning. Griffin knocked unconscious by striking a rock.

The ink had barely been dry on those pages when Liz McKinley's piece broke over the wire services. The truth. How Blane and Marish willfully prosecuted Dunbar Waddy—the wrong Bright Eyes—four years ago. Jamie Brooks verifying Blane's order to conceal Exhibit A, fingerprints that would have pointed to another suspect, not Waddy.

The truth flew across the air like an angry buzz of hornets shaken from their hive, and the sting was potent.

Marish and Blane were immediately suspended from the CA's office amidst talk of state and federal grand jury investigations. Civil rights violations. Perjury. Obstruction of justice.

Even if Marish and Blane managed to escape prison, they'd do so without their license to practice law. The Ethics Committee wanted them badly.

The only problem was, Liz's wire service editors cut all references to Jack Karupka as unsubstantiated. Griffin hadn't talked directly to Karupka, had no hard evidence of his involvement—had only heard Rawley Jenkins talking to *someone* named Jack.

And Rawley Jenkins? His blood was on the motel room floor, but Rawley himself? He was nowhere to be found.

Epilogue

Griffin felt odd seeing all his possessions in boxes stacked on the living-room floor. Surprised there wasn't more to it. Realizing, bit by bit, Carla had been "moving him out" while they were still together, always encouraging him to give away his old clothes and possessions to Goodwill, and never buying much new.

She left him a note, actually, more of a proposal, written in quasi-legalese, like the briefs she prepared for downtown law firms. Suggesting they have Alex Cooper come in and auction all their joint possessions—furniture, kitchenware, appliances—and they'd split the proceeds. List the condo with a realtor, price it "to move fast," and divide the equity. Carla leaving a line for him to initial if he accepted those terms, so he scratched his name and figured that was that.

He didn't want any of this stuff, and wished it would be as easy to get rid of bad memories as the sofa and love seat. Carla had lied to him; she had used him; and now seemed to be walking away as though it wasn't his spirit she threatened to snap, but a fallen twig she'd stepped on. It was unconscionable and he was without recourse other than to fight her in a divorce. But fight over what?

Sure, some hungry lawyer could drum up a lawsuit—couldn't they always?—claim intentional infliction of emotional distress, Carla lying about Cassie, letting Griffin believe she was his daughter, sue for the suffering she'd caused him. And to what end? A possible money judgment? Forget it. Nothing was going to turn back the clock and make the past different, and settling scores with an exchange of money was an empty alternative. Some wounds couldn't be healed, or dressed. They left scars you learned to live with. Maybe, somehow, he might get to see Cassie. That would take time to figure out. And paramount was what would be best for her.

Griffin resigned from the CA's office and headed for Florida to be with his parents, who were even more devastated about Cassie than he was—if that was possible. Charlie Griffin raving angrily about having been right about Mickey Blane all along; the rich boy who used everyone around him, friends included, as rungs on a ladder he was so eager to climb. And that Blane ended up corrupting Carla so she was just like him: a user.

Griffin worried the incident might tumble his father back into the bottle, but Charlie Griffin stayed stone sober.

Griffin visited Liz a few times in Atlanta, tabloid Liz enjoying newfound respect for breaking a legitimate news story. She was covering the grand jury hearings in Baltimore for AP, Blane and Marish facing certain indictment.

Griffin waited in Florida to be called as a witness, pending notification from the Attorney General.

The pain of his physical injuries lessened even while the hurt of his life remained persistent.

It was going to take time and there was no guarantee he'd ever feel whole again. A big chunk of him had been taken away. By Mickey Blane. By Carla. By the system he'd once believed in and the crimes he'd committed in its name.

He hoped Jenkins was okay. A man he'd grown up

hating and come to, in an unsettling way, respect despite all his obvious faults. Jenkins had been there to help him, serving his own interests, but also Griffin's.

Dunbar Waddy and Stevie Deke kept him awake at night and stirred his thoughts during the day. His first impression was that justice, in some perverse way, had emerged from injustice. Only he later came to consider the system so corrupted by its own malfunction that justice was now an anomaly. Something often grabbed for and never grasped, like dithering images in the mist.

Griffin debated with himself whether he was so different from Marish and Blane, and that maybe he should be punished, too, for killing Dunbar Waddy. If he'd captured Waddy four years ago, not killing him, perhaps Waddy would have been tried for murdering Blane's wife and son, and evidence of the real Bright Eyes might have surfaced.

Had Griffin, by killing Waddy, contaminated the process? Made the case so impure it was impossible to filter the evil from it? Or had Waddy's crimes been answered with the only true punishment there was?

These events set into play by a sexual deviant, Stevie Deke, Bright Eyes, who was now also dead. Griffin having seen to that, too. Griffin realizing during his entire chase of Deke he'd never once identified himself as a police officer or investigator. Because that's not what he'd been. Deep in his soul, from the moment he saw evidence Bright Eyes might still be alive, he'd felt—if not admitted—the urge to kill him. Now that it was done, it was very difficult to live with that realization.

He'd stepped off the page that contained the law within its four corners, and wandered into the abyss where morality was a swirling dark cloud that drew unclear distinction between right and wrong.

Some days, the guilt was tremendous, yet other times, Griffin justified it all. It was maddening.

The afternoon he was finally put to an eerie peace, Griffin was alone at a "shack-style" restaurant on the beach; one of three customers on the wood deck, sitting on a plastic chair at a plastic table in the shade of a striped umbrella. Griffin in his shorts and T-shirt, looking over the Gulf of Mexico, eating a fish sandwich, still struggling with what he'd done.

So often now feeling the urge pull him toward confession. That he had to somehow be absolved. That what he had done was right and deserved, and yet wrong and without due process. Concerned most of all with how easy it had been when he was in the thick of it. That the last four years only seemed wrong from a distance.

Tormented by this when a voice behind him said, "Kid, you gotta let it go." Griffin started to pivot in his seat. "Don't turn around, kid, this is a stickup." Rawley Jenkins kidding with him.

Griffin exhaling gratefully. "You're alive."

"Yeah, I gotta stop hanging around with the Griffin family. Hazardous to my health." Jenkins was tanned, tourist-attired: panama hat, baggy green shorts with big pockets, yellow polyester shirt, dark socks, white shoes. Saying of his outfit, "Color-blind nightmare, ain't it?"

They went for a walk on the beach. The sun was hot on a spring day. Late April, Fort Myers into its shoulder season as snowbirds headed north to thawed-out homes. No one around to hear them talk, to hear Jenkins tell of getting his "shot-up self" out of that motel room, needing to put distance between his ties to Jack Karupka and Stevie Deke; getting "private medical care" from Karupka's doctors; recuperating in Europe, first palling around with the girls vacationing there who lived in his carriage house, then going on to the Mediterranean, taking in the sights.

There was something different about Jenkins, a confidence, arrogance almost, a man who was in on a secret. A man who'd been living very high for a cop on disability.

A man who put his hand on Griffin's shoulder, squeezed his neck as though giving a roughhouse massage, saying, "You know, Jimmy, I think you'd like Jack Karupka if you met him, gave him a chance. He's a really good guy to work for. I mean, you're not doin' anything else, right? Hanging around, watching pelicans. You're too young to be geezing."

"I'm scheduled to testify in front of the grand jury. I'm telling them everything. Karupka's going down."

"You don't want to do that."

"Yeah . . . I do."

"You sure?"

"No doubts."

Jenkins's hand came out of his pants pocket, holding a small .22 pistol, jamming it into Griffin's ribs, pulling the trigger three times. Snap-snap-snap. Firing pin sticking into an empty chamber. Jenkins saying, "That's how fast it would happen, kid. You want to testify against Jack Karupka, you gotta take care." Jenkins slipped the gun back into his pocket. The hand that had been on Griffin's neck messed Griffin's hair. "Take care, kid. Take good care." Jenkins walked off, leaving Griffin standing there.

And then, he knew:

He had gone across a line and left his imprint, not like Jenkins's footsteps along the beach, which would be easily erased by an incoming tide, but like carving his initials into the granite walls of hell.

The answer to his dilemma couldn't come from within

the confines of the law, because he'd left that place and couldn't return. His actions had dispatched him to a purgatory between law and chaos. An unsettling thought, but one that gave him sudden clarity of vision.

It wasn't that he felt guilty for killing Dunbar Waddy and Stevie Deke, but felt guilt because there was no remorse. Not a single shred of it trickling through his veins. He had killed two ruthless criminals and could do it again. A frightening thought, but one with which he could be at peace.

The trial was impossible to deny. Impossible to rationalize.

A man, Raymond Jarvis, forty-seven, a farmer, indicted by a grand jury for the murder of Colleen Baker, seventeen, who disappeared one night last July after working her summer job at an ice-cream parlor on the highway.

Witnesses put Jarvis's truck in the shopping-center parking lot about the time the store closed. And Jarvis had a thing for high school girls. Blondes. The pretty ones. Tall. Liked them with long, straight hair, and straight teeth. Straight hips, too. Not too curvy for Jarvis. Breasts were okay, but not too big. Liked them with "nice titties," Jarvis's cellmate had testified, enough size to get his rough hands full of them. Hold on while he sodomized them.

My God. My God! Trial attorney Terry Moore suddenly jumped up out of the chair he'd positioned by the window, upright so quickly he knocked it over. Haunted by Raymond Jarvis. The trial. Colleen Baker. He paced by the window, no longer looking outside.

Not seeing the man cross the lawn, going to the side of the house. Covered access to the basement there: concrete steps beneath a pair of metal hatch doors. Terry never locked the hatch—wasn't that paranoid about locking doors, either. Other lawyers in the office told him he had a death wish. So many crazies in the world. Crazies like Raymond Jarvis.

The girl who testified at the trial, Susanna Lavetik, sixteen, blond like Colleen Baker. Straight hair, straight teeth, straight hips. Susanna shook on the witness stand, crying, struggling to recount a time Raymond Jarvis accosted her in a shopping-mall parking lot.

Jarvis had followed her out to her car. Jarvis in his truck, the old red one she said looked like an antique. The engine made a rumbling sound, like it might quit any minute.

Jarvis drove by her once, smiling at her, giving her "the creeps" by winking at her.

He had a hat on. A baseball cap, with a logo from a farm feed company. The hat hid his eyes, but Susanna said she could feel him looking at her. Very scary.

She hurried to her car. The parking lot had been more crowded when she'd arrived. Only about twenty cars remained now. No one else around except a couple way on the other side, and they weren't looking her way. Raymond Jarvis was.

Susanna wished she'd left the mall earlier, hadn't stayed to hang out with her friends. She should have been home an hour ago. . . .

At that point in her testimony, she'd looked for her parents in the gallery, burst into tears, telling them she was so sorry. Her father crying, too. Her mother shaking.

Susanna's cheeks streamed with tears. Terry Moore patiently asked her to continue. Stood there firmly, but patiently, pretending the whole process wasn't tearing him up inside, that his heart wasn't pounding. Ignoring the rage he felt, having to focus that for the courtroom. Get the evidence in. Keep logical. Organized. Present the case.

Susanna was unable to speak for three minutes. Her head stayed down, hiding, telling about Raymond Jarvis's red truck pulling up beside her. That he got out. A tall, rangy, skinny man. Leathery face creased with age and overexposure to sun. Raymond Jarvis grabbed her hair with one hand, wrapping his other hand around her mouth. Smothering her scream with a hand that smelled strongly of onions.

Strong hands. So strong, Susanna whimpered quietly. So strong.

And again, Terry Moore had to prompt her to go on. Susanna sobbed so painfully, as though Raymond Jarvis wasn't seated at the defense table, but was attacking her again. Tearing at her with those hands that smelled ripely of onions. Strong hands.

He held her hair and pulled her off her feet, Susanna said. He banged her head against the door of his truck. Once, twice, and then she blacked out. The next thing she remembered was waking up in an abandoned barn. Naked.

Shivering on a pile of wet, decaying straw smeared with mud. A terrible sharp pain in her head. A worse feeling between her legs.

"Do you mean your vagina?" Terry Moore had to ask.

"Yes . . . yes . . . my . . ." Susanna couldn't say it—that her vagina felt as though it had been torn open. Couldn't say that in front of fifty people in the courtroom. Her sobbing father. Her mother looking as though in shock.

Susanna struggled more desperately to continue testifying as Terry Moore tried to establish rape. Defense counsel objected when Terry's questions became leading, but Susanna was falling apart on the stand. Head down. Hands clutched over her face so it was difficult to hear her speak. Susanna crying loudly, not able to say much more than she wanted to go home. The judge convened a recess.

Susanna Lavetik never returned to the stand. She'd been fragile before trial, in the nonconfrontational atmosphere of the prosecutor's office. Her therapist had been there with her. Susanna believed she'd be able to do this—testify against the man who knocked her unconscious, abducted her to a barn, and raped her. She could consider this a rehearsal for a later trial, one twice scheduled and as many times postponed. Her testimony was to be used to establish a pattern of criminal activity—Raymond Jarvis's dangerous sexual proclivity for young blond girls.

The State needed that because they didn't have Colleen Baker's body. Jarvis had a record of similar assaults in his native Georgia, seeming to have decided not to chance leaving live witnesses to testify anymore. Colleen Baker disappeared. So did Leslie Henryton after her. Only no one could place Raymond Jarvis and Leslie Henryton together like they could Jarvis and Colleen Baker.

The ice-cream store owner where Colleen worked testified that Jarvis came into the store a couple times. Colleen would talk to him. She was very friendly that way, would talk to anyone. But she did later tell the owner she was uncomfortable working nights anymore. The man in the red truck was making her feel scared. Not because of anything he'd done. No. Just the way he looked at her. The way he smiled. And his hands, they were so ugly, and smelled so bad. Onions, the owner said. He'd come into the store stinking of onions. The smell was even on the dollar bills he passed over the counter. A smell so bad other customers would leave the store. The man didn't seem to notice.

Onions. Stinking of onions.

Terry Moore knew he'd never be able to eat onions again. Never be able to see one or smell one, and not think of Raymond Jarvis, the man acquitted of the murder of Colleen Baker.

Now Jarvis was out. He was free. Raymond Jarvis was free because the State couldn't produce Colleen Baker's body. The defense counsel, so slick, had painted her as a free spirit, said she may have run away, not been murdered. Not enough evidence. And enough reasonable doubt.

Now, Terry Moore was left with the horrible thought of another girl having hands stinking of onions pressed to her mouth, and it seized him with rage. And what could he do? My God! What answer was there to this madness?

He paced the bedroom, heart pounding hard in his chest. Terry Moore screamed silent thoughts to his heart. *Go ahead. Take me. Kill me. Explode. End this!*

The first he saw of the Angel was a presence of whiteness, a motion detected in a corner of his eye. He thought at first it was another throb of infuriated pulse forced into his vision. He turned then, seeing the figure standing in the darkened hallway outside his bedroom. Light from the lamp at the window didn't reach that point with much strength, yet the figure seemed to emit its own light.

Terry stopped, staring. Strangely not afraid—as though a soothing benevolence radiated from the figure he now saw was a man. Terry could not determine his age or see his face. A man no more than five-seven or eight, medium build. Dressed in white: a heavy wool sweater, heavy pants like those sold in outdoor magazines for carpenters who worked outside, pale hiking boots. Holding a satchel.

The man spoke in a calming, almost lyrical voice, saying, "Fear not." The words resonated strength and understanding. Terry Moore felt weak and disoriented. This was not possible. This could not be so. It had to be a vision. Or perhaps he was dying. He shivered as hairs rose along the back of his neck.

The man said again, "Fear not." He paused, then: "You tried the case too soon. It wasn't ready for trial. You were too eager." Not scolding, but teaching. "You should have waited. Let the police work longer trying to find the girl's body. Raymond Jarvis is not that smart. He made a mistake that would have led you to her, but you needed to be patient, to uncover that mistake."

"I know, but—"

"You let others make decisions for you. Others hastily decided the case must be tried quickly because of public outcry and demands for justice. Yet those who decided when the case would be tried left the responsibility upon you. And now put this suffering upon you."

Terry Moore didn't question how this man knew so much. He didn't want to question. He wanted to believe.

When the man said, "Close your eyes," Terry Moore closed his eyes. Clamped them shut because he so desperately needed an answer for what had happened today. And if this was some madman who'd broken into his house, to torture him further, perhaps this was what he deserved for Raymond Jarvis going free.

When Terry opened his eyes, he felt lightheaded and unsteady, unsure of what had happened. The man in white was gone. Terry listened for him, heard nothing.

The satchel that had been in the man's hands was left behind.

Terry picked up the satchel, unbound the crude rope that tied it shut. Even before he looked inside, he smelled onions. And when he saw the severed hands, he dropped the bag and screamed.

Hands that smelled of onions flopped out of the bag onto the floor. Raymond Jarvis's hands. Sawed off from his arms. Drained of blood. Drained of life. Drained of evil. Raymond Jarvis would molest no more young girls with those hands.

The Angel had seen to that.